SOLDIER OF THE SECRET WARS

SOLDIER OF THE SECRET WARS

KENT WALKER

This is a work of fiction. While inspired by true events and featuring real figures from history, it is not intended to be factual. Some persons, locations, and events have been altered for literary effect.

ISBN 978-1-7329958-1-9

For Evelyn Baker, my twelfth-grade English teacher, who softly encouraged me to write. Though it's been sixty years, her words have stayed with me and motivated me as only a great teacher can.

PART I

CHAPTER 1

At ten thirty on the morning of November 24, 1963, Milton Stack and his wife, Mary Jane, made their way from Dupont Circle to the funeral parade route. They had a long walk to St. Matthews, and Stack's feet were already frozen. He stomped his boots on the sidewalk to drive the blood into them. They were going to watch the parade, but not trek to the Capitol Rotunda where JFK would lie in state.

Stack feared for the future of the country, if differences were being settled with killing.

Thousands had come to view the president's casket on parade, virtually faceless and huddled in their heavy coats. The horse-drawn caisson carrying Stack's friend came around the corner, preceded by the solemn US Army Band.

There—just for a moment, popping up among the others like a jack-in-the-box—a familiar face. Valzic Krewcheski.

Stack froze and Valzic turned. The two men stared at each other for a moment, then Valzic continued walking.

Mary Jane laid a hand on her husband's shoulder. "What's wrong?"

"That man." She turned and followed Stack's line of sight. "The tall one with the beard—do you see him?"

"Who is he?"

Stack started moving again, trying to keep his eyes on Valzic.

What the hell is a Soviet sniper doing here?

Valzic had held whole battalions of Nazis at bay single-handedly. Yet many Jewish leaders had fallen to his aim as well.

If Valzic was here, he was here for a purpose. The trick would be to track him down before he left the country and disappeared completely.

A tourist taking Polaroid pictures stepped in front of Stack, blocking his line of sight. Stack grabbed the man's arm.

"Excuse me, sir," Stack said. "I'll give you a hundred dollars if you take a picture of that tall man with a beard standing over there, waiting to cross."

"You're nuts," said the tourist. "For what?"

"Just take the picture." He yanked his wallet out of his coat pocket and held out a bill. "Please."

"Okay, what the hell?" said the tourist. He lifted the camera, snapped a picture, and handed it to Stack.

"Thanks." He gripped the photo so tight his wrist ached.

Milton Stack knew who'd killed Jack Kennedy.

CHAPTER 2

January 1937

"Hey Stack! Stack, boy." Milton Stack had been addressed as "Stack" since he was a very young man. In the farm community of Carthage, Illinois, shortcut names for almost everything made it a lot easier to communicate, especially in the fields.

Stack stopped and waited for Judge Schofield to shuffle up the newly poured concrete sidewalk. Judge Schofield and Stack's dad were the only lawyers in the region, and both traveled from time to time throughout Hancock County to plead cases and dispense justice. Winter wind had kicked up on the Midwest prairie. Judge Schofield rarely wore a coat unless he planned to be out of doors for some time, and for the most part, he made sure that this didn't happen.

Catching up to Stack, the judge said, "Your dad told me that you were waiting to hear from Darrow about a job in Chicago." Stack had recently graduated from Carthage College and felt a strong desire to expose himself to the larger world beyond the middle of Illinois.

"Yes, Judge. I'm sitting on pins and needles," said Stack.

"I don't think you'll have any trouble, knowing how devoted he is to your dad," Schofield said.

The two men turned into the boarding house that Stack's mom ran. Midday dinner was a healthy affair with plenty of hot food, lots of hungry men, and stimulating conversation. The Stack family farm was managed by fifteen loyal employees, Stack himself being one of them. Most of the employees lived in the Stack Boarding House and were like a large family. Stack had worked on the farm since childhood when he wasn't in school, and it had made him a strong, muscular man. He was highly intelligent to boot. His straw-yellow hair contrasted with his father's and grandfather's dark hair.

"Got some good news for you, Stack," said his mother. Her smile was so wide that the news was sure to be good for everyone in the household.

"Your dad came by on his way to Quincy to say you have a job with Clarence Darrow."

"Holy cow!" said Stack. "That's wonderful!" The dinner table burst with applause, and Stack blushed.

"Well, that's great news. I told you not to worry," said the judge.

Stack shook the judge's outstretched hand. "When? I mean when do I leave?" asked Stack.

"Wait till your Dad comes home, and then you can get all the particulars," said Stack's mom. The rapid-fire questions and congratulations that followed were a kind of attention Stack was unaccustomed to.

Later that day, his father returned home. "Clarence is ready for you to come right away and will pay you a living wage, as long as your living is not too high on the hog. On the other hand, there's gracious plenty to do here, and if you leave, I'll have to hire another hand for the farm and probably in the near future another attorney. You could be that man."

"I know, Dad. But I've never been anywhere outside the county. I want to see more of the country, and maybe be part of moving it in the right direction."

"If things keep on the way they are, we may not have a country. Especially if Germany keeps moving around. How about if I take you with me tomorrow to Keokuk and you can sit in on a trial that's about to wrap up?" asked Mr. Stack.

"Come on, Dad. That's just across the river," Stack said.

"But you will see life being played out. There's also your mother to think about," said his dad. "She is strong from all appearances, and she will hold up without you, but her life will be complete if you stay."

"Dad, I'm sorry. I can't stay. I've got to go and make the best out of this opportunity," said Stack.

••• •▬▬• ▬•▬▬

The train from Springfield to Chicago was packed, a miserable 248-mile ride that bumped and rattled under cold and gray Midwestern skies. Stack had managed to grab a seat and a place in the overhead netting for his single suitcase, but he was on the aisle, which meant he was constantly being stepped on. In the window seat beside him was a young lady barely out of her teens. She stared straight ahead, back stiff. Maybe she was anxious. Stack wondered if it was her first trip to the big city too.

"Excuse me." A tall man with a mustache pointed to the aisle seat facing Stack's. "Is that seat taken?"

"I'm afraid it is," Stack said.

"I see. Thank you." The man smiled at Stack and half-bowed to the young woman. Then he placed his hat in the overhead bin, set his suitcase on the floor, and sat on it.

"Will this be okay?" he said.

"Fine, sir." Stack forced a smile—the air was so full of smoke his eyes were watering. "Do you folks feel stuffy? Maybe if we cracked a window, we could make the ride tolerable."

"I'd like that, if nobody else minds the cold," the girl said. "I'm feeling a little ill."

"I have nothing against raising the window for a short period to clear the air," said the man on his suitcase.

They all glanced at the man in the window seat across from the lady, but he was asleep. With a shrug, Stack leaned over and cracked the window.

Soon a lean young man in a canvas hunting coat made his way toward them. He flopped down into the seat across from Stack. "Whew! A rodeo cowboy couldn't stay standing on this train."

The door at the far end of the car opened, and two men began to work their way down the aisle, one selling beverages and one sandwiches. They stumbled as the car swayed and shuddered over the rails. Eventually they reached Stack's row.

"I don't care for anything," the young woman said. Even though the air had cleared, she looked a little pale.

"It's a long trip," Stack said. "You could take something now and eat it later."

"I can't . . ." Her cheeks turned pink. "I'll manage, thank you."

Before she could protest, the man on the suitcase rose, paid for a sandwich, and handed it to the young lady.

"Thank you so much," she said, lowering her eyes.

"That, sir, was a generous gesture," Stack said. "I'm guessing you're a minister?"

The man looked surprised. "How'd you know?"

Stack shrugged. "I make a hobby out of observing people."

"I was a Baptist pastor in Nauvoo, but the farmers went under, and the congregation couldn't pay me," he said. "So now I'm a drummer, traveling through Illinois and Iowa. It's lonesome, I can tell you."

A voice came from just behind the man, in the aisle. "Well, you couldn't have better company than this pack of rascals."

Stack turned and broke into a smile. "Hank! Where did you come from?"

"Stack, ol' man. Long time, no see—it's been, what, a year? What fate do you suppose brought us together today in this ton of steel? Come on over, and we can get caught up. I'm sure there's an extra seat on this train somewhere."

Stack stood up, grabbed the back of the seat to steady himself, and retrieved his suitcase.

"Here you go, sir," he said to the minister. "Why don't you take my seat?"

Stack and Hank wove their way through the cramped aisle and found two comfortable seats in the next car forward.

"So," Stack said. "What have you been doing since dear ol' Carthage College?"

"I've been in working on a small weekly in Davenport," Hank said. "But now I've got an opportunity to hack with the mighty *Chicago Tribune*. What about you? What brings you to the windy city?"

"You're not going to believe this, but I'm going to practice law with Clarence Darrow's firm."

"Perfect!" Hank cried. "I always pictured something like that for you. Hey, maybe one day we'll work together for the good of mankind," he grinned.

"Got to pass the bar first," Stack said. "You married yet?"

"No. You?"

"Not even close," Stack said. "You found a place to live?"

"The *Trib* said they keep some space for single reporters," Hank said. "Dormitory-style. How about you?"

"The firm said they'd help me get acclimated. I assumed that meant helping me find housing."

"Well, at least now each of us knows somebody in the city."

"Righto," Stack said. "So, is it just me, or are you nervous at all?"

"I am, Stack. I put up a strong front, but truth be known, I don't know if I'm afoot or on horseback."

"I've never known you to be unsure of yourself."

"I know, pal." Hank sighed. "There's a lot riding on this, though. We've never paddled on this river before."

"Well, you're one hell of a writer, and that's where you'll shine. The only safe room I have is that Dad knows Darrow really well."

The hiss of the engine and the screech of steel on steel drowned out the chatter as the train slowed, then stopped. Everyone stood up at once, suitcases tumbling from overhead bins as passengers crowded the aisle, shoving their way toward the exits.

Stack was relieved when he and Hank finally squeezed out of the car and onto the platform.

"I guess this is it," Hank shouted over the bustle. "Call me at the *Tribune* if you want to get together. Until then, I'll see you around!"

The two young men managed a brief handshake, then went their separate ways.

Stack swung his suitcase to clear a path off the platform. He was damp with sweat, despite the cold. He was wearing his best clothes, hand-me-down wool pants and a jacket from his father, but a quick look around told him he'd need to upgrade soon.

The passengers climbing down from the train were colliding with those trying to board. Paper boys ran up and down the platform, shouting, "Over 700,000 killed in Russia!" Stalin was killing anybody who could be viewed as "opposition."

How the hell will I find my ride in all this?

Stack finally stumbled, blinded by the sun, out of the terminal onto the street. As he did, he heard what sounded like a shot, followed by the shriek of a horse. His eyes adjusted in time to see a chestnut-colored horse rear up right in front of him. Its hoof slammed into his shoulder and knocked him to the ground.

He rolled out of the way and saw the horse was pulling a

delivery wagon. Cartons of produce had tumbled out the back and onto the street.

"Shit!" Before he could pick himself up, he was almost hit again, this time by an automobile—the same car, he realized, that had backfired and caused the horse to panic. It was now in reverse, and as it swerved to avoid one of the spilled cartons, it swung around and nearly clipped Stack a second time.

He scrambled under the wagon and into a slushy puddle, knocking his forehead on the rim of the wagon's wheel in the process. He saw a large man in a bloody apron reach his thick arms through the open window of the car, trying to grab the driver's jacket.

"Keep that fucking car out of the packing district!"

Stack, now bleeding from his head, slowly pulled himself out from under the wagon. He was stunned, and everything seemed fuzzy.

The car had finally stopped. A woman opened the door, stepped out, and grabbed him by one arm. She wasn't strong enough to move him, but it was obvious she wanted Stack to get into the car.

Stack shook his head at the chaos, then turned back to the woman.

My God, what a beautiful creature, he thought.

Before he knew it, two large men had him by the elbows and had hustled him into a car.

"Where are we going?" he asked. The answer came in the form of a steel-toned order.

"Take this guy to the hospital, Charlie."

"Why?" Stack said with a touch of irritation, "I'm fine. Wet, maybe, and cold, but I'm all right."

"Why don't we check you out to be sure?" The steel voice belonged to the lady in the car.

... .--. -.--

The hospital was just as chaotic as the platform had been, but at least his room was quiet, which gave Stack time to collect himself. He was all right, just shaken and bruised, with a small cut above his right eye.

"Nurse?"

The woman checking the clipboard at the foot of his bed looked up.

"Ma'am, I'm due at the Darrow law firm," Stack said. "Will you call them and tell them where I am and that I'm okay?"

"I've already done that," said a different voice, one with hints of steel.

Stack looked to the door. It was the pretty girl from the car accident.

"Hi," she said. "I'm Mary Jane Armstrong. I work at the firm."

"Wow," Stack said. "I'm, ah, really delighted to meet you. This farm boy could use a little guidance."

"Milton Stack!" Someone in the hall bellowed. "Stack!"

Mary Jane leaned back out the door and waved. "In here, Uncle Clarence!"

Clarence Darrow stepped into the room, hung up his hat, and planted his hands on his hips. His pockmarked face and heavy eyebrows made him seem even older than his eighty years. His gray seersucker suit was made for summer wear, and badly wrinkled. Thinning gray hair flopped across the right side of his forehead.

Darrow looked at Stack but spoke to the room. "Is he seriously hurt?"

Stack straightened himself up. "I'm fine, sir. Just some bumps and bruises, and a little damage to my dignity." He wasn't sure what else to say to the man who'd won the Scopes "Monkey

Trial" and defended Leopold and Loeb.

A doctor stuck his head in the door, then stepped into the room. He took the clipboard from the nurse and flipped through.

"Young man," he said, "you're as sound as a dollar. I think we can let you go."

Stack turned to the doctor. "Thank you, Doctor, for such speedy service."

The man grimaced. "Purely self-preservation," he said. "Mr. Darrow has very little patience, as you might've noticed. Nice to have met you."

The doctor left, and Stack realized he was alone in the room. At the desk in the lobby, Stack asked about the bill and was told there wasn't one. He hurried down the hall and he found both Mary Jane and Darrow.

"Uncle Clarence thinks we should run by the office before going home. I've already asked Mom if Stack can come to dinner, and she went one up and suggested he spend the night," said Mary Jane.

"Ann got him a room, but I can't remember where," said Darrow. "Let's go to the office and see what Ann's done and get a quick look."

"Well, okay, let's get going," said Mary Jane. "Don't want to miss dinner."

The three pulled up at the door of the Wrigley Building and got out, leaving the car with the valet service.

Stack stopped to look at the list of tenants of the large building

"My God. Is this the chewing gum company?" asked Stack.

"Among other things," said Darrow. "They are clients of ours." He waved his hand for Stack to hurry up.

"I've got to get off on five, but I'll be right up," said Darrow in the elevator.

On the top floor, Mary Jane opened the door from the elevator hallway to a beehive of activity. Standing in front of Stack was a woman who looked to be in her late fifties, with a pencil in her hair.

"Oh, sorry. I'm afraid we didn't hear the door. Hi, Mary Jane."

"This is Mr. Stack, the new lawyer Uncle Clarence hired. He had to stop at the railroad office but he'll be right up."

"Well, my name is Ann, and I work for Mr. Darrow."

"And everyone else in the firm," said Mary Jane.

Stack stood there, awkwardly waiting, not sure what to do with himself. Ann said, "Mr. Darrow said for me to show you to your office."

He was escorted into a room with wood floors and wood paneling from floor to shoulder height, and then frosted glass to, he guessed, about six feet. There were wooden chairs and a wooden rolltop desk and a telephone. Stack had never had an office or a room solely for himself. There was only one window, which bothered Stack not a bit.

"How many offices does the firm have?" Stack asked Ann.

"Twelve, as of right now. You make thirteen. Hope you're not superstitious," Ann said. "The bulk of the work is civil litigation—a lot of research and an all-hands-on-deck mentality."

"I'm up to the task," Stack said.

••• •▬▬• ▬•▬▬

Mary Jane stuck her head in the door, with a look that might have been disdain for a back-woods youngster being invited into a prestigious Chicago firm. "I don't think you've given much thought to what your next step is, have you?" she said.

"You got me," Stack said. "What do you suggest?"

"I don't know. You're not my problem," said Mary Jane. "You have had a little bit of a whirlwind day. Sorry, I guess that's partly my fault, when I bungled picking you up in the car. So the least we can do is give you dinner. You'll get a chance to talk to Uncle Clarence, too, since he eats most of his meals with us."

"Well, I should warn you," Stack said, "I haven't had a lot of meals outside of my family home, and I'm pretty hungry. I hope I can remember my manners."

"It's just a home-cooked meal," Mary Jane said. "Nothing fancy. But it is a bit rude to assume there won't be enough to eat." She was smiling for the first time.

"I didn't mean to imply that," said Stack. "I just meant that I may be awkward," he said.

"Well, you've already hit the bull's eye there," Mary Jane said.

"Sorry," Stack said sheepishly.

... .--. -.--

"Tell me about your uncle," Stack said as he rode with Mary Jane to the Armstrong house. "I know all about his cases, but what's he like deep down? How does he run his firm?"

"Let's see," Mary Jane said. "Uncle Clarence is for women's rights and abolition, and against capital punishment, obviously. He's very emotional and has a wonderful imagination. Being around him is a treat. Everyone adores him."

That's a relief, thought Stack.

"What about you? What area of the law do you concentrate in?" Mary Jane asked.

"Well, I . . . I'm just starting out," said Stack

"What? Uncle Clarence never hires rookies. What makes you so special?" Mary Jane asked.

"Well, my dad and your uncle Clarence are associates. Dad works downstate as a practitioner and a judge."

"Say no more," said Mary Jane. "I guess you'll find out fast how good you really are."

"First I need to pass the bar," said Stack.

"Wow! You have bitten off a big chew. Darrow Law Firm and the Illinois Bar all in a few weeks?"

"Why in a few weeks?" asked Stack.

"Because Uncle Clarence won't give you more than that."

"But I haven't had any experience—I don't really know what I want to specialize in."

"Well, you better start thinking, cause the fire hose will be coming out quicker 'n Billy B. Damned."

"I think I have to take things one step at a time. I'm supposed to look over Mr. Darrow's shoulder for a few weeks and see what he sees and how I fit in here."

"How will you know—if it's right for you, I mean?"

"Well . . . I don't know that yet," he said. "I can get a little impatient when it comes to details, but if I decide this is the right profession, I'll just put in more effort to overcome that. Like I said, I'm just taking things one step at a time."

"Hmm," Mary Jane said. She still looked skeptical.

Stack wondered if Uncle Clarence had asked Mary Jane to feel him out. And whether he'd passed the test.

••• •▬▬• ▬•▬▬

As soon as they pulled up to the Armstrong home, Stack found himself staring. It was an old three-story Federal, fully restored.

"Man, this is beautiful beyond description. I wish I had a picture to show my folks."

"I'm glad you like it," Mary Jane said, walking up on the wooden porch. "My grandfather bought it in 1890. We're right by the lake, see? And Northwestern University's not far from here."

"Well, I'm honored to be here."

The screen door creaked open, and a slightly older, more solid version of Mary Jane stepped out.

"Mother," Mary Jane said, "meet Mr. Stack, your brother's new hire."

"Well, I know his folks, and if he's cut from the same cloth, he can move right on in."

"No, no," Stack said. "I don't want to intrude on your household."

"Silly man," said Mrs. Armstrong. "You're welcome here for as long as you like. Come on, let's go inside."

For the first time since boarding the train back in Springfield, Stack began to feel more comfortable, and was able to relax as he took in his new surroundings.

Five o'clock was suppertime on the farm, but Stack had assumed big city folk ate much later. Dinner was served at six, however—and at a table far too large for five.

"I'm terribly embarrassed," Elizabeth Armstrong said when she saw Stack trying to decide where to sit. "We had a faculty dinner last night, and we neglected to remove the table leaves. I think it's so awkward to be sitting so far apart. Amos, will you move your place setting over to Clarence's side of the table?"

They ended up with Elizabeth at the head of the table, Stack and Mary Jane on one side, and Darrow and Professor Amos Armstrong—Mary Jane's father—opposite them.

"So, Stack," Professor Armstrong said. "What sort of law are you looking to practice?"

"Mostly civil, I think," replied Stack. "Right now, I'm still in awe of being here in Chicago."

"Don't let the city scare you," Darrow said. "It can take some getting used to, but I'm sure you can handle it.

"Maybe so. But the city is awfully intimidating. I've never seen a building more than two stories, much less an office building."

"You'll do fine," said Darrow.

"Well, not if this morning is any indication," Stack said, eliciting a chuckle from the professor and smiles from Mary Jane and Elizabeth. "But I'm very grateful to have you as a mentor, sir."

"I'm sure the firm, and the family, will be glad to have you here," said Darrow. "But tell me, Stack, why civil law? Are you one of those boys who wants to change the world?"

"I don't really know. I've just left Carthage, and haven't seen much of the world. But I want to."

"Maybe this is the best way," said Darrow, "through your work."

"I guess so, sir."

"Clarence is eighty years old, and he's still trying to change the world," said Professor Armstrong.

"So, do you think your passion for something makes it worth doing?" Darrow held up a finger. "Better question—how can you be sure that you're making changes for the better?"

Stack hesitated. "I'd have to think about that, sir, but I feel it's best to evaluate anything on a case-by-case basis." He wasn't entirely sure what the right answer was, and he didn't want to cause an argument. "My dad always told me to ask myself: what would you give your life for? I figure whatever the answer is, that's something worth working toward."

Darrow helped himself to the green beans. "In the face of Hitler, Americans are going to have to answer that question sooner rather than later."

Stack leaned back a little in his chair and faced Darrow. This wasn't the kind of how-was-your-day dinner-table discussion he'd been expecting. "I admit, sir, I haven't given that much thought."

"You should." Darrow walked around the table and extended

his hand to Stack. "I'm happy to have you on board, Stack. I know I can be a little blunt. I just haven't had a tutorial environment in ages." He returned to his seat. "This is a fine dinner, Elizabeth. As usual."

••• •▬▬• ▬•▬▬

After dinner, Darrow left. Mary Jane took Stack into the living room, where she guided him to the divan. As they settled in, she gave him a penetrating look.

"That's about as bad as it gets," she said. "Don't worry, he's much more easygoing in the office."

"It wasn't all that bad. I just wasn't quite expecting so many questions." Stack said. "If we'd been in the office, he might've thrown me off stride, but I'm feeling very comfortable with you and your folks. You all make me feel so welcome."

"I think it's more you than us," Mary Jane said. "I don't know anyone else who'd have bounced back so fast from a first day in the city like you've had."

"Hello! Are you children out here?" Elizabeth stuck her head into the room. "Don't stay up too late—you've had a big day, and you'll have an even bigger one tomorrow, so get some sleep!"

Elizabeth showed Stack to a second-story bedroom, complete with fireplace. He sat in a high-backed chair and began to read case summaries he'd brought home from the office.

CHAPTER 3

Early the next morning, Stack made his way through a cold, misty rain to the office. He was hoping to be the first one there and impress the others. No such luck. Ann was already making the coffee and made no fuss over his early arrival. He went straight to his office, still not believing he didn't have to share the space. He felt like a king in his castle.

"Phone call for you, Stack," shouted Ann from down the hall. Stack instantly felt a rush of optimism, as if a phone call indicated that he had arrived. "Just pick it up at your desk," she said.

"Hello?"

"Stack, this is Hank. Catch you at a bad time?"

"As a matter of fact . . ."

"Okay. I'll ring you later. Got some good news."

"No, no. Tell me now," said Stack.

"Okay," said Hank. "I think I've met the girl of my dreams! What a knockout!"

"That's really fantastic," said Stack. "How about we discuss it over lunch?"

He'd just hung up when he heard a sharp rap on the door, and in walked Darrow, all smiles.

"Are you getting organized?" Darrow asked.

"Yes, sir," Stack said. "I love it. Can't wait to get to work."

"Already got a client?" Darrow asked, winking.

"That was a friend of mine who's working for the *Tribune*," said Stack.

"Well, good. You don't need to be dealing with clients just yet anyway. Your first order of business is to study for the bar exam and pass it."

Darrow walked away, and another man stood in the doorway. "Hi there! I'm Jerry Wells; I'm in litigation. Just wanted to welcome you to the justice factory."

"Hi, Jerry. Call me Stack."

"Where you from, Stack?"

"Downstate in Carthage."

"Hey, that's great. I'm from Springfield. They say the best people are from downstate."

Throughout the day, others dropped in to welcome him. Stack saw no signs of resentment or backbiting—they all really seemed to like each other. And they all looked alike, with black suits and white shirts. Stack felt out of place in his wrinkled hand-me-down suit, but no one seemed to notice—just as well, since he had no money for buying new clothes just yet.

Looking out the window at the swirling snow, Stack felt he was right where he was supposed to be.

... .--. -.--

"Ahem!" Stack stood at the door to Mary Jane's office around noon the next day. "Are you available for a consultation?"

"Sure," she said. "What can I help you with?"

"I need to find some quarters that aren't part of the Armstrong house," Stack said.

She looked amused. "Getting sick of us already?"

"Never," he said. "But I hate to keep imposing on you folks."

The truth was, living at the Armstrongs' was comfortable—too comfortable. Practically speaking, though, Stack thought he should have his own platform to build a life.

Mary Jane smiled. "Let's go." She rose and pulled her coat off the rack as Stack ducked into his office to get his ragged one.

"Stack, wait a minute," Clarence said, poking his head out of his office. "When you get back, get the Illinois Railroad v. the Railroad Union files from Ann, and start familiarizing yourself with them. This is coming to trial soon, and I want you as co-defense. That is, if you pass the bar."

"Yes, sir," he said to Clarence, and Clarence went back inside.

Looking sleepily at Mary Jane, Stack said, "Damn. I'm sure your uncle is not happy that his prize rookie is not in the office, grinding away."

"Well," said Mary Jane, "why don't you order something to go and bring it back to the office?"

"Good thinking," said Stack. "Here's the list of apartments that Darrow's secretary put together—would you mind looking at them for me?" Stack asked. "I figure a little local knowledge might help."

"I'll review that and add some," said Mary Jane. "I assume you want to live somewhat near the things to do, close to the office, and affordable?"

"You got it, lady," Stack said.

••• •▬▬• ▬•▬▬

For the next two weeks, Stack spent every lunch hour looking at apartments. Once he'd narrowed it down, he put in a call to his buddy Hank. "Are you still living in the dorm?"

"Indeed I am," said Hank.

"I've found an apartment close to our offices."

"Whoa! What do you mean 'our' offices?"

"Come on, Hank," said Stack. "You bitch about living like you're still in college all the time. And this is a steal: $25 a month. Split!"

"But Stack, ol' boy. I'm paying zero now," said Hank. "Let me think about it?"

"You've got two minutes."

"Okay, okay, I'm in," said Hank.

"Great!" Stack said. "I'm excited."

"Good," said Hank. "Got time for lunch?"

... .--. -.--

The Southie Dog Deli was loud and crowded when Stack pushed open the doors. From a high table near the window, no chairs, he saw Hank waving him over.

There was nowhere to hang his coat, so he left it on.

"The *Trib* is like a frat party," Hank said. "Lots of silly jabs and lots of jokes. They're great guys, but I'm relieved to be moving to a place where I can think."

"I can't wait for you to see the apartment. It's at the rail end on the North Side. Close to the office and not far from the college girls."

"Wow, home run!"

"Actually, that's . . . sort of the problem," Stack said. "I've been staying with Darrow's sister and brother-in-law . . . and their daughter." He hesitated. "She's a great girl, Hank. But a bit of a sourpuss. I like her—she's smart, funny, caring, and yet she pisses me off at the same time."

"Well, at least you know someone," said Hank.

"I guess you're right," Stack said. "But when I'm with her, it's hard to explain, but it's like I'm all hers."

"Stack, you need to cool down! You just got to Chicago—it's much too early for you to settle down. Has she given you any hints as to how she feels about you?" Hank said

"No, but she would be naturally cautious around her uncle," Stack said.

"Hell's bells, Stack, at this time in our lives, we don't need to be tied down with women, no matter how smart and attractive they are." The arrival of their food stopped the conversation.

"It's good I'm moving in with you to keep you out of the ditch. So, sign me up with a contract that gives me rights to criticize," Hank said.

Stack ignored him. "Damn good chow."

"Depends on how hungry you are," said Hank.

After their lunch was done, Stack followed Hank out of the deli. The wind was harsh, even with a new topcoat he'd gotten on a shopping expedition with Mary Jane. "So do you want to run over and take a look at the apartment?"

"How far is it?" asked Hank.

"Not far. Follow me."

The young men got let into the building, a five-minute walk from the deli. "This place is perfect!" said Hank.

"I've made a list of things we need. You look it over and add or subtract."

"What about we dedicate evenings and weekends to shopping around?"

"That's a good idea," said Stack. "But I was thinking we might enlist Mary Jane to tell us where to go."

"You're gonna get that girl deep under your skin," said Hank.

"No, sir. I'm keeping it professional."

Hank just chuckled and shook his head.

••• •▬▬• ▬•▬▬

"Stack!" Darrow called down the hall. "Where the hell are you?"

"Right here, boss."

Darrow spent as much time as he could training Stack, but his responsibilities to the firm prohibited total dedication to any kind of real preparation program. Generally, he just drafted the first person he saw each morning to keep Stack in tow and show him whatever they could. No one seemed to mind; if anything, it meant they had Stack as an assistant for the day.

But the closer the Illinois Railroad suit came to trial, the more Darrow depended on Stack.

"Great job, son. I just might put you on your feet at the trial," said Darrow, grinning.

Occasionally, Hank was invited back to dinner at the Armstrongs. Walking down the sidewalk, Hank said, "Boy, they have given you the maximum encouragement with Mary Jane."

••• •▬▬• ▬•▬▬

Stack was sweating as he kicked open the apartment door.

"Well, hell. Come on in," said Hank.

Stack dropped his briefcase on the floor and sank into a chair.

"So I'm guessing the bar exam was not a piece of cake," said Hank.

"Shit, some of it was like a first-grade spelling test," Stack said. "But a lot of it was on agriculture law and human rights. I don't know shit about agriculture law." Stack shook his head. "But I passed."

"How the hell do you know you passed?" said Hank.

"They graded right there, and when you reach the acceptable number of right answers, you're in."

"Damn," said Hank. "I ought to do a story about that."

The roommates celebrated that night by cracking open some beers and telling stories about their college days.

••• •▬▬• ▬•▬▬

Now that he was an official member of the Illinois Bar Association, Stack spent his days helping Darrow prepare for the Illinois Railroad case.

"By the way," Darrow told him during a lull, "if you're going to appear in court, you'd better get a new suit. Looking at you, the opposition will think all they have to do is stall until we declare bankruptcy."

"Oh." Darrow's bluntness left Stack nowhere to hide. "Sorry, sir. I'll get something today."

Darrow nodded, already busy poring over another file. "Just get a nice dark suit and some white shirts. Shoes too. Have the bill sent to me, and I'll see you're docked for it."

"Thank you," Stack mumbled.

••• •▬▬• ▬•▬▬

"This should knock off the rough edges," Stack said as he and Hank looked over several suits in the haberdashery.

"You're coming along," Hank said. "Little by little you're kicking Mr. Rural out the door."

"You've been a real help, Hank. I can't thank you enough."

"That's right, Stacko, you can't." Hank seemed to have a constant smile. "I think we can adjourn for now."

••• •▬▬• ▬•▬▬

By March, the eighty-hour work weeks were taking their toll. Stack needed a quiet evening, something restorative. So he asked Mary Jane if she'd like to join him for an early dinner.

"I know just the place," she said.

The restaurant was upscale, small, and intimate. It was the perfect fit after a long day at the office.

A waiter materialized at Mary Jane's elbow. "Cocktail before dinner, madam?"

"What?—Oh. No, thank you."

He turned to Stack. "Monsieur?"

"You sure?" Stack said quietly to Mary Jane.

"Oh . . . all right. How about a beer?"

"Make that two," Stack said to the waiter.

"Very good."

As soon as the waiter left, Mary Jane's eyes dropped back to the table. "You know, I've lived here all my life," she said. "And I've found there are several Chicagos. Southside is a completely different town—you saw some of that in the stockyards the first day you came here. Polish, Irish, Italian—there's a little of everything in Southy. But the largest ethnic population here in Cook County is German. That'll become a real part of the dialogue as Europe gets hotter, don't you think?"

"Probably," replied Stack. "A lot depends on how deep-seated the nationalist feelings are. I'm afraid we'll get into the war anyhow and it'll be a disaster."

"But we may have to just to save the world from itself." She looked up at him. "What happens then?"

"I don't know what the future holds, Mary Jane. I feel rumbling under my feet and conflict in the air, but right now all I can think about is a settlement with Illinois Railroad written all over it," said Stack.

"I'm in the same place," she replied.

CHAPTER 4

August 1937

Hank and Stack had fallen into the routine of having lunch together every Monday. The conversations about the situation in Europe grew more intense, though Hank always seemed to be in a good mood. The lunches moved to white-tablecloth restaurants as their paychecks began to fill their bank accounts. The one who suggested the place on any given Monday usually paid.

Chicago has a habit of picking up spring winds and saving them for the early summer. Stack was windblown and tousled by the time he arrived at the restaurant of the day, Nick's Uptown.

"Glad we're indoors today; the damn wind is a bother," said Stack.

"No kidding. But Stack, sit. I've got some good news." Stack pulled out his chair and sat.

"What the hell is it?" asked Stack.

"You remember the feeling for advertising I thought I had?" asked Hank. He was grinning.

"Sure. I always thought you were a very conceptual person."

"Well, the paper has moved me into the advertising department, which at first sounds ominous. But there's just some salesmen and my boss in the whole department. The sales guys are gone all day, and my boss thinks advertising is a dead end, so I'll have the operation to myself." Hank was so excited that he brushed off any negative traps that might lie ahead. "I know I could become the whipping boy who gets blamed for everything. But, hey. I'm going to dazzle them, so no problem."

"Well, let's have a drink to your success," said Stack.

... .--. -.--

"Stack!" Darrow stuck his head into the hall. "Could you come into my office for a minute? There's someone here I'd like you to meet."

Stack followed Darrow into the office, where another man stood waiting for them. He had salt-and-pepper hair combed back, broad shoulders, and a slim waist.

"Stack, this is Colonel Bill Donovan," Darrow said, closing the door to his office. "He practices law in New York, and as a hero of the Great War, is a consultant to President Roosevelt. He has a proposition I think you'll find quite interesting."

After a firm round of handshakes, the men all took a seat—Darrow behind the desk, Stack in front of it, and Donovan perched on the edge.

My God. What have I done? thought Stack.

"Mr. Stack," Donovan said, "I'm here as an emissary of President Roosevelt. I and a few other fellows are working with the British to develop an international information agency. This is to be an effort to develop and grease channels of information. This is top secret, and should you become involved, you can never speak of it to anyone outside the operation. Having said that, we would like you to join us."

Stack, rattled at this sudden proposition, stared back and forth between the two men. "I'm sorry, sir," he said. "I'm not sure I understand what you mean."

"Now Stack," Darrow said, "this isn't something you can talk about—with anybody." He gave Stack a severe look. "Only a very few people know about this. The government has great confidence in you."

"I know this is a shock," said Donovan. "You sure as hell weren't expecting this when you got up today. But we haven't got much time, and you passed all the vetting we could do without your knowledge. You're valuable to us because you're an unknown; no one in Europe has ever heard of you or seen your face. Plus, I'm partial to farmers." Donovan smiled. "Have you ever heard of Professor William Dodd?" he asked.

"Should I have?" asked Stack.

"Not really," said Donovan. "Dodd was a professor of history at the University of Chicago. In '35, the president appointed him ambassador to Germany. It's been a disaster, and now FDR has decided to replace Dodd with a fellow named Hugh Wilson. The idea is for Wilson to get on over there and help Dodd clean up his act paper-wise, then take over in the fall." Donovan was now up and pacing. "I want to send an unknown to Berlin under the guise of helping Dodd pack up. This operative will observe the situation, assist with correspondence, and keep an eagle eye out for anything and everything to do with the Nazis. Plus, he can keep us informed on the actions of the new ambassador. Wilson has made some very disturbing statements regarding a need to emphasize the positive aspects of Nazi Germany."

"Excuse me for interrupting, sir," Stack said. "But what does this have to do with me? Or Mr. Darrow for that matter?"

"Why, Mr. Stack, you're going to be our operative." He smiled. "A spy."

Stack jerked backward, nearly knocking over his chair. "You want me to be *what*?"

"We could have gotten a military man, but they tend to be chain-of-command guys, and I need this person reporting directly to me," said Donovan.

Stack took a deep breath and straightened himself. "Sir, I'm flattered, but I wouldn't even know where to start."

"The president and Winston Churchill, a power in Parliament, believe the Nazis won't stop until they *are* stopped. Mr. Stack, we have a chance to help save the world. That doesn't come along every day."

Stack looked at Darrow. "Where do you figure into all this, sir?"

"Donovan is a longtime friend of mine, and he asked me for a recommendation. I chose you."

Stack stood and paced, trying to grasp some of the repercussions of what this job would entail. Then he looked back at Darrow.

"What happens if I don't want to go?"

"Actually, my young friend, I'm strongly suggesting you accept." Darrow looked up at Stack from under his bushy eyebrows. "You're perfect for this: you're sharp, you've got good perspective, and you're observant. I believe you will grow in the job, and you'll gain a level of experience a man five times your age wouldn't have. And when all this is over, you'll still have a job here if you want it."

Slowly, Stack sat back down. "What exactly would you need me to do?"

"Just take the job, and let the embassy people tell you what they need. Keep your eyes and ears open. Take notes. You'll go from here to New York, where you'll meet with my associate Stephenson, and from there you'll go straight to London for a bit of training—you'll meet the rest of the team over there."

"Where will I live, and on what?"

"Stephenson will give you the details, but rest assured, you'll be paid handsomely. We'll advance traveling funds for you, and there are rooms at the embassy in London."

The whole idea was . . . exciting. Crazy, but exciting. And he'd be paid, and trained.

"Can we discuss this, sir?" Stack asked Darrow. "In private?"

"Certainly." Darrow stood. "Let's step into the library."

As soon as the door closed behind them, Stack collapsed into a chair.

"Mr. Darrow, I don't know what to say. I've just gotten settled at the firm and passed the bar. And, while Mary Jane and I are enjoying each other, marriage is out of the question at the moment because I'm so busy with my career, and I think she agrees," said Stack. "So I don't know what to think. Tell me, sir, what to do."

Darrow nodded. "I'm glad you cleaned romance off the plate. You have to look in your soul for the answer to this one. But I believe our country will be at war pretty soon, which means you'll be heading over there anyway, one way or another. Going with Donovan gives you some options."

Stack hadn't thought about that. This sure sounded safer than the front lines.

"As to your responsibilities," Darrow said, "I've always felt that every man's responsibility is to maintain the integrity of our country." He paused. "I know we told you not to discuss this with anybody, but I think for Mary Jane you'll need to make an exception. You don't need to give her any specific details, and don't talk to anyone else about it. But there's no way she's going to understand if you don't tell her something."

"You're right," Stack said. He really didn't want to leave her, but . . . he knew he'd never forgive himself if didn't grab this opportunity.

••• •▬▬• ▬•▬▬

Stack and Mary Jane had been seeing each other steadily for nearly six months. This was momentous news, and he felt he had to break it to Mary Jane personally. They met on Wood Island, in a small inlet off Lake Michigan, and walked around to the wind shelter.

"I've got something to tell you." Stack faced Mary Jane squarely and forced himself to look her in the eye. "I've got an opportunity to help our country in a pretty big way, but it'll mean relocating. To England."

"What?" she was stunned. "When? Stack, what's going on?"

"We both know Germany is rearming," Stack said. "Britain may well be invaded. After that, who knows where this stops?"

She folded her arms. "And what can you do to prevent that?"

"The way I understand it . . . and this is all top secret . . . Britain and the US are setting up a joint intelligence operation. They're looking for young men to be a part of it."

"I don't understand." Mary Jane bit off the words as if she were spitting. "And even if I did, why you?"

Stack suddenly realized how silly this must sound. A top-secret organization no one's ever heard of wanted him, a farmer-turned-lawyer with no experience to speak of, to move halfway across the world and be a spy? He hadn't even started the job, and he'd already spilled the beans to Mary Jane.

"Your uncle recommended me." He hesitated. He wasn't sure how much to say and how much to keep quiet. "But mostly, they wanted someone nobody would recognize. Someone who'd never be suspected."

"But why *you*?" He'd been expecting her to cry, but instead she looked furious. "With all the other smart, strong men running around this country, why the hell did they pick the one I care about?"

"I don't know," Stack said. "But this is an honor, you know. To be trusted with something like this."

"I'll worry about you. How can I be sure you'll come back quick and safe?"

"I will," Stack said. He grabbed both her hands and looked her in the eye. "My God, Mary Jane, I'll miss you so much."

"Then don't go!"

He shook his head. "There's something in me that tells me I have to honor my country." He pulled her into a strong hug.

Choking back tears, she whispered, "I love you, Stack. I love you so desperately. I don't know if I can make it if you go."

"Of course you can, Mary Jane. You're the strongest woman I've ever met. Remember, weakness of the will affects individuals as well as nations."

··· ·−−· −·−−

The conversation was light-hearted and casual at dinner at the Armstrongs' house, but when the table had been cleared and kitchen chores had been done, the discussions took on a more serious tone.

"Clarence," said Professor Armstrong, "have you heard anything more about Lindbergh's effort to keep us out of the conflict?"

"Nothing unusual," said Darrow. "But I did hear—"

Mary Jane threw her napkin on the table.

"Can't we sit down for one meal without hearing about Hitler? Can't we talk about anything that doesn't reek of war? What's wrong with the damn Cubs—couldn't you talk about them?" She shoved her chair back and stormed out of the dining room.

Professor Armstrong looked worried. Stack pushed his chair back as if he were going to console Mary Jane.

"Leave her alone for a while," advised the Professor. "She'll cool down soon enough."

Nevertheless, Stack got up and went after her.

"We're all part of this nation," Stack said. "If America gets in it, that means all of us are in it too."

"Go on," Mary Jane said. "Go home. I can see you don't want to hear what I have to say." Then she looked right at him, her gaze so direct Stack almost took a step back. "You think I don't understand, but I do. I understand much more deeply than you do how real the chance is that you won't come home."

Stack met her stare. "Okay," he said. "I'll go."

He headed toward the door but stopped when he felt Mary Jane grab his arm. She stood in the middle of the study.

"What do you want?" she said. "You want me to be happy about this? To smile when I kiss you goodbye?"

"That'll be the day," said Stack.

"What? Do you think I'm not capable of understanding world politics?" Mary Jane said with that old steel in her voice.

"No," said Stack. "I was referring to the possibility of your not kissing me at all, not to mention at the train station when I leave for Berlin."

"I want you to understand, that's all."

"I'm not the only one, you know," Stack said. "I know I might not come back. But a lot of future husbands and fathers might not come back either, and I'm not going to be the only one who stays behind, dammit!" said Stack.

"Don't you dare cuss at me." She rose and pushed past him. "I'm going for a walk."

Damn, damn, damn! What could he do? They'd talked about this till they were blue in the face, and if she wouldn't see it, there was nothing else he could say or do.

"I think I'd better go," Stack said when he returned to the

dining table.

"Cooler heads will prevail in the morning," said Darrow.

"Women are maddest when they lose something," said Professor Armstrong. "This is the first time that my daughter has had something to lose." He paused. "And I don't mean a war."

PART II

CHAPTER 5

December 1937

Once he boarded the train to New York City and heard the piped-in Christmas music, Stack was overwhelmed by anxiety and loneliness. Going from Carthage to Chicago to New York in less than a year, he felt like he'd barely found his feet in one city, and now he was on his way to another. He longed for the sound of the river back home, and the smell of dry hay in the barn.

The train was packed with men caught in the teeth of the Depression. Farms were going under, and everyone hoped to find jobs in the big city. The smell of men's sweat mixed with livestock reminded him of home again. After all, these were his people. It wasn't just Mary Jane he was leaving behind—it was his home, his family, an entire way of living.

"You ready to turn in, mister?" said the porter. Since he'd had to take the night train, Darrow had reserved him a berth in the sleeper car.

"No, not yet," Stack said. "I'd like to write a letter. Do you have any paper?"

"Yes, sir. I'll get it for you right now."

With so much to write about, Stack decided to keep it upbeat. Emotions would come later.

Dear Mom and Dad,
I'm doing fine and loving my work. But now I'm traveling East on a real secret case. I won't be writing frequently but will try to keep you up to date. . . .

"Best turn in soon. Your light is the only one on, and you'll soon be keeping folks awake," said the porter.

"Oh . . . I hadn't thought of that."

"That's all right, mister," the porter said. "Just keep it in mind and let me know when you're ready."

"I'm ready now," Stack said. "Sorry, I guess I was just lost in thought."

"Livin' in this messed-up world, every man on this train is lost in his thoughts," the porter said. "Go on, stand up, and I'll make your bed up."

... .--. -.--

When he woke the next morning, Stack rubbed his eyes and looked around, trying to remember where he was. When it hit him, the wave of emotion he'd kept in lockup since leaving Chicago was set loose. Sorrow sat so heavy on him it was hard to breathe. Each mile took him farther from home, and he saw clearly how alone he was. He twisted in his seat and tried not to cry, but with little success.

... .--. -.--

About noon on the second day of travel, the train stopped inside the largest building Stack had ever seen. Grand Central Station.

In the hubbub, he saw a sign that read West Forty-Eighth Street. His meeting with Bill Donovan and Bill Stephenson was at 45 Rockefeller Center, but he had no idea which way to go from here. He spotted a policeman in the crowd, and stopped and asked directions. The policeman smiled and said he needed to go one street up, walk west, and he'd get where he was going.

After walking for a block, Stack began to relax. The hustle and bustle of so many people was strangely comforting, not too different from Chicago. As far as he knew, there was no time set for the meeting—Donovan told him they'd start whenever Stack arrived—so he took his time, trying to absorb a little of the city.

The minute he saw the skating rink and the statue of Atlas, Stack knew he'd arrived. He took one of the elevators up, his stomach doing a little flip with every floor he passed. When he stepped out into the corridor on the forty-fifth floor, he took some deep breaths, then looked for a door labeled EAST WEST TRADING COMPANY.

He found an office, and when he gave the woman at the desk his name, she told him Donovan and Stephenson were in meetings. She offered him a cup of coffee while he waited, which he accepted.

Stack shrugged out of his top coat and took a seat.

It was late afternoon when Donovan finally stepped into the waiting room.

"Welcome to New York!" His smile was wide. "I'm so glad you're here, son. Any trouble?"

"No, sir, but it was a long ride."

"No kidding! The train's a beast. Sorry to have kept you waiting—come on, let's not waste any more time."

He led Stack into the conference room just off the waiting area.

"Can I get you anything? Coke, water, coffee?"

"No thank you, sir." Stack looked around. "Where's Mr. Stephenson?"

"Right here." The door behind them barely closed before a

man stepped in after them. Stephenson was handsome, a little short, wearing a dark charcoal suit and starched white shirt. "Sorry about the delay. We're two men running what should be a fifty-man operation." He looked Stack right in the eye, slowly raising his chin. "But I guess now there's three of us."

"We'll have to skip the getting-to-know-you stuff; we just found out there's room on board a troop ship headed to London," Donovan said. "We've reserved a ticket for you."

"When do I . . . ?"

"You leave in one week," said Stephenson. "Until then, you'll be staying in the Roosevelt Hotel next to the train station."

"So let's hit the books," said Donovan. "You need to master German, explosives, codes, and infrared cameras. You won't be able to cover everything here, of course, but you need to get started. We just want you as prepped as possible. The only thing Britain does better than us is intelligence, and if the US is forced into the war, superior info will help that effort along."

Stephenson spoke up. "We have some excellent people in place, and a sound organizational structure. We've also got some damn good men in the field, and we always need more. You'll be focused on Germany. The ambassador's move is an unprecedented infiltration opportunity."

"We'll talk details over the next couple of days," Donovan said. "Meanwhile, go to the hotel and get some rest. We'll meet tomorrow at nine."

"Yes, sir," Stack said. Things were moving quickly, but maybe that was for the best—it gave Stack less time to second-guess himself.

... .--. -.--

A week later, Stack boarded the troop ship, excited to be underway. This excitement lasted less than a day.

Shipboard accommodations consisted of hammocks stacked one on top of the other, close enough to squeeze in a thousand sailors and soldiers. Six inches separated Stack's face and the hammock above, and there were two more hammocks below his. Getting out to pee was a problem—you had to clamber out of the hammock without disturbing the men above and below. Consequently, most men just held it, or lay down on the wet deck and went back to sleep rather than wake their shipmates. Stack was seasick early on, but quickly rode it out. To avoid the stench from the head, Stack spent most days topside, in the salt air. The ship was part of a convoy—sailing the North Atlantic was dangerous. German U-Boats considered any and all ships to be fair targets.

"Why so many soldiers?" he asked some of the men he'd become friendly with. "I thought this was a resupply convoy."

"Well, pal," said one scruffy man in a uniform, "don't know if you noticed, but there's a war going on."

"I know that, but I didn't know the US was in it."

"We're not yet—we're just going to let the Krauts know the rest of the world is fed up with their antics. Me and my buddies are going to show the Brits how to run things."

The convoy was guarded by US Navy destroyers, which dictated practice maneuvers every day, adding to the time at sea. New uniforms and equipment had been issued to the men, but they preferred to wear their old tattered clothing. Stack had come on board wearing a new wool suit and didn't take it off for the duration of the trip because of the cold winds. He also suspected he'd be the butt of jokes if he unpacked a suitcase, when the men all had duffel bags.

An old sailor approached Stack, who was topside walking the deck.

"You look like a character out of a spy story, mate."

"I feel like one," Stack said, "especially in this thick fog." He felt a little rattled but tried not to show it.

"How come you're in civvies?"

"Duffel's in the hold and it's a royal pain in the ass to get it out. Suits me to float and soak while the weather stays socked in."

"U-Boats'll come out of hiding if the weather clears up," said a sailor who was working nearby.

"Aye," said the old seaman. "Right you are."

"See you around," Stack said as he turned into the wind and walked away. As soon as he rounded the corner of the cabin, he stopped, leaned back, and took a deep breath.

"Watch out for that bloke in the civvies," he heard the old seaman say. "I got a feeling about him. Looks like a German spy."

Of all the luck. Standing out like a sore thumb already—just what he didn't need. He needed to make an effort to blend in. There was always a card game below decks . . . maybe he could start there. Besides—the wind was turning raw again, and he couldn't spend all night topside.

••• •▬▬• ▬•▬▬

Below, with some hesitation, he allowed the men to teach him to play poker. He had only $500 that Darrow had advanced him, and fear of losing it made him cautious. A little luck resulted in modest winnings—enough to stay in the game on most nights, especially when the sea was calm. His intuition told him winning big would be a disaster—better to lose money and be liked than win the pot and unwanted attention.

"You still with us, partner?" asked the dealer.

After waiting a bit, Stack nodded. "Sure." He'd won a little and lost a little, and generally felt the sailors were good guys, at least to play cards with.

The Marine master sergeant sitting across from Stack had won a lot of money, but he'd been drinking beer all night. He beat the table with his fist. "Deal the goddamn cards. I want to see what the cowboy can do in a real man's game."

All five men around the table, including Stack, were dealt five cards each: two cards face up and three cards face down. The dealer bet $10. By the time it got to the master sergeant, the pot was $100.

The master sergeant squinted at Stack, who was thinking hard about the possibility the sarge might have three aces. He had two showing, and now he bet the pot and raised $100.

Everyone folded except Stack.

Seeing Stack's suddenly pained look, the sergeant, smiling smugly, called for him to show his cards.

Stack flipped his last card, and the master sergeant roared like a lion. All he'd had was a pair—Stack had two.

"You asshole! You suckered me!" The sarge walked around the table and grabbed Stack by his shirt and lifted him out of his chair. "I ought to throw you overboard."

"Sarge!" one man said, half rising out of his chair. "Cool down!"

"Yeah!" said another. "It's only poker. Besides, at the rate you're going you'll make that pot back in a couple of days."

The sergeant dropped Stack back into his chair.

"Better stay away from me topside, asshole." He stomped out.

••• •▬▬• ▬•▬▬

To Stack's surprise, most of the enlisted men on board were under twenty years old. Many had enlisted to keep from starving, and most of them had never been more than twenty miles from home. It began to dawn on Stack that this journey had a purpose, beyond just getting him to London. The two Bills wanted to expose him as quickly as possible to the realities of war.

Stack befriended a young man named Tony, a fellow Midwesterner. Tony was eager to please, with puppy-dog eyes and a kind face. He was always smiling. Stack joked that it was because he didn't have to worry about a job or food for the next few years, but the truth was, Tony was proud of being in the army.

"Think we'll get torpedoed?" asked Tony as they walked topside.

"Naw," Stack said with a sense of confidence that he didn't feel. "Old timers always try to impress new boys by talking about all the danger they've faced. It's just talk."

"Don't they know that if we go down, they go down?" Ahead, two seamen had just come around the bulkhead. One snickered at Tony's comment.

"There's a couple of newly minted pussies."

"Fuck you," said Tony. Stack stared—he'd never heard Tony say anything so harsh.

The seaman came directly to Tony and stopped in front of him.

"Well, tough guy," said the seaman, "how'd you like to kiss my ass?"

In the blink of an eye, the seaman was flat on his back on the deck, the victim of a lightning-quick left hook from Tony.

Stack sized up the situation. He could probably defuse it right now if he thought quickly.

"How about it, asshole?" Stack said. "Any other comments? No? Well, how about apologizing to the US Army lightweight champion?" He smiled.

"Ahhh, shit," said the sailor, as he staggered to his feet and rejoined his friend. "Sorry. I didn't know."

As soon as they were gone, Tony looked wide-eyed at Stack. "Stack, where in hell did you get that bullshit? I ain't no lightweight champ."

"No, but they think you are, and that might keep you out of trouble. Nice left hook, by the way."

"I'm just left-handed," Tony said. "Back home you could make a little money in fights like that. It ain't like a regular job, but you can get by."

Stack was about to say more—about his own hometown, which probably wasn't that different from Tony's—before he stopped, exhausted. He reminded himself of his top directive for this voyage.

Don't be memorable.

CHAPTER 6

The ship reached Portsmouth soon after dawn under cold gray clouds, in high seas and spitting rain. Disembarking required balance and volunteers to supplement the cargo crew. The navy and marines were put on the job. All the confusion did nothing to heighten Stack's spirits. The dock was like a kicked anthill—everywhere he looked he saw men pushing carts filled with grain, cloth, and other essentials, people scurrying to and fro, running into the carts and each other.

Stack decided he had to get out of the crowd before he was run down, or someone grabbed his suitcase and made off with it. He'd been told that someone would meet him, but he had no idea who or where to make contact.

Figuring he had to start somewhere, he began walking away from the wharf. That got his blood flowing, but not enough to really warm him. If he could find the American embassy in London, surely someone there would have information for him.

But how do I get to London?

"Stack! Milton Stack!" A young man in a black suit and navy-blue top coat was waving his arms, looking toward Stack but not at him. "Here!" Stack waved his own arms overhead. "Here!"

After a few moments, the young man saw him and made his way through the crowd. "Milton Stack?"

"Yes. You from the embassy?"

"Sure am. Jack Kennedy here."

"Glad to meet you."

Kennedy was immaculately dressed and wore a big smile, as if life was dessert and he was looking for a fork. His hair had a bit of a wave that tended to fall down over his forehead. Dressed in the same black suit he'd been wearing for two weeks, Stack felt a wave of embarrassment.

"Where in the hell have you been?" Jack said. "I've been all over the docks looking for you."

"Have you been here a while, then?"

"Of course not," Jack said. "But I do like to get the job done. That makes me your guide, and that makes you my first customer."

"So you're going to charge me?" Stack was having trouble keeping up.

"Hell no!" Jack laughed. "I just know where the good bars are." He looked Stack over. "We need to get you out of that suit—you look like a rat from the docks. And trust me, that isn't the kind of place you want people to think you're from."

"This is my only suit. I've got nothing to wear till it's cleaned."

"Wow! You're a po'bucker, aren't you?"

"What's that?"

"That, my friend, is a poor person. I thought they were sending a lawyer."

"I've only been lawyering for about a year," Stack said.

"Not a Harvard man either, I'll bet."

"No," Stack said. "But I've got good dust on the brain. Which, my learned friend, means I have great understanding of people and their problems."

Jack laughed and slapped Stack on his back as he guided him out of the crowd and toward a black limousine.

"Well, we've got to go shopping, then! Jesus! Look at you." In the car, he tapped the driver's shoulder. "Change of plans, Berkshire. On to Savile Row, first to Frederick Scholte and then the drycleaners. We need this suit cleaned right away."

Stack settled himself in the backseat. “Gee, thanks. I guess I should have been more prepared.”

“Don’t worry. They told me you were a native of downstate Illinois, and that’s all I needed to hear. But Stack, old man, not to worry—I’m going to put you at the lead of the fashion parade,” Jack said.

Don’t be conspicuous. “Are you sure that’s . . .”

“Fredrick Scholte is the most famous designer in London. If you show up in Berlin wearing one of his suits, the Nazi brass will know it. Trust me! We need you to look prosperous.”

··· ·−−· −·−−

When they arrived at Scholte’s shop, Jack had Stack fitted for a sport coat, slacks, and another suit, and picked out some shirts and ties. A gray snap-brim fedora topped off the look. Meanwhile, Jack picked out a jacket for Stack to wear while his suit was being cleaned.

“How do we pay for all this?” Stack whispered to Jack.

“The embassy will take care of it. You’re a very important person to the foreign service—they want you commanding respect.”

During the ride to the US embassy, Stack learned that his brash new friend was a son of the soon-to-be US ambassador to Britain. Jack was younger than Stack, which came as a surprise—he’d struck Stack as older, more worldly. “I’m working on a book,” Jack said. “We should talk about it after dinner. It’ll be part of your European education 101.”

“I hope you know what you’re talking about, because I’m way behind on the subject.”

“Relax, I’ll get you going before I have to go back to the States. And the good old US of A has a heavy contingent of people over here—you'll be in good hands. What d'ya think of a plate of oysters and lunch? I know the best places. Get cleaned up and we'll be off," Jack said.

Stack unpacked, washed the grime off his face, and took a deep breath. He was exhausted and did not want to go out for oysters. But not going would be shortsighted. Back in the embassy car, Jack began to outline the situation in Europe. It was a short ride, so he promised to get into it more at lunch.

"How about a good gin martini, mister farmer?"

Stack agreed, although he knew little about the drinks of the world. Wiltons Restaurant had been open in London for nearly two hundred years and had not lost its popularity. The Victorian motif was stunning to Stack.

"Two dozen oysters on the half shell and two martinis straight up, my man," Jack told the waiter.

"Damn good food and drinks, don't you think?" asked Jack once they'd dug in.

"My first oyster is smashing. But the martini is built with fire," said Stack.

"A true connoisseur." Jack laughed.

"Tell me what your mission is here."

"You tell me yours," said Jack.

"I'll hold back on a firm commitment to disclose all," said Stack.

"Oh hell! Everybody in Europe knows what everyone else is doing," declared Jack.

"Are you still in school?" Stack asked.

"Hell no," said Jack. I'm the advance man for my dad, who will be appointed ambassador soon. He and Roosevelt have it all worked out."

"Okay, I'm confused," said Stack. "I thought this guy Wilson is the new ambassador."

"Well, he is," said Jack. "But he's just keeping the seat warm."

"Oh shit, oh dear," said Stack.

"More drinks," said Jack. "I'll get it all straight for you." The waiter appeared, and Jack promptly ordered two more martinis. Stack's red light came on and he switched to alert/caution mode.

"I'm writing this book on the state of Europe and how vulnerable Europe is to Hitler and the Nazi regime. I'm also am amateur people observer. I look hard where ever I go."

"Sounds exciting," said Stack.

"I guess," said Jack. "But I'm much more focused on my book in hopes that Roosevelt will read it. The truth is that England is running away from every shadow, and everyone is scared to death, which makes them deny Hitler's horrors."

They finished up their drinks and recognized the conversation was going uphill. They prudently rose and moved to the door.

"Thank you for coming in, Mr. Kennedy," said the maître d'.

"Holy cow. I'm too dizzy to walk," said Stack.

"And I need a nap," said Jack.

They went back to the embassy, where Stack attempted to meet the staff, but his mouth was so dry he needed water every fifteen minutes, and he had the worst headache of his life.

••• •▬▬• ▬•▬▬

"I tossed and turned all night," said Stack in reply to Jack, who, bright-eyed, had asked how he slept.

"Don't worry," said Jack. "The real fun is found in German beer, not English martinis."

"Jack, let's go somewhere where we can continue yesterday's conversation," said Stack.

"Yeah," replied Jack. "But first we have to see what Donovan has in store for you. He's the man with the iron balls around here."

Stack spent the rest of the day meeting the embassy staff and settling in. The subject of war almost never came up—everyone seemed to be more concerned with their social status, or standing within the diplomatic corps. He doubted any of these people had ever done so much as one day's hard labor.

Donovan showed up during predinner cocktails. Stack was eager to get some answers; so far, he'd been afraid to ask too many questions. He got the impression that not everyone knew exactly why he was there, and until he heard otherwise, he decided he'd better keep it that way.

Before he could approach Donovan, though, someone called his name.

"Stack! I say, Stack, old fellow, over here." Stack turned and saw an immaculately dressed bearded gentleman standing at the bar. He gave a quick wave, and the man strode over to him.

"So very pleased to meet you, Mr. Stack." The man gave him a wide smile. "I look forward to working with you from time to time. Believe me, we need all hands on deck to handle the crush. Ambassador Dodd is out of town right now, but he'll be back in the next day or two. Perhaps we can get together for a little chat. I wouldn't be out of line if I said that a good many British statesmen don't believe that Hitler can make it across the channel—and that even if he did, we'd turn him right back around."

"Ah . . ."

Suddenly, Jack was at Stack's elbow.

"Sorry about that, Stack, looks like I missed introducing you to some of the staff," Jack said. "This is Gerald Fletcher, the undersecretary to Ambassador Dodd."

"Pleased to meet you, sir," Stack said. "I'm sure Mr. Donovan has a pretty rigorous schedule for me, but I'd love to talk with you and the ambassador as soon as they let me."

Fletcher chuckled. "Too right, my boy, too right! And do let me know if anything comes up that I can help with."

As Fletcher moved back toward the bar, Jack patted Stack's shoulder.

"Donovan wants you to start first thing in the morning," he said. "Orientation, then after that, we'll start on the heavy stuff. But don't worry about all that tonight—come on, it's time for dinner."

When they were seated, the conversation continued, but on more mundane issues, like the weather, the royal family, the latest hits at the theater. Again, Stack didn't hear a word about the current situation with Germany, at least not from the embassy staff. Fletcher was the only one who'd even mentioned it so far.

"How people can live so close to the Nazis and not talk about it?" Stack asked Jack.

Jack put his arm around the top of Stack's chair and leaned into him.

"Denial," he said. "Take my dad, for example. I don't know if he's a Nazi sympathizer or just trying to give big business a reason to rebuff Roosevelt."

"That's a terrible reason to support Hitler," Stack said.

"Let's leave it alone for now." Jack pulled away and stabbed at his plate.

··· ·−−· −·−−

After dinner, Jack, Fletcher, Donovan, and Stack retreated to the drawing room for cigars. The men pulled off their jackets and settled in.

"Fletcher, will you summarize our current situation for the benefit of Mr. Stack?" Jack asked.

"Certainly, Mr. Kennedy. And if, in an attempt to be brief, I overlook a thing or two, please don't hesitate to cut in." Fletcher leaned back into the sofa, cigar in one hand and brandy in the other. "So, as I'm sure you know, the Treaty of Versailles, which ended the Great War, was especially brutal to Germany. As the proudest of the world's nations, their resentment ran quite deep, and inflation was at an all-time high. The German people were primed for a payback. All they needed was a rallying cry and a charismatic leader."

Stack leaned forward. "Hitler?"

"Precisely," Fletcher said. "Churchill's been twisting the American arm, while Chamberlain is stuck in the mud hoping against hope. Over half your lot was strongly against the idea of engaging in another war, in another country. The easiest way for FDR to get elected was to be a noninterventionist."

"Too bad the clearer minds of free Europe and America can't get their heads together to work on a defensive policy," Jack said.

"I suggest you talk to your father about that," Fletcher said.

"Oh, I will," said Jack. "But with Chamberlain believing that Hitler will stop when Germany and Czechoslovakia are reunited, there's little room for logic."

Fletcher continued to outline the situation, and despite his promise of brevity, it was late by the time Donovan finally stood up.

"It's been a busy day, and it'll be an even busier one tomorrow," he said. "I suggest we all get some sleep—especially you, Stack."

••• •▬▬• ▬•▬▬

Rising early, Stack put on his new suit and went downstairs. Since he was staying in Winfield House, the ambassadors' official residence, he was a bit out of the loop on embassy activities.

Best way to get up to speed is dive right in, he thought.

It was a short walk to the embassy proper in Grosvenor Square. The place was alive with activity, and Jack was already up and waiting for him in the library.

"Come on," he said to Stack. "I want to introduce you to a few more people."

"I can barely keep straight the names I've already learned."

"Don't worry. You'll get to know everyone as time goes on."

Stack gave Jack a curious look. "As I understand it, I'll be in Berlin before long."

"Sure, but you'll be in and out of London too," Jack said. "All in good time—first, how about some breakfast?"

"I'll be glad to fix my own."

Jack stared at him, then burst into laughter.

Stack blushed. Once he took a closer look around, he realized the room was full of servants, one of whom Jack flagged down.

"We'd like to be served in the pantry, if you don't mind," said Jack.

"Won't that be a little crowded?" Stack said.

This time there was an embarrassed air as the staff looked away. Jack was now nearly helpless with laughter.

"The pantry is perfect for getting us out of the way," Jack finally managed. "More private. In addition, the full English breakfast is delicious, and I recommend it wholeheartedly."

"Well," Stack said, "I can't pass that up. I'll have it."

Jack nodded at their waiter, and guided Stack into the pantry—now he understood the laughter. It was a whole room, with its own table and chairs, hardly the cramped cabinet he'd been picturing.

They settled in.

"So what do you mean, I'll be spending a lot of time in London?" Stack asked. "That wasn't my understanding. What's changed?"

"Damned if I know," Jack said. "Just a comment I overheard. Donovan should be here in a few minutes; you can ask him."

Shoes clicked on the hardwood floor, and the door opened to reveal Donovan.

"Good morning, gentlemen."

"Bill," Jack said. "Come on in. We're just about to have breakfast."

In short order, a tray of eggs, dry toast, tomatoes, fried mushrooms, black pudding, boiled potatoes and marmalade was delivered to their table. Donovan stuck to coffee.

"Sir, a little bird told me I may be spending a lot more time in London," Stack said. "What's changed?"

"Nothing's set in stone just yet," Donovan said, "but a Polish Nazi agent may be coming over to our side. We don't want to drop two relatively new agents into Berlin at once." He sipped his coffee. "Then again, this may be an opportunity to slip you in under the radar. We'll just have to see."

"No offense, sir, but it all seems a little . . ."

"Seat of the pants?" Jack said.

Donovan glared at Jack, then focused on Stack. "We have intel that says Hitler plans to move on Czechoslovakia and the Rhineland, but nobody in France, Poland, or the Baltic states seems to know anything about it. We need a hell of a lot more information before we act one way or the other. Information and imagination—both are essential in this line of work." Donovan slapped the table and stood. "Come on, time for training exercises."

"Where do we start?" Stack said.

"Language is key, so we'll start with German. At the same time, we'll be teaching you how to work a wireless, codes, and a little more history. Eventually we'll have you memorize photos of the Nazi brass and known agents on the loose in Europe." He smiled. "Then it's time for some of the fun stuff."

"Fun stuff?"

"Parachute jumps, explosives—all sorts of things."

Holy smoke! Stack let out a long, slow breath as he followed Donovan to the front door. "Sir," Stack said. "I thought I'd just be keeping an ear to the ground and an eye on the ambassador's correspondence." He paused, but Donovan didn't slow down, and he was forced to jog to catch up. "I think I'm in a little over my head."

"I didn't pick you for what you know; I picked you for what you could learn." Donovan glanced over his shoulder and met Stack's gaze. "And believe me, you'll learn fast."

••• •▬▬• ▬•▬▬

"Colonel Springer," Donovan said, "meet Stack—your next victim."

Straight as an arrow, Springer stood over six feet tall and had a white moustache drooping across his upper lip.

"Good morning, Colonel," Stack said.

Springer nodded, then looked at Jack, who'd tagged along behind them.

"Mr. Kennedy, I believe someone from the embassy's been looking for you. And don't bother checking back in—Mr. Stack and I will be busy the rest of the day."

"Fine, I can see I'm not wanted," Jack said. He grinned at Stack. "See ya later, victim."

Stack spent the rest of the day with the colonel. Springer ran him through a set of cardio machines in the weight room. He was coached through legs, chest, back, and arm exercises. By the time he got back to the embassy, he was completely exhausted.

"Well?" Donovan asked. "How'd it go?"

"You'll have to ask Colonel Fatigue," Stack said. "I don't have a basis of comparison, but I feel like my brain's been hit by a truck, then it backed up over the rest of me."

"You've got time for a short nap before dinner," Donovan said.

"My brother Joe will be here by then," Jack said as he tipped his hat to Stack. "I think you two are really going to hit it off."

Though he wouldn't be assuming the role of American ambassador to Britain until next year, Joseph Kennedy Sr. had sent some family over early to shape the embassy up—and to control any statements that came out of it in the meantime.

"He's damned hard-headed, though," Jack said. "I wish I could hear what you two have to say to each other."

"Wait," Stack said. "Are you leaving already?"

"Soon," Jack said. "Come on, pal, let's take a look at your new quarters."

Stack had spent the last couple of nights in a previous staffer's room. Now he was shown to a more permanent room: cherrywood floor covered with Oriental rugs, ceilings of well over twelve feet, and a massive king-size bed. He caught his breath as he thought of the family farm and his modest room back in Carthage.

"Is this for me?"

Jack laughed. "Enjoy while you can. Don't forget, your real digs are in Berlin."

A butler appeared, with all of Stack's luggage in tow.

"Dinner will be served in one hour, gentlemen," said the butler. "In the main dining room to the right at the bottom of the stairs." He set the suitcase on the floor and withdrew.

Stack just nodded. That nap was sounding like a great idea.

"See you at dinner," he told Jack. After unpacking, he lay down and slipped into an exhausted sleep.

••• •▬▬• ▬•▬▬

"Where's the new guy?"

Stack was woken by a loud voice from down the hall—not Jack, but the same strange accent. *I still can't believe they talk like that in Boston.*

"You'll meet him at dinner." That was Jack. "I think you'll like him."

"We'll see."

CHAPTER 7

Not fully rested but definitely refreshed, Stack came down for dinner. As he rounded the door and entered the dining room, he was shocked to see just four people seated around the massive table.

"The family's still in the process of moving in," Jack said. "Haven't had time to get rid of this thing. Here, come meet the family—this is my sister Eunice and my brother Joe."

Both smiled and came forward with strong handshakes. Joe and Jack had on dark bespoke suits and white shirts. Stack was glad Jack had pushed him to purchase something similar—he fit right in.

"How are you, Mr. Stack?" Eunice said. She looked young, still in her teens, but she didn't seem at all cowed by this gathering of men.

"Yes, Stack," Joe said. "How are you, and who are you?"

"I'm just an errand boy," Stack said. "I work for Bill Donovan." He smiled at Eunice. "And there's no mister there—it's just Stack."

"And where are you from, Stack?"

"Illinois," he said. "Carthage."

"Well, we Kennedys are Irish," said Joe. "And as I'm sure you've figured out, that's a much more serious ailment."

Eunice laughed and stuck out her tongue at her big brother.

"Hello, everyone." Donovan appeared in the room dressed in a tweed Shetland wool jacket. "I'm sorry to be late."

As everyone grabbed a chair, Stack wondered how in the world they'd communicate—the table was so huge it felt like Jack and Joe were in another room.

Servers in formal clothes brought plates of food, mainly large slabs of beef.

"So, Stack," Eunice said. "What brings you all the way to England?"

"I'm going to Berlin to assist with the transition from Dodd to Wilson."

"And what did you do before that?" Joe asked.

"I've been practicing law in Chicago with Clarence Darrow."

"Seems to me you're a little overqualified to stuff boxes for an ambassador," Joe said.

"We're in a precarious position," Donovan said. "Europe is changing right before our eyes, and we need someone to keep us up-to-date on those changes—culturally, geographically, economically, and politically."

"So what does that mean?" Eunice looked curious. "Are you going to be a spy?"

"Anything said at this table, or in this embassy, for that matter, is highly confidential," Donovan said. "Any leaks could cripple our efforts." There was a long, terse silence. "I suggest we continue this discussion over coffee."

"And cigars," Jack said.

"I'm coming too," said Eunice. "If we have a spy under our roof, I want to know all about him."

Donovan frowned and opened his mouth to speak, but—

"That's our girl," Joe said. "Come on, Stack. We want details."

••• •▬▬• ▬•▬▬

Now in the library and settled in front of the fireplace in a wing chair, Stack was feeling more comfortable.

"You know, Jack," he said, "all your talk about a book had me thinking. Maybe while I'm in Berlin I could keep a journal—nothing top secret, but something I could turn into a book of my own someday."

"Historians often make strong cases for someone or other's bad judgment."

Several memo pads had been placed in the center of the table along with pencils. Each person took one and looked up to see if Donovan was ready. When the coffee was poured and the servants had retreated, Donovan began to speak.

"Information gathering is what we're all about. Several countries in Europe are already doing this, but they're god-awful at it. Most of what we've achieved is by luck. We have a good guess as to where Hitler goes from here, though he's said that the Czechs are German and so are those Rhinelanders, so we expect activity in those arenas. His romance with Stalin is on and off, but Russia will be a big player either way. What we desperately need to know are the details of their armaments, supplies, and production rates. That'll tell us a lot.

"Everyone here is a cleared for classified information. Joe, since you're flying with the Brits, you can be a great source of rumor or, if we're lucky, fact. Same with Jack on the home front. But both of you need to be alert and *think*!"

"We'll do our best," Jack said.

Donovan continued. "Our most valuable asset will be Stack, who, as you've all correctly guessed, will be the ground operator."

"We can't put out hell with a bucket of water," Joe said. "England's been asleep since the end of the Big War. They're consumed with Russia."

"So's Washington," Jack said. "I'm going to tell whoever will listen that the US needs to start making serious plans for war."

"But how do you get folks' attention?" Stack said. "You're not an expert. What makes you think people will listen?"

"It's not hard to influence public opinion," Donovan said. "Jack, if you make any headway there, it could be a real help to us."

It suddenly occurred to Stack that Jack was playing on a much bigger field than he'd realized.

••• •▬▬• ▬•▬▬

The conversation continued for another hour before Donovan told them all to get some sleep. Even though it was getting late, Jack and Stack decided to take a head-clearing walk in the park.

They walked with hands clasped behind their backs. Jack held his hat in his hands, Stack wore his. Both men looked—and felt—pensive.

"You really think you can change people's minds?" Stack said. "Just you on your own?"

Jack smiled slightly. "You worry about Berlin. I'll worry about things back home."

••• •▬▬• ▬•▬▬

The more Stack worked alongside Donovan, the more impressed he was. It seemed as though America's intelligence efforts were fragmented—each branch of the military, the FBI, Department of State, and other outfits ran their own operations, and none of them had any interest in sharing what they found. But Donovan was creative, and humble when he had to be, and as far as Stack could see, he was the only reason they had any intelligence at all.

He was also teaching Stack as much as he could: operations, techniques for opening locks and safes, photographing documents, story fabrication. The man was a master of tradecraft. But the most interesting for Stack were the language lessons.

Stack had an ear for languages, and the US government had a language school in the Manchester region that could turn one fluent in a foreign language quickly. "The language school gave me a sense of confidence that I never had before," Stack reported to Donovan.

"Uh-oh, now it'll be a challenge to keep you from getting too cocky," said Donovan with a chuckle.

As Stack was gathering materials for his German language class, he heard a soft rapping on the door.

"Stack." A soft voice. "Stack, it's Donovan."

Stack opened the door and invited Donovan in. "Have a seat."

Donovan went straight for the chair behind the desk, leaving Stack to sit on the bench before the bedroom fireplace.

"What's up, boss?" Stack said.

"I'm supposed to interview a double agent, someone we're hoping will join our operation." Donovan pressed his fingertips to his temples. "While setting up the meeting, he let it slip that Hitler wants to move on Czechoslovakia immediately. Of course, I'm not sure how reliable this guy is."

"Was that the tall, scraggly looking guy I saw heading into the meeting room earlier?"

"That's the one. Name's Valzic—I think he's Russian, possibly Polish. But I felt shaky about him." He pulled a few papers out of his coat and dropped them on the desk. "I want you to add his face to the stack you're memorizing."

"Will do." Stack picked up the photo and studied it for a moment. "Should I file him under friendly agents, or hostile?"

"Neither," Donovan said. "Not yet."

••• •▬▬• ▬•▬▬

Tension rose as Stack waited for transportation to Berlin. He had been in London three weeks, and the routines were getting stale. The potential double agent Valzic had disappeared, and no one knew where he was now or whose side he was on.

Talks and training continued as snow flurries began to fill the English air.

Donovan dropped a new bulletin on his desk every morning. What few facts they had seemed to shift almost daily, and with them, Stack's perspective. The only consistency seemed to be that things were getting worse.

Stack's stomach turned when he read the brief on German concentration camps. People were being herded from Czechoslovakia to Poland and then had to live on the frontier. Stalin, in a fit of paranoia, had sought out and purged everyone who might be a threat to him—at least two hundred thousand people, mainly scientists, teachers, and key military figures.

"Hey, boss," Stack said, pulling Donovan aside after reading the latest bulletin. "What's going on in Russia? Why are they all turning on each other?"

"Stalin's cleaning house," Donovan said. He looked grim. "Susan Ashton's coming for dinner. You might ask her about it."

"Who's she?"

"She's the one who tipped us on the Hossbach Conference."

"That's the first I've heard about it." Stack frowned. "What is the Hossbach Conference? Anything else you're not telling me?"

"No," said Donovan. "We need to become authorities on Nazi behavior, and that was a pivotal event. Late last year, Hitler stated his willingness to go to war if he was not able to reunite Czechoslovakia and Germany. That is the platform for all relations with Nazi Germany, Look, it'll all be different once we have our own people in Berlin." Donovan smiled, but didn't look particularly cheerful. "In fact, based on what Colonel Springer has told me, you're about as ready as we can make you. As soon as we talk to Susan, I'm planning to send you over."

This is it.

Stack knew there was a world of knowledge out there he wasn't privy to—but soon, he would be. Finally, he could stop relying on scraps of information from Donovan.

Finally, he'd see what was going on for himself.

••• •▬▬• ▬•▬▬

Jack leaned back and put his feet on his desk and his hands behind his head.

"Looks like we're abandoning ship," he said. "You'll be reaching Berlin around the time I'm back in Boston."

The door opened. Donovan entered, stopped, and looked sternly at Jack. Jack promptly yanked his feet off the desk.

"Be glad to be out of the cover of the military," said Jack.

"Let me remind you," Donovan said, "that from here on out, you have no identification, and your best friend here will not express recognition. Be thankful," said Donovan, setting his coat over a chair. "So how're the young firebrands doing? Who's done what to whom?"

"I was just telling Jack that I'll be heading over to Berlin soon."

"We still need to talk about Anton," Jack said.

"I'll tell you over dinner," Donovan said.

••• •▬▬• ▬•▬▬

"This is what you could call classified information, but use extra caution," said Donovan.

They'd just finished dinner. The whole meal had been

awkwardly silent. Susan Ashton had said very little. She looked like a tired but regal woman who knew a great many secrets.

Now, Donovan took the floor, pacing as he spoke. "As you know, the White Russians and the Communists, or Red Russians, haven't had an efficient government since the revolution in 1917. The tsar and his family were killed, but of course they had some relatives who survived. Anton, the operative we've been watching, is some sort of cousin to the tsar. For years, he's been working his way down the Romanian coast doing odd jobs. He was captured by the Nazis, whom he managed to persuade that he was not a Communist. His education and language skills landed him a job with Hermann Göring, who's running the Luftwaffe—which, in violation of the Versailles Treaty, is rearming."

"Better if that treaty had never been written," Ashton said. "The Germans lost vast amounts of land, and with it the raw materials for industry. Anyone who didn't see this coming was a fool." It was the most Ashton had said all evening, but she was not finished. "In any case," she continued, "we're told that Anton has a photographic memory, and has been exposed to all the rearmament efforts of the Nazi war machine, especially air power. We have good reason to believe he's not sympathetic to the Nazis, and we're hoping he agrees to come to London and share his information with us."

"British intel is comical," Donovan said. "They get a report the Nazis are leveling off airplane production, assume the war is off, and then switch strategies. Then they find out production's not leveling off at all, and everybody panics." He huffed. "They need information, and Anton has a head full of it."

"What's the current estimate of ships, foot soldiers, tanks, and planes in Nazi inventory?" Stack asked.

"As far as we know, they've got three thousand planes of all types. They've given a few to client states, such as Italy. But right now, we don't know about anything but aircraft."

"How'd we find out about Anton in the first place?" Stack asked.

"Martha Dodd, the ambassador's daughter. She, by the way, is on romantic terms with Rudolph Diels, the head of the gestapo."

Jack scoffed. "A party girl?"

"Everything she's sent us has been accurate," Donovan said. "According to her, the Nazis' success in moving out the Jews has given them the hubris to attempt the same with all Eastern Europeans, hence our urgency in extracting Anton. We need to get him on our side and send him back with a structured mission—and you," said Donovan to Stack, "are just the cowboy to rope this steer."

Donovan stared out the window for a while. Finally, he turned and faced the two young men.

"Any questions?"

"Why do we need Anton to come back to London?" asked Stack. "How about setting up an information exchange at specific drop-off points and have him bring the info we need? It'd be a lot safer than moving him in and out of Berlin, wouldn't it?"

"Good thought," said Donovan. "I'll bring this up with Stephenson. But let's not get ahead of ourselves. Over the next few days, we'll develop a plan and give you the prerogative to execute it," said Donovan. He fixed his gaze on Stack until the young man shifted in his seat. "There's no official sanction on this. If anybody gets caught, there's no exchange, no negotiation. You'll be disavowed."

There was a brief pause.

"I understand." Stack had a momentary swell of panic but managed to tamp it down. "Jack . . . why don't you stay in England and help me?" He was having that feeling again, the one that had plagued him on his voyage to England—an overwhelming sense of isolation, of loneliness. "With your family connections and knowledge, you would be a real asset."

"No can do, pal," Jack said. "We leave for the States next week, and Dad damn well wants me home."

"I think that's about it," Donovan said. "Stack, I'll have the details for you first thing tomorrow." He nodded to Ashton and Jack. "Anything else?"

As Ashton and Jack stood and made their way out of the dining room, Stack lingered with Donovan.

"Stack, as you will see over and over again, the European spies are renegades from hostile countries and believers in freedom first. The countries that have been under dictatorial rule the longest have the most capable spies. What they don't have is organization and direction. Ashton and Anton are both from that background. We hope to have many more working for us as time goes by."

"Sir?" Stack tried to catch the other man's gaze, but Donovan was staring out the window again. "I understand this is all necessary. You don't have to sell me on that." He frowned, trying to find the right words. "I understand the risks, too. But . . . I don't want to participate in a mission involving needless death."

Donovan turned. For the first time, Stack thought he looked almost . . . disdainful.

"Are you saying you're a conscientious objector?"

"No sir," said Stack, "but I was raised to respect life. Hell, I've never even shot a deer."

"Don't worry," Donovan said. "We're on the same wavelength. While you're in Berlin, you keep a sharp ear open. Some of the tradecraft you've learned won't take hold until you practice it, and you'll get that practice in the field."

"Are you going to be coming over?" Stack was feeling uneasy

again. "You know, to the British Embassy? To coach me or something?"

"I can do that," said Donovan. "But you have to understand, Stack. There are going to be times when you have to make a decision immediately, right there in the field, without me or Jack or Stephenson or anyone else to help you. Are you up to the task?" asked Donovan.

"Yes, sir," said Stack. He was torn with the thought of what Hitler had already done in Germany and Poland. But knowing and accepting were two different things.

CHAPTER 8

February 1938

Berlin was freezing and covered in snow when Stack finally landed. It soaked right through his shoes, and by the time he'd reclaimed his luggage his feet were numb.

Out in front of the airport, he looked around. Someone from the embassy was supposed to be there to meet him.

"Herr Stack?" A man in a Nazi army uniform clicked his heels and half-bowed.

"Yes, I'm Stack."

"Follow me," the soldier said as he picked up Stack's two bags.

It was about a thirty-minute drive from the airport to the American embassy, and his driver was giving a passable travelogue—Stack was already thankful for the German lessons as well as the immersion environment. But why was a Nazi soldier was picking him up at the airport? Maybe it was an exercise in building personnel files on the American embassy staff. Regardless, Stack felt tense the entire ride.

When they arrived at the embassy, the driver opened the door, retrieved Stack's luggage, and set it on the curb. With that, the soldier clicked his heels, saluted, and drove off.

A white-haired man in formal dress emerged from the front door, followed by a stunning young woman in a white skirt with navy checks, and a navy blouse. Her dark brown hair was wrapped in a white head scarf.

"Oh! Mr. Stack!" she said in an excited voice. "Please, let me show you to your room."

Stack nodded. "Thank you very much," he said in German.

The American embassy was a four-story sandstone building located on Bendler Street in the center of the city, about a half of block from the Tiergarten. Once he'd passed through the massive front door, Stack was warmly greeted by another lovely girl with ruby-red lips, a tight wool skirt, and a tighter wool sweater.

She kissed him on both cheeks. "Hi. I'm Martha Dodd, the ambassador's daughter. I'm so glad to finally meet you." She grinned. "You're every bit as handsome as advertised."

She turned on her heels and clapped at the nearby servants.

"Please fetch Mr. Stack's bags and bring them to his room." The girl in the checked skirt stepped forward. "Mr. Stack, my name is Becky, and I'm here to see to your needs." She gave him a wide smile.

"Pleased to meet you," Stack said. "But you can skip the mister. I'm just plain Stack from Chicago."

"Well, plain Stack from Chicago," said Martha, "as soon as you get settled in, we'll give you a tour of the embassy, so you'll know where and who to speak to."

"Thank you, Miss Dodd, that'd be most kind."

"Call me Martha." She tilted her head, still smiling. "On second thought, how about you let Becky show you your room, and if you come right back down, I can give you a tour of the embassy now."

"I'd like that."

... .--. -.--

Upstairs, he took just enough time to splash some water on his face before going back down, where Martha slipped her arm under Stack's and nudged him along on a tour.

"This is the grand ballroom," she said as they swept through a set of double doors into the large open area. "I think it'd be such a thrill to get married here, with all the European nobles jostling each other just to get a view of your dress!"

Before Stack could answer, she tugged him forward.

"Of course, you'd be introduced as you came down the grand staircase, which is here." She swept her arm at the stairs and bobbed a quick curtsy.

"Are you engaged?" asked Stack.

"Silly boy!" She laughed. "But you can bet I'll be ready when the moment comes." She dragged him forward again. "On to the embassy proper!"

Martha showed off every nook and cranny of the grand old building, with the exception of the top-floor apartment.

"That's where the Jewish family who used to own the house lived," she said, breezing by and on to the next attraction.

"No one told me how perfectly luscious you'd be," Martha said, still clinging to his arm. "You'll do very nicely as an escort. In fact, unless you have an objection, I think I'll take full responsibility for your Berlin education. How's that sound?"

"Um . . ." Stack felt like his face was on fire he was blushing so deeply. "If it's okay with the ambassadors, I suppose."

"Wonderful," Martha said. "How would you like to go to a party with me this evening? It's at the Reichstag in honor of the recent marriage of Field Marshal Werner von Bloomburg to Eva Gruhn."

"I don't know if I should go without an invitation . . ."

"Not to worry," she said. "You're invited by me, and that makes everything all right. Besides, everyone's dying to meet you, or they will be. You'll be the hit of the party! And," she said, lowering her voice, "you can meet people tonight that you might not meet in six months on your own." Then, her voice became loud and cheerful again: "As for clothes, a dark suit, tuxedo, or uniform should work. Got anything close?"

He certainly hadn't packed a uniform as he was not in the military. "I might have a suit."

"Well, if you don't, just tell them you arrived ahead of your trunk." She laughed and threw her blond hair back over her shoulder. "See you in the parlor at seven!"

••• •▬▬• ▬•▬▬

Promptly at seven, adrenaline pumping, Stack descended the sweeping staircase. He was wearing the new charcoal suit Jack had gotten him fitted for, and his hair was somewhat tamed by a side part.

Martha was standing across the hall amid a cluster of British and American diplomats, easy to spot in a black-and-red cocktail dress. She was in deep conversation with a young man in a tuxedo. He was smoking a cigarette, carefully blowing smoke away from Martha as she hung on his arm.

Stack took a moment to study her. She was beautiful and she knew it.

She spotted him standing at the foot of the stairs. "Come on, everyone!" Martha raised her voice and clapped her hands. "Time to go. There are cars waiting to take us to the Reichstag."

The party was underway when they arrived. It took Stack a few minutes to get his bearings. He'd never encountered such opulence and tried hard not to look overwhelmed.

"Stack, do come over here," Martha said, waving him over. "I want you to meet one of my dearest friends, Anton Nikoshevki."

Anton. From his file, Stack knew they were the same age, but Anton hardly looked it. He looked sophisticated, and very European: black hair oiled and combed back, and exuding a quiet confidence.

Anton looked at Stack with a bit of a curl to his mouth. He did not offer his hand.

Before he could think the situation through, Stack felt a hand close around his wrist. When he turned, he was looking into the eyes of another lovely lady.

"Let's dance, young man." And with that, she half dragged him onto the floor.

"I saw you come in with that awful tramp, Martha," she said. "I just knew I had to rescue you. You're Stack, is that right?"

"Yes, ma'am." Good grief, so much for keeping a low profile.

"And you are an American?"

He nodded.

"Goodness, a real American right here in my arms. What shall I do with you? I know—sit!" He stumbled back into a chair, and his dance partner planted herself on his lap.

"Don't worry, I won't seduce you—unless Hans says it's okay." She snuggled closer, the warmth and weight of her right breast pressing on his arm. "My name is Greta Oster. My husband is second in command of the Abwehr."

Married—too bad. Greta was a fine-looking woman. But even if she weren't married, Stack's sexual world had never extended beyond Mary Jane—how would he even proceed? Besides, he had responsibilities, commitments. He needed to keep a clear head.

"Thank you for putting up with my poor dancing," he said. "That's very kind of you."

"Nonsense, Mr. Stack. Our husbands are so busy conquering the world that they leave their wives in need of a little company." She smiled. "So far, I think you're an excellent find. Of course, Martha always snatches up the most desirable men, damn her."

The music ended. Greta got up from his lap, gave a slight bow that displayed some wonderful cleavage, blew him a kiss, then turned her back and walked away.

He'd lost track of Anton. Damn it.

Standing just off the dance floor, Stack scanned the crowd until he spotted him, then picked his way back toward his target.

"Anton," he said, "pardon me for getting pulled away so suddenly. I've met so many people in just one day, I don't know how I'll remember all their names. How do you do it?"

"I've been here for a while," Anton said. "It gets easier with the passage of time."

"I'm sure it does."

"Your German is quite good," Anton said. "What is it you do for your Uncle Sam?"

"I'm here to help smooth the transition from Ambassador Dodd to Ambassador Wilson," Stack said.

Anton shot him a sideways look. Anton knew immediately that Stack was a spy. The path was too worn. "You must think me a, how do you say it, a dumbbell?"

"Not at all," Stack said. "Most government employees are slow to action. I'll be the prod, that's all. Thinking on multiple levels is not natural."

"I believe the British airmen would call that 'kicking ass,'" Anton said as he gave Stack a sly smile, then said in perfect English: "I can anticipate that we will be seeing a lot of each other. Now please excuse me, Herr Stack—I promised Martha a dance, and there she is standing with one of Berlin's biggest bores."

Even the German Embassy was not immune to Europe's fuel shortage, and the temperature in the grand hall was kept at a bone-chilling low. It only seemed to stimulate the guests, who became more raucous as the evening passed.

The party to celebrate the Bloomburg wedding was Martha Dodd's natural habitat.

"I think everyone here knows you," Stack said.

"Well, when it comes to society or the military, Berlin is a small town." She gave him a sly smile. "And of course, the fact that everyone knows you're here with me makes it that much more interesting." Then she patted his arm. "If you're feeling bored, though, you're welcome to leave any time."

"Oh . . ." He scanned the crowd. He could learn a lot here, but not if he hung on Martha's elbow all night. "I'd love to stay, but I feel bad keeping you all to myself . . ."

As he debated, Anton reappeared at Martha's other elbow. "Anton!" she leaned into him. "Where have you been?"

"I went to refuel," he said. "Now I'm ready to fly." He gave Stack an amused look. "I would be happy to keep the lady company, if you desire to mingle with the other guests a while."

Stack hesitated.

"Oh, don't you worry about me," Martha said. "I'll be just fine with Anton. Besides, we live in the same house now, Stack." She winked. "I'm sure we'll be seeing a *lot* more of each other."

Now that he was free to roam, Stack wasn't sure where to go. He'd been intrigued by his encounter with Greta, though, so he looked around for another woman with whom he could dance or talk.

He was approached by a tall man with a stiff military bearing. "General Walther von Brauchitsch at your service, Herr Stack!" The general smiled, but his eyes pinned Stack to the floor like a pair of daggers. "Have you only just arrived in Berlin, or have I been missing you for months?"

"It's an honor to meet you, General," Stack said, intentionally stumbling over his German a bit. "Seems like word gets around fast. This is actually my first day in Germany, and everyone seems to know my name already."

"Yes, yes," von Brauchitsch said. "This is a small town in many ways—is that the correct way to say it?" Stack nodded.

"Well then, can I assume that you are an American?"

"Yes, sir."

"And what brings you at this time to the future center of the world?"

"I'm here to help Ambassador Dodd move out and Ambassador Wilson move in. Mostly paperwork. They're giving me room and board."

The general tilted his head. "What is this 'board'?"

"In the US that's slang—it means they provide my bed and my meals."

"And do they provide you with a mistress as well?"

"Ah . . . no." Stack smiled. "I'm afraid I have to make my own arrangements there."

Von Brauchitsch laughed. "Well, be sure to let me know if you need anything while you're here." Another cold smile. "Not an American spy, are you?"

Stack felt his pulse jump, but he kept smiling and shook his head. "No sir, I'm just a country lawyer helping out the ambassadors."

"What country do you lawyer for?"

"Oh, sorry—that's another American expression. It means we don't work in big cities."

"Very interesting. Perhaps we need to have some in our country." With the click of his heels and a brisk "Heil, Hitler!" von Brauchitsch pivoted and marched toward his wife.

Feeling slightly rattled, Stack decided maybe it was time to head home after all. First, though, he had to find Martha.

When he finally spotted her, she was caught up in an animated conversation with several Nazi brass, all of whom seemed to hang on her every word and gesture.

Stack caught her eye and pointed to the door.

"Good night, darling!" Martha called, giving him a little wave and drawing envious stares from several of the other women.

Stack was almost out the door when Anton stepped in front of him.

"Are you returning to the embassy, Herr Stack?"

"I've had a busy day," Stack said. "I'm a little tired."

"I also am tired." Anton said. "May I walk with you?"

"If you like," Stack said.

Outside, Anton moved slowly down the sidewalk, as if it were a summer day. Stack matched his pace, even though his feet were already numb from the cold.

"I must say, I find your situation a bit strange," Anton said. "One would think that a man with a law degree, a citizen of the United States, would be an ambassador himself, not a file clerk. How did you come into such a position?"

Stack was on edge, and unsure of himself. He had to make a decision—should he come clean with Anton now, or feel the man out some more? If he was wrong, the whole operation would crater right here and now, on his first day.

"You're right," Stack said after a while. "It is strange. As for how I got the job . . . like I said, I'm here to help the ambassador. I'm also here to keep an eye on things." He looked squarely at Anton. "It's hard to know which way to go without good information. The clearer the information, the easier it is to make decisions. I'm told you're a man with a lot of information."

"You didn't hold back," Anton said. "I'm surprised."

"What do you think?"

"I may be able to help." Anton lowered his voice. "These Nazis, they're barbarians. What is it you want to know, exactly?"

"Not here," Stack said. "For now, just watch and listen."

"Who is it you represent, then?" Anton asked. "England? Or America?"

"Think of it as a joint operation." Up ahead, Stack could see the lights of the embassy. "Looks like this is my stop. What do you say we meet after breakfast and take a walk in the park? We can talk more then."

"Wonderful," Anton said. "I will meet you at the steps to the Tiergarten at ten."

CHAPTER 9

Stack awakened the next morning to a new blanket of snow that quickly turned black in the heavily trafficked streets. Only the Tiergarten, with little traffic except on the footpaths, maintained its fresh beauty. Stack rushed through breakfast and arrived a few minutes before ten.

"Herr Stack!"

Stack looked around.

"Over here." Anton was standing in front of a rock wall farther down in the Tiergarten, barely visible from the street. Stack waved, and Anton gave a slight salute.

"I think you're a born spy," Stack said. "Keeping a low profile seems like it's a natural impulse for you."

"I could be one of the first to be shipped back to Russia," Anton said. "The last thing I need is to be noticed."

"You mean no one knows who you really are?" asked Stack.

Anton shrugged. "I have a German birth certificate and passport, and I do a lot of critical work for the engineers at Luftwaffe. I haven't done anything to arouse the interest of the Nazis."

"That may change," Stack said. "I know you've suffered at the hands of the Communists, but this is all pretty dangerous stuff. If you're not comfortable with the risk—"

"Do you have any idea how brutal the Nazis are?" Anton asked. "If they found out who I am, they would have me shot in the street and get a medal for it." Anton gave him a sickly smile. "Nothing is safe, Herr Stack. But don't worry—I am still prepared to help. Depending on exactly what it is you need."

"You know," Stack said, "in peaceful times, I think you and I could be good friends."

"I agree," Anton said.

"So call me Stack."

Anton bowed slightly and gave a small smile. "Are Americans always so informal?"

"No," Stack said. "I've been called just Stack for practically all my life. Nobody ever calls me mister—or herr, for that matter."

They turned down a new path. For a little while they only sound was the quiet crunch of their boots in the snow.

"Stack, I have spoken with Americans and Englanders before," Anton said. "They gave me hope. But nothing ever seemed to stick—contact soon fell apart, or became too dangerous to continue. I can get data—but I want to see what you have in mind for getting it out safely."

"That's understandable," Stack said. "The way I see it, the safest way to get the information out might be to get you out—we'd go to London, and you could meet my people."

"You've got to understand," Anton said. "London is a very dangerous place for me. No one must know who I am."

"I'm aware of that," Stack said. "I can promise to keep your identity a secret and your visual exposure limited to nonexistent."

"For now, that's enough," Anton said. "But the Nazis make a lot of noise about the Communists, and right now any Russian is automatically considered a Communist. Now, I am not a member of the Nazi or Communist party. But they can and do arrest people on any charge they can think up, and send them away or execute them. At least I'm not a Jew, and that can be proven."

"I've just arrived," Stack said, "but it looks like you're

in a damn good position."

"In the five years I've been in Berlin, I've never seen so much frantic movement by the military and the diplomatic corps." Anton kicked at the snow as they walked. "It's chaos—we could be shot any day, and the explanation would be that we just disappeared. Before, the Nazis were just another political party, but now . . . they're moving so fast you need to check who's in charge every morning."

Stack looked uneasy. "What do you mean?"

"Bloomburg was just married," Anton said, "and now someone has come forth saying they have seen his wife in pornographic photos. Depending on how seriously Hitler sees this, Bloomburg will be forced to divorce his new wife or be executed. No questions, no defense, no verification. Did you know Hitler just sacked most of his military advisors? He thinks they're unsympathetic to his policies."

"I thought that was just a rumor." Stack stamped his feet to keep them warm. This was the type of information that needed to be in Donovan's hands, soon. "I'm freezing—why don't we head back over to the embassy and talk there?"

"Is it safe?"

"Well, I was up half the night searching my room for bugs," Stack said. At the look on Anton's face, he smiled. "I didn't find anything, don't worry. I think it'll be all right."

••• •▬▬• ▬•▬▬

Back at the embassy, the butler took the two men's topcoats, and Stack led Anton into the grand meeting room.

"You said you'd been in touch with other Americans, other British agents," Stack said. "Do you have a handler? Someone you report to?"

"In Moscow," Anton said. "And I only forward information I receive from other engineers in Europe. Communication backup is the use of cables, wireless, and diplomatic pouches. Any international movement requires a passport and other documents that have to carry Göring's signature."

Stack was wide-eyed. Direct communication with the Kremlin—that was more than he expected. But could he trust Anton? And more importantly, could he trust that Anton's information was sound?

Hell, we won't know until we've run with it.

"I think we can get around the passport," he said, remembering the packet of documents Donovan had given him before he left London. "Not too sure about the signature from Göring, though."

"Who is 'we' exactly? Were you trained in the US?"

Stack took a deep breath. "I'm the furthest thing from trained. I'm a small-time lawyer, raised on a farm. I was asked to help out."

"Help out in what? Stack, look at this from my perspective. All of a sudden you drop in out of nowhere and tell me you want to take me to London. You obviously know who I am, so you must have been following me for some time. Who do you work for? How do I know you won't just put a bullet in my brain?"

"I could have done that in the Tiergarten."

There was a heavy pause. Stack hadn't meant it to come out like that, but strangely, it seemed to reassure Anton.

"Can I at least have a name?" he finally said.

"A man named Donovan. Sound familiar?" When Anton shook his head, Stack continued. "Britain and the US are trying to put together an intelligence organization in Europe." He leaned forward. "We can beat this ball back and forth all day long, Anton, but the only real question here, it seems to me, is whether you'll agree to come back to England and meet with us."

"It's not that simple," Anton said. "I'm working for the Luftwaffe, my sister works in the American embassy, and I talk to the embassy staff almost daily. Why the urgency?"

"Think of this as a joint operation between Britain and the States," Stack said. "We're playing this as if the US is already in the game, and this isn't just about a single mission—we're thinking longer-term than that." Stack frowned. "Wait a minute—you have a sister working here? What's her name?"

Anton grinned. "You met when you first arrived. Becky."

"Damn! What a great spy I turned out to be."

"No one knows we're related. She's also very, very smart and strong under pressure. If I go to London with you, I want her to come as well. It's not safe for her here."

"Why, is she a spy for Russia too?"

Anton went white. "You mustn't say that. No one must know!"

"Easy, your secret's safe with me." Stack lowered his voice. "We can get you out, Anton, you and Becky both. But I need to know you're committed to this. We want you on our team, for the long haul."

Anton stared at the floor for a long moment, then nodded.

"All right," he said. "I agree. But you must get Becky out as well."

"Like I said, there shouldn't be a problem with passports for both you and your sister." Stack hoped to hell he was right about that. "What about work? Won't they notice you're gone?"

"I'll just say I've got to supervise the testing of the new Messerschmitt Bf 109. This usually takes a week. A beautiful reason to miss work." Anton said.

"I'm pretty sure you're more important than you realize," Stack said. "But for now, wait for me here—I'll be right back."

Stack left the room and went directly to the office of the undersecretary, Gerald Fletcher. According to Donovan, all coded messages were to pass through him.

Before Stack even reached the door, it swung quietly open.

"Mr. Fletcher."

The man nodded. "Good to see you again. Come on in."

Stack followed Fletcher into the office, then across the room to a portrait of FDR. Fletcher pulled the painting away from the wall to reveal a safe door. Stack had been told the combination back in London.

"Write your message quickly, leave it with me, and I'll code and send it," Fletcher said. He patted the safe. "We'll keep everything in here until it's ready to go."

Stack scribbled a message and slipped it into the safe. If he was going to extract Anton and Becky, he'd need those passports soon.

He returned to the meeting room.

"I'm starved," he said to Anton. "What do you say we get some lunch?"

Anton and Stack left the embassy and went to a small restaurant near the Tiergarten. There was no more talk of spies or information—they shared casual conversation over a warming lunch. That was fine with Stack, since his mind was racing with all the information Anton had already given him.

As they left the restaurant, Stack said to Anton, "How soon can you be ready to go?"

"I'll let you know by tonight."

"Dinner at Tim Raue?" The moment Stack said it, he had second thoughts. If the Nazis saw him with Anton . . .

It's just dinner—I'm the new guy, after all.

"I've got to make a call," Stack said. "We just passed a park bench—why don't you wait for me there until I'm done?"

He trudged through the black slush. He needed to get Anton

in front of Donovan as soon as possible.

I'm miserable, cold, and out of my element, Stack thought.

Huddled in the phone booth that sat like a snow-covered soldier in the center of the park, he asked the operator to put him through to Donovan in London, reversed the charges, and was eventually able to get through.

As expected, Donovan picked up his own phone. "Hello."

"Stack here."

"How's business?"

"Brisk," Stack said, trying to reassure himself that there was no reason a public phone would possible be bugged. "I have most of what we need to know for phase one."

"Good man!"

"But," Stack said, "I felt I needed to break a rule. I explained our process to Anton. It was very much a spirit-of-the-moment thing. He was right on the edge and I pushed him over. He's ready to join the team."

"Jesus!" screamed Donovan. "We have a thorough process to analyze a potential agent—"

"Don't holler at me, Bill. You're the guy who preaches thinking on your feet. Besides, his sister is over here—I think she might have some useful information for us too. I already sent you the details."

"Well, hell," said Donovan. "Let's get on with it, then. One week from today. Confirm back to me."

"We also need to move on an alternative communication system."

"We've got people on the ground," Donovan replied. "They're working on it now."

"Where the hell are they?"

"Now who's hollering?" said Donovan. "The three of you come on over and we'll see what we've got."

Stack struggled to maintain his composure. "Okay. You square it with the new ambassador, sir, and I'll get them there."

Stack held the phone receiver in a death grip after Donovan hung up.

"Damn it to hell." Stack bit off the words and yanked open the phone booth, nearly hitting a man who happened to be walking past. The man was short, maybe five foot three, with a felt Alpine hat and a smart navy-blue topcoat.

"Excuse me," Stack said in German.

"Certainly," the man replied in perfect English. "Are you quite all right?"

Stack froze. "Please excuse my lack of manners," Stack said. "I'm surprised you speak English."

"And I'm impressed you speak German so well," the stranger replied. "Are you American?"

"Yes," Stack said. "And you?"

"No, I'm not so lucky to have been born in the USA, though I have always wanted to visit there. I'm told it is truly magnificent. And what creativity! A wonderful country to be sure."

"Yes," Stack said, wondering where this was going, "though it's very different from Europe."

"Oh yes, I've seen the pictures!" the man said. "The great plains, the huge rivers, two oceans, wonderful lakes. It makes this bitter cold seem awful in comparison. Will you walk with me, sir? I would enjoy your conversation."

Stack glanced back up the path, toward the bench. Anton was now walking toward them. But even though his feet were frozen and he felt a cold coming on, Stack's instincts were on full alert. There was something odd about this man.

"I'd be very pleased to walk with you. Just give me a moment to speak with my friend and let him know I'm leaving."

"Ah yes, I see that cold gentleman."

Stack stepped over to Anton.

"My instincts tell me this guy could be important to us," he whispered. "You go on home. I'll see you at dinner."

Anton nodded, turned, and walked away.

"I hope you didn't send him away on my account," said the little man when Stack returned.

"No," Stack lied. "I have a meeting in thirty minutes and I'll see him there."

"May I know your name, sir?" The smaller man wasn't quite smiling, but there was a sense of humor riding just below the surface.

"Milton Stack from Chicago, Illinois. But you can just call me Stack."

"Wonderful!" said the man. "You are certainly easy to know in more ways than one. My name is Eric Wilhelm. Would you care for a spot of tea or coffee? There's a café just around the corner. I highly recommend it."

"I'm at your mercy, Mr. Wilhelm," Stack said. "Just as long as I make my meeting."

The two men entered the café and sat at a small table in the rear, just past the bar. The Tiergarten was only a half block away, and children laughed and screamed as they ran toward the park with sleds.

"Tell me, Mr. Wilhelm, what is it that you do for a living?" Stack asked.

"I work for the government."

"That must be very interesting. In what capacity?"

"Security," Wilhelm said. "And you, Stack, what service do you supply?"

"To my government?"

"That's very humorous. No, since the United States has refused to become involved in events here, I doubt you do anything that would interest the Führer," Wilhelm said.

"I'm sorry, said Stack. "I hope I didn't offend you."

"No, I find you quite refreshing."

"Well, to clear the air, I do work for the US government, but in a very low capacity. I'm a lawyer with an interest in European history. As you probably know, our Department of State is changing Ambassadors, and I'm here to help with that transition."

"I see," said Wilhelm. He suddenly stood. "Well, Stack, it may be better that we part now. I have noticed you trying to warm your feet; they must be aching from the snow. I am at the Reich Chancellery, if you would like to have coffee another time." Reaching into the breast pocket of the suit jacket he was wearing under his topcoat, Wilhelm pulled out a letter-sized folded piece of paper that he handed to Stack. "I look forward to visiting with you again, and soon."

Touching his Alpine hat with a modified salute, Wilhelm turned and made his way through the café.

Stack let Wilhelm get to the door of the café before he looked at the paper he'd been handed.

The letter was a word-for-word record of Stack's telephone conversation with Donovan, seconds or so before he had bumped into Wilhelm.

Stack felt a chill that went beyond his wet coat and hat. He had no idea who Wilhelm was or how he'd spotted Stack so quickly. He was a very dangerous man, of that Stack was sure.

CHAPTER 10

"Damn," Stack muttered to no one in particular. "The temperature must have dropped thirty degrees in the last hour."

He'd sent Anton and Becky on to London, but he'd stayed in Berlin to try to get to the bottom of the mysterious meeting with Wilhelm. He needed to talk to Donovan. This time however, he used the phone in Fletcher's office.

"Eric Wilhelm?" Donovan said. "I've never heard that name before."

"He said he was attached to the Reich Chancellery."

"Well," replied Donovan, "from your description of him, I'd say you've made yourself known in record time."

"What do you mean?" Stack asked.

"Ah, I believe you made friends with Wilhelm Canaris himself. The head of the Abwehr—Nazi intelligence."

Stack swallowed.

"I'd like to bring your visibility down a notch," Donovan said. "Get your ass over here and we'll work it out. I assume you got Becky and Anton out okay?"

"Not a hitch," Stack said. "There were just too many people leaving Berlin for the gatekeepers to be thorough with every passport."

"What do you make of your meeting with Canaris?"

"Are you sure it *was* Canaris?"

"Of course, I'm sure," said Donovan in his most confident tone.

"Look, that meeting wasn't accidental. But it doesn't make much difference. They showed us what they can do, and they verified that an intelligence operation has opened up in Berlin. Canaris is among the best and most disciplined. My guess is he's playing for time, trying to figure out where we fit in and if we're going to be a problem for them."

"What action do you think the Abwehr will take?" asked Stack.

"Could go either way," said Donovan. "They also have double agents. That's a game we need to play."

"How do we get in the game?" Stack asked.

"I'd guess we already are, considering the way you were approached. British field agents have been hearing rumors that Canaris might have been involved in a plot to kill Hitler. That's really good news."

"So . . ." Stack tried to put it all together. "Him reaching out to me may confirm those rumors. He may not be a true Nazi."

"Right, my boy," said Donovan. "But why was Canaris making personal contact, against all rules of tradecraft?"

"Sounds like you're changing your mind about my role," Stack said.

"I am," said Donovan. "You've proven to be much more effective than I'd anticipated. I think you can run a whole group, once we get it organized. What do you think of you, Anton, Becky, and two or three communications guys from the British? Then we can add as we find obvious candidates."

"Sounds smart," Stack said.

··· ·−−· −·−−

His new role in the operation, along with Donovan's strongly worded directive, made it essential for Stack to travel back to London so he could assemble his group and formulate a game plan. But it wasn't long before Stack and Anton were able to fly directly back to Berlin, again using the fake passports. They arrived back in Berlin just in time for Stack to receive the full blast of Martha Dodd's temper.

"What in the hell have you done with my maid? She's nowhere to be found, and the staff said she was last with you. Answer me—what have you done with her?"

"Martha, she's okay!" Stack glanced at Anton—he hadn't thought about what to tell her. "She's fine, she's just . . ."

"She ran off with an Argentinean who owns a leather shop in Hamburg, and maintains an apartment in Berlin," Anton said. "I have discussed the dangers with her, but one cannot hope to control young love. Don't worry, she'll be back in three or four days, weeping about a love affair on the rocks. She can't go for a week without a lover."

"I'm sure you can get someone to cover for her?" Stack said. "Just for a few days?"

"Of course I can, but it's a pain in the ass." Martha planted her hands on her hips. "Stack, do you have a girlfriend?"

"No," Stack said, wanting to keep his relationship with Mary Jane to himself.

"You're not any help." She threw up her hands. "Someone get Fletcher to get a maid for me, pronto!"

"Let me ask you a question, Martha," Anton said. "Now that Ambassador Wilson is taking over, are you planning to go back to America?"

"Oh, I'm staying here. I'm having too much fun to leave."

"What if there's a war?"

"There isn't going to be any war. But if there is, then it depends on who's fighting whom."

"So, if some Polish prince were to show up and sweep you off your feet, you'd be a Pole by sunset?"

"I'm having a damn good time and not hurting anyone," Martha said. "What about you? Are you going to hang around Berlin now that Wilson is in?"

"That's my job," Stack said. "You do realize if you stay here, you could be shot?"

"I'm not stupid, fella." Martha frowned at him. "Why do you think I've cultivated so many relationships with powerful people in the Communist *and* Nazi sectors?" she said.

"No Americans, though?" said Anton.

Then she gave him a smug smile. "Don't you worry about me, Stack. I have an ace in the hole that can't be matched by the likes of you and Anton."

"What's that?"

"I have a lovely warm spot in my pants that has control written all over it." She looked hard at Stack.

"Could spell slavery if the wrong guys get control," Stack said.

Martha rolled her eyes. "Look, Stack, I know you're up to something, something more than just helping out. The ambassador's already asked Daddy if he had to keep you on staff after we leave. What should I tell them?"

Stack felt real anger. "You scare the hell out of me, Martha. You know what's going on, but as long as you're not threatened you don't seem to give a damn—and you've got no loyalty that I can see." He let out a long, hard breath. "Just do me a favor and let me know if you see anything dangerous going on, okay?"

Martha's face softened somewhat. "I have noticed the whirlwind of movement among the military. But you're right—that doesn't affect me. We don't mix with the herd. We live with the beautiful people."

"You're a real peach," Stack said with disgust. "Just steer clear of me, all right?"

"You little punk!" Martha hissed. "My boyfriends could throw you out the window with one hand."

The phone rang, ending their conversation. It was Ambassador Wilson calling for Stack.

Stack covered the mouthpiece and spoke in a low voice to Anton. "Call me in the morning?"

Anton nodded, then left.

••• •▬▬• ▬•▬▬

The moment Stack entered the ambassador's office, he was handed a stack of papers.

"What's this, sir?"

"It's a copy of the Nazi Case Green memorandum, which has kept Hitler from invading Czechoslovakia."

Stack stared. "How did you get this?"

"Martha. They thought she and her boyfriend, the Nazi field marshal, were out of town, so they left it on his desk. Martha has security clearance, so she went in and got it."

"My God." Stack thought of everything he'd just said to Martha. What courage . . . maybe he'd been wrong about her.

"Note that the memo is signed by all the major Nazi generals," said Ambassador Wilson.

"Sir . . ." Stack scanned the memo. "Do I understand from this that the Nazi plan to invade Czechoslovakia was tabled by a unanimous vote of the Nazi generals?"

"They finally understood they couldn't win a war, at least not now." He settled back into his chair and peered at Stack. "What's next?"

"I think we need to contact Donovan," Stack said.

"I certainly think so, if he's the man running this operation," said Ambassador Wilson.

"May I use your phone?"

Wilson nodded, and Stack dialed. He quickly brought Donovan up to speed.

"Is Martha manageable?" was Donovan's first question.

"Well, she got us the memo," Stack said, glancing at Wilson. "At personal risk, which I didn't think she was capable of."

"Well, that's not any reason to trust her," Donovan said. "We need to know how volatile she really is. I'm coming to Berlin immediately, so let's keep her as an ally till then—we really don't want her to be an enemy. We just have to evaluate the situation."

"See you then."

Stack hung up and turned to the ambassador. "Remember that our goal is to get as much information as possible on the Nazi progress in war preparation. Planes, ships, trains, and fuel."

"I can't believe things will go that far," said Wilson.

"Believe it, sir. I'm afraid that most countries are ill-prepared to face a mobilized Hitler, including England and America."

"It seems to me America doesn't want any part of another land war, even to save our first cousins," said Wilson.

Pressure from both sides of his head was exhausting Stack. Another cold walk might clear his head or help him figure out what Canaris was thinking.

"If it's all right, sir, I think I might step out for a while."

"Be my guest," Wilson said. "You don't answer to me, do you?"

••• •▬▬• ▬•▬▬

Stack realized he was too tired to even brave the cold, so instead of taking a walk, he went to his room and lay down, exhausted. But sleep was elusive. He carried a weight that sat on his chest and kept him staring out the window at the raw, gray day. His mind was swimming. *How did I become a leader instead of a follower?*

Stack realized how deeply he missed his parents—especially his mother, who would have told him to get up, take one day at a time, and to do the right thing. She also would have told him to fight for justice and to love others.

Thinking of love brought Mary Jane to mind. He missed her terribly, but he'd barely had time to think about her. Did he love her? Hell, yes. But she was so far away, and if he lost his focus here for even a moment, something awful could happen. He forced her to the back of his mind once more.

Stack finally drifted off to sleep.

He rolled over and woke at six the next morning. His nervous energy hadn't diminished, but he was rested. The gloomy weather matched his mood.

He sat at his desk and wrote Mary Jane. He tried to give her an understanding of what he was doing but doubted it would pass the censors. His guilt somewhat alleviated, he tried to focus on the day's challenges.

The success of the whole operation depended on Stack getting another face-to-face with Canaris. Another conversation with him would give Stack an opportunity to feel Canaris out about the Nazi party and Hitler—assuming Canaris would discuss these things with a young American.

Well, he'd run into Canaris in the Tiergarten once. Maybe that would work a second time.

Out in the open air, he felt better. He kept to the path's edge, leaving his footprints in the day-old snow as he used to do when he was a young boy.

"Good morning, young man. Do you remember me?"

Startled, Stack almost fell into the snow as he quickly turned to see Canaris.

"Of course," Stack said. He recovered his composure. "However, the last time we met you didn't have a military uniform on."

Canaris smiled. “I have been in the service all my adult life. Have you provided such service?”

“I’m afraid not. I was born too late to fight in the Great War, and we don’t have a tradition of military service in America.”

“Are you terribly busy?” Canaris said.

“Not at all.”

“Then come, walk with me a while.”

They walked slowly, looking at the fallen leaves in the snow. Stack’s stomach was tight as a drum, but he felt capable. Whatever Canaris had in mind, Stack hoped he was up to it.

“Tell me, Mr. Stack, do you have children?”

“No, I’m not married.”

“That may be a blessing. The danger in these times is beyond comprehension,” said Canaris.

“As we say in America, things are certainly hopping in Europe,” Stack said.

“Yes! Not just ‘hopping,’ but deadly. You must have heard that Hitler changed his mind about moving on Czechoslovakia.”

“I don’t know much about German politics,” Stack said, trying not to think of the memo Ambassador Wilson had shown him, “but wouldn’t that be a decision for the general staff?”

“Would you like a coffee, Mr. Stack?” Canaris smiled as his put his hand on Stack’s elbow.

“Yes, that would be good.” Stack managed to return the smile.

“Come with me to my office,” said Canaris. “It’s warm . . . and close by.”

The heat from the first-floor office hit them in the face like a warm blanket when Canaris opened the door. Stack walked in first, even though being followed by Canaris made him nervous.

In I go. This is the job.

On his way in, he nearly bumped into a tall man with no uniform, only a long coat and a scruffy beard.

"Sorry," he said, but the man was already gone. "Who was that?" he asked Canaris.

"His name is Valzic," Canaris said. "He's our special projects man."

"What does that mean?" asked Stack.

Canaris's eyes were cold gray. "He kills people."

In the office, both men chose chairs that gave them a view to the door and the windows. They removed their great coats and sat angled toward each other. Canaris picked up the phone and ordered coffee.

He looked at Stack with a friendly smile, but a sharp eye. In a full Nazi uniform, Canaris looked sinister, even at his diminutive height.

"You remind me of Alan Ladd," Stack said, hoping to break the tension. "He's an American actor."

"Very flattering, for sure. I'm a great lover of American films, and Alan Ladd and I are about the same height." Canaris smiled. "How do you like Berlin so far, Herr Stack?"

Stack smiled back. "I like it, but I've seen very little."

"Well, Mr. Stack, you certainly impressed one member of the Nazi general staff."

"Who's that?"

"General von Brauchitsch, who is due to become commander-in-chief of the German Army. I believe you met him recently."

Stack was shaken, but held tightly to his composure. "Oh yes. We spoke briefly at the party for the newlyweds, the day I arrived in Berlin."

"The general was also very curious about you. It seems he can't get comfortable with the idea of a smart young American coming to Berlin to accept such a menial job at this time. Frankly, he suspects you of being a spy."

"Good lord!" Stack said, forcing out a laugh. "How did he ever come up with that idea?"

Canaris took a cigarette from a gold holder, tapped it twice on the table, lit, and inhaled.

"You will have an opportunity to disabuse him of that idea," he said. "The general's army is quite different from the Abwehr or the SS, but we all work together for the good of the whole. And now the general has a suspicion, which I share. I think it's time to clear it up."

"I agree," Stack said. "And I promise it's not complicated. Folks just thought that to send a senior officer over here would have ignited rumors about America's intentions regarding entry into any European war. So they sent me instead."

"It sounds credible," said Canaris. "But it is an act of negligence to allow an inexperienced young man to exist in Berlin in these days."

"Well," Stack said, "too late to do much about that. What do you do, Wilhelm? Where do you fit in?"

"I am in charge of Abwehr, the intelligence arm of the Third Reich."

"No wonder you're so curious about me." It was warm in the office, and Stack felt overdressed. "I hope my explanation satisfied you. Because I don't want to be the subject of interest to the Abwehr. And I want to get out of here as soon as I can before any war starts."

"Ah yes . . . the war," said Canaris. "Tell me, Stack, how do you see the situation now?"

Stack said with a quizzical look, "Me? I really don't know."

Canaris leaned forward and lowered his voice. "As much as I love my country, I think Hitler is unstable. The danger to human life is huge. What can be done to prevent this?" Then he leaned back. "Stack, do you know a man named Donovan?"

"Yes, somewhat. Do you?"

"Only by reputation and intercepts of messages, like your call from the Tiergarten. I would very much like to speak with him directly, and you clearly have a line of communication."

My God! "Well, I might be able to arrange that. But first you need to understand the American view," Stack said. "An element in the US is against war because it seems so far away. When they start to read about the realities, the decimated cities, people in chains, they will react like a hive of hot hornets."

"So you are saying that if the reality of Europe and Hitler becomes an emotional feeling, Americans might be motivated to enter the war?"

"That's my thinking," Stack said.

"That is something to think about."

"Wilhelm, what are you doing?" Stack leaned into the table. "Trying to make me comfortable because we believe the same things? You can't want the US in this."

Canaris crossed his legs and leaned back. "My friend, you are quite young and new at this. I am old, and experienced. Your keen observation would, most of the time, be on target. But today, mad men are running things, and there is no greater good to be achieved by their rule. It is going to take an imposing power to stop the fascists. We don't need war. Russia will be fighting us before long, and the carnage will rupture the world. The people will feel better about themselves if we take on the big, old countries—they want to forget the humiliation of the Great War. But living after *this* war will be horrible. The music will stop. The beer in the halls will not flow. There will be no jobs, and even if there were, we will have no more young men to fill them."

Canaris paused to take a deep breath then continued. "We can't change thinking, but we can alter events. And you, my young friend, can play a key role." He paused. "You find it strange that I should be talking this way? When you know me better, you will come to understand that I have a deep love for my country. But I and some others think Hitler will destroy Germany, and perhaps Europe as well. Never have I seen or known such a man. He acts on a whim, refusing any information that is contrary to what he wants to hear or believe. But if he is stopped . . . how well do you know Bill Donovan?"

"You already asked me that."

"I asked if you knew him. Now I ask you this: are you working for him?"

One wrong move and he could be expendable. But Canaris already knew—he'd heard them on the phone. So, was this a test of his honesty, or something else?

"Yes."

Canaris took a sheet of paper and began to write. After writing, he folded the paper and gave it to Stack, who read it.

We can work together to stop a war and Hitler.

Stack nodded, rose, and began to pull his topcoat over his shoulders. The suddenness seemed to disorient Canaris, who rose quickly and hurried to catch up as he followed Stack back into the hallway, out the door, and onto the narrow cobblestone streets.

Stack finally turned to Canaris. "Why aren't you worried about my turning you in as a traitor?"

"No one would believe you, Mr. Stack. No one in the Nazi family would even know who you are. That's one reason you are perfect for our plans." He beamed. "Consider our conversation, and I will be in touch."

The small, erect Nazi officer turned to walk away.

"Wilhelm," Stack called after him. "Was your office bugged?"

Canaris walked on as if he hadn't heard the question.

Stack was beset with a bag of emotions, not least fear. Stepping farther into the cold, he started across the Tiergarten on one of the winding walking paths.

CHAPTER 11

Stack returned to London in May of 1938. He was elated to have received a letter from Mary Jane, though she sadly reported that her uncle had died in March.

How painful for her and her family, and how lonesome she must be. He felt a profound loss over his mentor, and a need to be with Mary Jane. She made no mention of his letters, probably because they hadn't yet reached her—her own letters had taken two months to reach him. He thought about writing another, but if she hadn't even received what he'd already sent, what was the point?

••• •▬▬• ▬•▬▬

He met Donovan and the rest of the team in a brownstone not far from 10 Downing Street. Donovan sat at the head of the table in a white ribbed turtleneck sweater with a shoulder holster and pistol strapped to his chest. Becky, Anton, and Ashton filed in shortly after.

Tension filled the room, but after everything he'd been through in Berlin, Stack felt strangely relaxed. He had several plans bubbling in his head and was eager to get to them.

As Becky and Anton pulled themselves up to the large conference table, two men arrived, one in a British Army uniform and one in an American GI uniform. Both had hair slicked back from the forehead, and were clean-shaven and alert. "Everyone, please welcome our technical team members," Donovan said. He gestured to the man in the US uniform. "This is Lieutenant Charles Graham, our chief technical officer. He's a Yale man."

Donovan turned to the other man. "And next to him is Lieutenant James Smathers, our communications officer. He's a graduate student at Oxford. Before that, he was an engineering student at MIT. Ashton will work cheek by jowl with them, but these boys will be in and out of our meetings as needed."

"Do you feel comfortable with that?" Stack asked Ashton. "I know you aren't used to working with a structured backup."

"I'll just be doing what I always do—gathering information and giving it a proper person," she said. "Are you comfortable with that, Stack?"

"Absolutely," Stack said. "Hell, I'm thankful for it." Then he turned to Donovan. "You wanted us here, so here we are. What now?"

Just then a man in a white jacket entered with a tray of coffee, tea, and cakes.

"All right everyone, drink up and let's make hay." Donovan gave them a minute to serve themselves, then got down to business. "Now, we need to concentrate on the most immediate problems. Code breaking is coming along nicely. But remember, we're not at war yet—we need to move carefully. We want to prevent incidents, not cause them."

At that moment the door opened, and a short balding man with his hands behind his back and a cigar between his teeth entered the room. Stack would have known him anywhere—as did the others, all of whom stood along with Stack.

"Sit, sit, please," said Winston Churchill. Churchill had given up his role in government to speak out about the dangers of the government in Germany and was beginning to fill the void when Chamberlain's tactics were not working. He stood behind the chair at the head of the table, leaning on its back. "I assume you've been discussing the wonderful start of Operation Inquire, for which I and everyone in Britain thank you." He paused, taking a few moments to lock eyes briefly with everyone at the table. "I understand we've already been able to make a contact or two in the German high command. These relationships will run their course fairly quickly unless they are supported by more and stronger relationships. So we must take advantage of as much as possible as quickly as we can. Something about early birds and worms and such." Churchill laughed, and Stack watched everyone around the table relax slightly.

"But back to the abominable Hitler," Churchill continued. "He's so terribly unpredictable that we need all eyes possible on his movements. Last month, as you recall, after giving all of us assurances that he would leave Austria alone, he unleashed his Anschluss, annexing Austria and condemning two hundred thousand Jews to prison and death. Do we want to live under this man? It is unthinkable, but possible." Once more, he paused, looking everyone in the eye. "I am extremely proud of all of you here. I have supreme confidence that this war is coming to us, and we can and will win it because of people like you, who love freedom. When you have finished for the day, pop over for a drink to seal the deal." He winked at Stack. "Sort of an American expression, what?" He turned to Donovan. "Oh—and we shall require copies of all reports that originate with you and your team members." Clasping his hands once more behind his back, he nodded to the group. "Until next time."

As he left, Stack took another look around the table. *God, what a man!* He saw pride and confidence where the mood had been so tense and uncertain just moments before.

Take life one step at a time.

"Well," said Donovan, "I guess we have a mandate, as well as an open door to the supply room, so we better get going. Ashton, anything to add?"

"My lord," she said. "I can't believe I was just sitting in a meeting with Winston Churchill. . . . I'm at a loss for words."

"Well, you can tune up over the next couple of weeks," said Donovan. "I have to agree with Mr. Churchill: our initial contact with Canaris looks very promising. He's all but asked us to partner with him. Plus, we finally have some solid intelligence on the military side of things." He nodded at Anton. "Why don't you fill everyone in?"

Anton cleared his throat. "Hitler does not have the firepower to back up his rhetoric. The Nazis are short on oil, and their efforts at creating a synthetic fuel haven't yielded the results they'd need to meet their goals. Air power has also been overestimated. But we need to know where they stand and what plans they have, so we can evaluate Hitler's next possible moves."

"That's where you come in." Donovan pointed at Stack. "If Canaris makes a solid overture, he can get information to us that may give us an edge, and that will go a long way to turning the tide of opinion back home." He frowned. "This may boil down to a double-agent situation. Be prepared! Anton, what's the Luftwaffe planning to do about their oil shortage?"

Stack looked forward, lips compressed. He didn't like the sound of being a double agent.

"They may plan to capture oil from countries they invade. If so, it'll make war with Russia prohibitive."

"Here's how we organize," said Donovan. "I'll be back and forth between here and the States. Long term, if worse comes to worst, we'll also be operating in the Balkans, and Scandinavia. That won't be our focus, but any of you may be asked at any time to assist with an op in one of these theaters."

Donovan stood up and paced at the head of the table, running a finger under the collar of his sweater.

"In my absence, Tar Robertson of the British Operation l Cooperative will be in charge. While you're in the field, your touch base will be Ashton. A good number of British agents are already out there, and some of them are double agents. It will be your responsibility to learn what we know about each of them." He nodded at Anton and Becky. "You two will go through more language and espionage training."

"That shouldn't be a problem," Anton said. "I already speak French, Polish, and some of the Balkan languages, as well as German."

"Anton," Stack said. "You were fearful of going in and out of Berlin. Is that still a problem? Can you still work at the Luftwaffe manufacturing facility?"

"Absolutely. They're so short of engineers right now that they can't keep up with demand," Anton said. "Eventually I will receive an assignment of importance."

"Until then, let's move on," said Donovan. "Stack, that puts you back in the file room of the American embassy in Berlin. Keep out of sight." He laughed. "You'll have to work out a way to meet and to communicate with Anton that won't draw attention. Do all the normal things that would bore anyone who's watching."

"I think I'm okay if I keep a low profile at the plant," Anton said. "Germans expect young people to party at night. So I can go places, see people without necessarily being seen. What about Stack?"

"It all depends on how his romance with Canaris progresses," said Donovan. "We'll see soon, I wager."

Stack felt as if Donovan was hanging him out as bait.

Becky spoke for the first time. "I think I can be of help. I also speak Russian and French, as well as German. I get a lot of calls from girls I know, looking for work. I can pick up loose conversation, documents, that sort of thing."

Donovan shook his head. "I've already got plans for you. You'll coordinate the communications and intelligence effort right here."

Becky frowned, but Anton kept his eyes on the table. Stack wondered if he'd suggested this to Donovan.

"Thank you, General," Becky said after a long pause. "I have been in the middle of the upheavals in Europe before. I think I can serve your efforts well and bring perspective to our operation."

"That I'm sure of," Donovan said. "With you here and Anton in the field, we'll have a stronger team than any currently in operation."

"Boss, I can see you're in a hell of a hurry to get this operation off the ground," Stack said. "But I hope we're ready both on our own and as a team."

"Thanks for the caution flag," Donovan said. "But I have complete confidence in all of you."

Stack smiled as he and the others watched Donovan's excitement grow.

"I think it best to move one at a time," Donovan said. "I'll go first and take the Lisbon route, since I have a diplomatic passport. Anton has a German passport, so he can go straight to Berlin. We can meet in the embassy there."

••• •■■• ■•■■

Travel was becoming more and more difficult. The route from Lisbon to Berlin and London was still safe, but little else. Lisbon was the most open city in Europe, and most of the world's diplomatic corps and espionage agents traveled through it.

A fat, mustachioed Portuguese customs officer studied Stack's passport. The passport was British, but his country of origin was listed as the United States. Someone putting the paperwork together had been sloppy.

"What makes an American come to Lisbon in such terrible international weather?"

"The world of business must go on," Stack said.

"Ah, so what is this very important business?"

"We export potassium and other chemicals for customers in Switzerland, Spain, and other countries."

"Do these chemicals go 'boom'?" the officer asked in a loud voice.

Stack looked and the officer and said softly, "No."

"Senhor, I must check something before I can allow you to proceed." He pointed to an outdoor café. "Maybe have some coffee or some American whiskey over there. Please be so kind as to not leave."

With that, the customs officer bowed, saluted, and left.

Stack sat at an outdoor table and sipped a cup of dark Lisbon coffee, growing more and more tense as time went by. Thirty minutes, an hour, two hours passed—he'd definitely missed his flight, and if he didn't leave soon, he'd miss the whole team reconnoitering at the embassy.

Finally, the customs officer returned.

"So sorry for the delay, senhor. I had to wait while the officer in charge contacted England. Have you missed your plane?"

"Yes, I have," Stack said.

"So sorry, so sorry. But there are excellent accommodations at the hotel adjacent to this building. Shall I arrange a room?"

"Yes," Stack snapped.

Despite his girth, the officer pivoted smoothly and was soon out the door.

"Do you require another coffee, senhor?" the fat man asked

upon returning. Without waiting for an answer, he went to the bar and returned with a fresh cup of coffee. Bending to set the cup and saucer on the table, he dropped a small piece of paper.

Discreetly, Stack picked it up.

Rt from café. Bar at first corner. Turn in. Go out rear.

Stack followed the instructions, and once behind the corner bar, he looked around.

A blanket was thrown over his head. He was shoved into the backseat of a car, where someone held a hand on the back of his neck, doubling him over.

"Stay down!" A voice said from the front seat, speaking German.

"What the hell is going on?" Stack screamed.

"Relax, asshole," said the man in the front seat. "We're on your side."

"So, who the hell are you?"

"Do you have a pistol?" asked the front-seat voice.

"No."

"Better get one. You know, fifty pounds to the bartender would have gotten you out fast enough to catch your plane. Everything is for sale in Lisbon." The voice chuckled. "You'll learn."

Stack wanted to scream and kick, but there didn't seem to be much point—no one would hear him, and for all he knew, they had a gun pointed at his head right now.

They drove for an hour. He felt the car darting in and out of small streets, until they broke into a clear stretch where the bumpy road smoothed out. When they came to a stop, Stack was dragged out and the blanket was removed. He was standing on the tarmac at an airport, with one twin engine plane on the runway.

The man who had removed the blanket grabbed his arm and pulled him toward the plane.

"I say, ol' chap. You certainly make it difficult to sleep." A man in an army uniform, speaking English, bent to offer Stack a hand aboard.

"What's this all about?" Stack asked.

"Look, pal," said another man. "We saved your life. Word came down that you were a VIP and we should activate our rescue mission. Remember us when you're in Southern France or Portugal."

"Let's make a dash for it," the first man said. Turning to face Stack, he smiled. "We like to keep things dramatic. Helps in recruiting. By golly, you must be an important bloke to get the main office all excited."

"Guess so," Stack said. He was just relieved that he was being taken out of Lisbon.

••• •▬▬• ▬•▬▬

Back in Berlin, Stack resumed to his walks in the Tiergarten as bait to draw Canaris out. Anton stayed in London for two more weeks to spend time with his mother and sister.

In the early days of June 1938, Stack had received two more letters from Mary Jane. She missed him terribly, and wished he'd find time to write. She sounded despondent, both over losing Stack and Darrow's death.

He penned a long letter, giving some details he was sure the censors would delete. He didn't know whether she was getting his letters at all, but he had to try.

Damn! Stack lay on his bed, recalling the face and mannerisms of Darrow, the old warhorse. There was a vacuum in his heart that he hadn't anticipated. He felt guilty, too—he could have written, but he'd always put it on the back burner, something to get to later on. He vowed to correct that.

Even in early June, there was a chill in Berlin. When Anton returned, Stack went to meet him in the Tiergarten.

"Anything changed in London since I've been gone?"

"The new estimates show a slowdown in British arms production," Anton told Stack. "They must be assuming there's less chance of a war because of the Munich Agreement. Donovan sent a note to Chamberlain telling him we think that's balderdash."

"Where's your place?"

"Viktoria Street, just behind the Hotel Esplanade," Anton said.

"Damn," Stack said. "You must love living dangerously. That place is packed with Nazis."

Anton gave him a wry smile. "I wasn't involved in the intrigue of the day when I rented it."

"Let's look for another location," Stack said. "Maybe even two apartments, in case you need to move around."

"There's no reason to think the Nazis are awake to our presence," Anton said. "But if they are, I'll hear it from the Luftwaffe plant."

In their training sessions in London, Donovan had acknowledged that the Nazis had over thirty spies in England, but the Special Operation Executive knew the whereabouts of each one and considered them harmless, and easy to round up and execute as soon as their usefulness to England had diminished. Until that time, they were considered a useful way to spot leaks and distribute misinformation.

"Do you think Canaris will see us out here?" Anton asked.

"If we're lucky," replied Stack. "His office looks right over this place . . ."

"Mr. Stack!"

They both looked up to see Canaris coming across the street. Stack turned to Anton. "Hang on; this is a biggie."

Anton nodded and began to fall back, turning onto a different path. "I'll see you later."

Canaris caught up. "Hello again, my American friend. Do you have time for a cup of coffee today?"

"Yes, of course," answered Stack.

"I haven't seen you lately."

"No reason you should," Stack said. "Most of my work is indoors."

"Have you been to meet with Donovan?" Canaris asked.

Stack saw no point in lying. "He sends his best."

Canaris laughed. "Very good, young Stack." He folded his hands behind his back. "Who was the young man talking with you just now?"

Stack had expected Canaris to know who Anton was, but remembered that, by all appearances, Anton was nothing more than an aeronautical engineer.

"I met him at one of Martha Dodd's parties," Stack said. "He's been a good tour guide."

Canaris nodded. "We've been working with several would-be double agents," he said. "I would very much like for you to review one or two of their reports for accuracy."

"I can do that," Stack said. A chance to verify reports coming from Eastern Europe was just what he needed.

"We talked to the Polish prince," said Canaris. "Subject to background checks and so forth, he could be a splendid asset for us both."

Stack smiled. "He's already spying for you, isn't he?"

"As a matter of fact, he is," said Canaris. It was Stack's turn to nod. "Come now, Stack." Canaris' demeanor hardened. "Let's abandon the cat and mouse and get right down to the brass basement. Is that the way you say it?"

"Close," Stack said. "But I get the idea." Time to outline the arrangement he'd discussed with Donovan. "You have an office that's close to all the embassies. Except for the gestapo presence, it's perfect for running the operation."

"Good idea," Canaris said. "But we are not to use gestapo or Abwehr funds."

"That's fair," Stack said. "We can get one or two of our people over here once we get set up."

"Is the man walking with you earlier one of the people you will use on this operation?" asked Canaris.

"Yes," replied Stack.

"Is that story about a tour guide is, how you do you say it . . . bullshit?"

Stack grinned. "One hundred percent."

CHAPTER 12

Walking along the Tiergarten paths, Anton and Stack felt the calm of the summer day, warm, breezy, and green. It was near noon and Stack was about to suggest they have lunch. He noticed that Anton seemed unusually upbeat.

"I ran into Martha yesterday," he said.

"Oh?" asked Stack cautiously. "Where?"

"The bus stop at the rail terminal, of all places."

"That's odd," Stack said. "Why were you at the rail terminal? A little out of your way, isn't it?"

"I went to find routes to the rest of Europe from Berlin." Anton shrugged. "As we go forward, I think we'll need the info."

"So how's Martha?"

"Very much the same," Anton said. "Still the sexiest woman in Europe. Train travel is the most efficient now, she says, and she's still working hard on her social life."

"Is she dating a Communist or a Nazi these days?"

"Likely both. She wants to get together for dinner soon. She said if we leave a message at the embassy, she'll get back to us."

"She must have a lot of clout." Stack felt uneasy. "I thought the Bolsheviks weren't held in high esteem in Berlin now."

"They aren't," Anton said. "I think she has a pass because of her playgirl reputation. But the worm can turn in a minute. If we're careful, we might be able to use her."

"Maybe."

"So, when do you want to get dinner with her?" Anton asked Stack.

"Slow down, Anton," Stack said. "I'm not one to get involved with your social life, but Martha's a loose cannon. You could get burned."

"I understand," Anton said. "But she is very attractive."

Stack shook his head.

... .--. -.--

Stack walked up the three stories to the Abwehr headquarters on Tirpitzufer Boulevard. The command headquarters of the German Army, Navy, and Air Force occupied the fifth floor. Canaris had engineered this arrangement so his people could see the comings and goings of the various military chiefs—who, in turn, wouldn't be able to observe the activities of the Abwehr.

An attractive lady in short bobbed hair opened the door and held it for Stack. "The admiral is expecting you."

"Stack. How are you?" Canaris rose with an upbeat smile. "Thank you for coming over. You are certainly responsive—it's only been minutes since I called." He indicated a chair. "Please, sit."

"I'm not as responsive as you think," Stack said. "I didn't even get your call. I just was looking at the apartments along the Boulevard."

"I hope the Americans don't question you as to the nature of your visits to our building."

"Not with so many other offices in the building—besides, no one ever knows where I'm going."

Canaris leaned back in his chair and took a deep breath.

"You look pretty comfortable," Stack said.

"I feel comfortable. Maybe it is because I finally have some bright people around me."

"I assume I'm included in that group."

"Of course. You are part of the atmosphere that breathes life over death." Leaning across his desk and motioning Stack closer, he said, "I think both sides can achieve a great deal. I'm convinced that without Hitler, the Nazi party will crumble and the world will become peaceful again."

"How would that work?" asked Stack.

"We already have assets all over Europe, Spain, and the Balkans. Another will not cause much notice or concern," said Canaris. "I'm thinking of pairing you with Johnny Jepsen, from Hamburg. He is smart but loves women and whiskey. I think you can keep him in line. But first, I have an idea that I think will pay dividends, and I wanted to see what you thought."

Stack unbuttoned his suit coat, crossed his legs, and waited.

"The possibility of bombing England is a constant subject of the general staff," Canaris said. "So I propose the following: we let it be known that we plan to attack the Netherlands and use their air bases to stage the bombing of London. That could push America to declare war. What do you think?"

"Well, sir," he said, "it's hard for me to judge. I've only been here a short time and can't predict the British reaction—or even the American one. Why are you asking me?"

"Because, young man, you are going to be the conduit by which Donovan gets the news." He pushed back his chair and stood. "Please be back in my office at three p.m. Can you do that?"

"I'll be here."

••• •▬▬• ▬•▬▬

At three o'clock sharp, Stack walked back up to Canaris's office and announced himself to the secretary. She once again stood and held the door for him to enter. Canaris was waiting for him—along with someone else.

The other man was slim and a bit taller than Canaris, but still shorter than Stack. He wore a thin mustache and was immaculately dressed in a tweed sport coat and wool trousers. He clenched an unlit pipe between his teeth.

"Stack, this is Johnny Jepsen," Canaris said. "He knows all about you. Johnny is a Polish Anglophile and has been an asset of ours since he graduated from the University of Freiburg. I expect you two to develop a strong working relationship."

Jepsen rose and extended his hand to Stack, then sat back down and began to light his pipe.

"I understand you have some contacts in MI6 that might help us," Stack said. "We need to sit down and compare notes. "

"Here's what I have in mind," Canaris said. "Johnny has read the false memo to let the British think we plan to use Dutch airfields to stage an attack on England. Like you, he thinks it may backfire. I'm not going to discuss the merits now. But with so much attention given to Czechoslovakia, the plan, if it got into British hands, might create a bit of havoc." Canaris pointed to an old tattered briefcase. "The memo is in this briefcase. I will leave soon. Johnny will pick up the briefcase and carry it out of the building. He will leave it on the bench nearest this office. In an hour, Stack will pick up the briefcase and take it to the British Embassy, where he can code and send the message to the British high command. You understand?"

The two men nodded.

"Stack, we have another situation I think you can help with," Canaris said. "There is a solid group of high-ranking officers who think Germany will be destroyed if it goes to war. We can't change Hitler, so we must remove him."

Stack was excited. "What about a strong PR campaign against him? Collect all the film you can and newspaper articles and photos." He suddenly thought of Hank. "I know a man who can put it all together."

"I doubt it would be effective," said Canaris. "The German psyche is still badly damaged and needs a heavy hand of the positive."

Getting up from his chair, Stack stretched. Looking out of the door he saw a tall, thin, bearded man wearing a rough leather jacket. Valzic, the man Canaris had called a killer. Stack felt his blood go cold.

Canaris joined Stack at the window and followed his gaze.

"He's very useful to us," he said, watching Valzic cross the street below. "He has several eliminations to his credit, including Huey Long in the US." He shook his head. "We wanted the American public to feel the consequences of nonintervention." Canaris paused and looked intently at Stack. "He is also the man who can make our attempts on Hitler a success."

••• •■■• ■•■■

After their meeting, outside on the steps of the Reich headquarters, Stack found his way blocked by a man a little over six feet tall, his sharp features and slicked-back yellow hair proclaiming him a true member of the Aryan race. He'd memorized the man's photo as part of his training: Reinhard Heydrich, head of the SS and one of the most powerful men in the Third Reich.

With a raised right arm, he saluted Stack, who responded with a half-hearted salute. Heydrich had sent over three hundred thousand Jews to the gas chambers. The only area over which he had no control was the Abwehr, though he dropped in on Canaris from time to time.

"Herr Stack," Heydrich said. "It is good to meet you. I was told that you were on the staff of Admiral Canaris."

"Sort of," Stack said, wondering why the hell Canaris hadn't told *him* that. "I'm only a private citizen who helps from time to time." His legs felt rubbery.

"If Canaris approves, I will take you to Prague tomorrow," Heydrich said. "You will be able to see more of our operations." He grinned. "Also, it is my favorite city."

Prague, a city-state much desired by the Nazis, was under Heydrich's control.

"Yes, sir. I would very much like to see more of the fatherland." Stack felt like he was going to throw up. Apparently Canaris had already put a cover story in place for him. Canaris, it turned out, was not eager for Stack to make the trip to Prague, but had little excuse to prevent it.

CHAPTER 13

Once airborne, in a twin-engine Ar240, Heydrich swiveled in his seat to face Stack. "What do you think of our new Germany?"

"I'm very impressed, Herr Field Marshal." Looking into the cold eyes facing him, Stack began to feel weak and uneasy. All Heydrich had to do was open the door of the plane and he was done. "I'm particularly impressed by the discipline and cleanliness of Berlin."

"Come, Herr Stack. I mean what do you think of the goals of our leader, to make the German nation as great as it once was?"

Stack struggled to find an answer—Heydrich couldn't just be flattered into submission. "You know, this is the first exposure I've had to Germany outside of Berlin," he said. "But then Berlin must be the German showcase."

"Well, now you will see a part of the German Empire that has hundreds of years of rich culture throughout the city," said Heydrich. "I love it."

"But is Prague a part of Germany?"

"We all share the same heritage," Heydrich said, "and soon will be reunited."

The plane droned on for a few minutes, during which neither man spoke. Finally, Stack gathered his courage again.

"I'm not fully versed in where the Third Reich is headed, but it seems that you're fully capable of achieving your goals."

"We are, Herr Stack, we are." Heydrich's eyes bored into him.

"If we have a war, on whose side do you think America will enter it?"

"Right now, I'd have to say we don't plan to enter on either side."

"But it is all subject to change," Heydrich said. "Don't you think?"

Stack summoned a small smile and held his tongue, letting Heydrich lead the conversation.

"Perhaps you will write a book about our new Germany?" asked Heydrich.

Stack's head bobbed.

"I hope you do. It would be a wonderful story," Heydrich said. "As you must know, we intend to take over Czechoslovakia and the Sudetenland, thus pulling the original Prussian-German country together once again. This will be a prelude to conquering Poland, and eventually . . ." He shrugged, smiled.

Eventually, the world. "When will all this be accomplished, Herr Heydrich?"

"Soon, my young friend, you will be calling me Herr Commandant of Prague. That's the purpose of this trip—to get prepare for the attack on Prague and Czechoslovakia." Heydrich settled further back in his seat and stared out the window. "Ah, Stack, wonderful days are ahead of us."

••• •▬▬• ▬•▬▬

Jackboots reverberated as soldiers marched over thick oak floors—the SS had taken over the Hotel Jakubska completely. Under orders from Heydrich, Stack was given a room key and instructions to be in the officers' mess for dinner.

"Are you not going to the great meeting?" said the bartender, a portly man with white hair and a thick white mustache.

"What?" Stack looked around and realized the room had emptied. "What meeting?"

"The meeting of all the brass in the room upstairs."

"I guess not," Stack said. "I wasn't invited."

"I've been told that these are the men who will run Prague after the Nazis take control," said the bartender.

Stack shrugged. *What the hell am I doing here? Am I supposed to just watch as Heydrich takes over the country?*

Stack saw a small group of senior officers enter a private dining room and slam the door behind them. Soon after, the door opened again, and Heydrich leaned out. He beckoned Stack over and waved him into the room.

"Gentlemen, please forgive me for neglecting to introduce my traveling companion," said Heydrich to the officers seated around the table. "Impress him while he is here, because he is going to write a book about the rise of the Third Reich. His name is Stack, and he is an American. He was recruited by Admiral Canaris himself, who thinks he has potential."

Sitting in fine cherrywood chairs, the junior officers stood and clapped, though all the senior officers remained in their seats. Stack allowed himself to be slapped him on the back and welcomed aboard.

"Why don't you tour the city, my young friend?" Heydrich said. "Our meeting here will not take long."

••• •▬▬• ▬•▬▬

The late dusk seemed an invitation for a walk. Several men were still sitting near the bar, so Stack asked if any of them wanted to go look at the city. No one did. They'd seen quite enough.

Heydrich knew Stack was working with Canaris, but clearly didn't know what his role was. He could never lose sight of the fact that Heydrich and Canaris were competitors within the Reich. They might even be outright enemies. One point, Stack now began to understand, was the Nazi orientation of "hang the man first and ask questions later." Heydrich was known as the Blond Beast because of his unyielding adherence to that principle. Misplaying this intrigue could be fatal. Stack had gotten himself into a hornets' nest. Back in Illinois, when he was twelve or so, he'd seen a hive in action. A frightening sight. The hornets here might be asleep, but they'd wake up eventually—and he'd need to be gone by the time that happened.

As he walked through the city, he stopped to look up at the ancient clock on a towering building that must have been erected in the Middle Ages. He had seen sights like this only in books and in school. He wondered at the skills these people possessed. Ironic that the ingenuity that had created these buildings was now being channeled into war.

He crossed the Charles Bridge on foot and wandered along several streets, absorbing the antiquity of the city. It occurred to him that no one seemed to be watching him, no one following. Did they trust him, or did they just want him to think they did?

His stomach rumbled. He'd probably overeaten, given the heavy German food and the nervous stomach, which had worked overtime all day.

Turning the corner, he caught a sound of—what was it? A strange noise, somewhere in the distance but not too far, in the direction of the rail station. Whatever, it carried a note of alarm. Was that wailing? Screaming?

He quickened his pace, following the sounds.

Moments later he emerged onto the rail platforms, the sound now loud enough to make him flinch. A frantic crowd of hundreds of adults and children—most of the children were young, some just babes in arms—yelling, screaming. Panic.

Some of the men and women were dressed handsomely in suits, topcoats, and stylishly cut dresses. Others were from factory labor, with dirty and greasy hands and in old, ragged coats. All had one thing in common.

They were fighting for possession of their children.

Stack stopped in the middle of the crowd and stood staring. *What were they doing*?

The children were being packed into railcars. SS troopers were pushing and kicking their way through the crowd, snatching the children from mothers' arms. The children screamed, shrill. The women attacked the railcars and were shoved aside by the SS.

Stack grabbed the coat sleeve of a nearby SS uniform. He pulled the guard around.

"What the hell is going on here?"

No answer, only a hostile stare. Stack realized he'd spoken English, and repeated the question in German.

"Ah," the man replied, "these parents are sending their children away. To keep them from going to a work camp."

"Under whose authority?"

The guard jerked his right arm up and saluted. "Heil Hitler!"

Stack could not speak. He felt light-headed and had to work to hold back nausea.

"But—how can Hitler dictate actions—in another country?"

"Sir, this is part of the fatherland. And by the end of the week, it will officially be part of Germany."

Heydrich had been right.

Another guard appeared, waving his arms and instructing this guard to "get the babies in the train now or leave them behind." Stack stood immobile, unable to believe what he was witnessing. What could he do?

The guards were throwing babies at the train. Some of the tiny bodies flew through the open windows, others smashed against the side of the railcar or fell between the tracks. Even the ones who landed in the train would die, Stack knew, for who would look after them?

The noise was paralyzing. Stack felt ashamed to be standing there. Was there anything he could do? He watched helplessly as one of the guards swung a child by the legs and banged its head against the metal black side of the railcar.

An SS soldier was standing in a ticket booth located on the platform and speaking into a microphone. "Cars two and three are now closed."

Stack focused on the man in the booth and fought his way toward it. He yanked open the door and jumped into the booth as the announcer turned from his high chair. The soldier was a beast. He overpowered Stack, who was pulling his pistol from his coat. But before Stack could defend himself, the soldier fell forward into his arms.

Stack looked up.

There was Valzic, switchblade in hand, motioning him to get out of the booth and run into the woods. "Go!"

Survival overcame surprise, and Stack followed Valzic off the platform.

"Tell Canaris he owes me," the assassin said before he vanished into the woods.

••• •▬▬• ▬•▬▬

What Stack had seen wasn't over yet—nor would it be for a long time to come. It was impossible to believe, yet here it was, and here he was. The shock that had taken all the strength from his legs began to subside, and awareness finally began to seep back into him, along with a strong sense of the terror he'd just witnessed. His needed to be more vigilant, to have more self-discipline. Wasn't that the first thing Donovan had taught him?

Weakened by nausea and despair, he stumbled away. Before he'd gone far, he understood: something inside him had changed. Sticky perspiration covered his skin, but he had no sense of heat.

He saw no SS troops after he got back into the city center, so he quickened his pace. *But what about Valzic? Where had he come from? What was his role*? Had Canaris ordered him to keep an eye on Stack, or had there been another reason for his presence at the train station?

The hotel lobby was vacant when Stack returned, some time before midnight. He guessed the troops were out on the town, so he went to his room to wash his hands and face. Then he went straight back down to the bar, threw his jacket over the back of a chair, and ordered a brandy.

The bartender was humming a tune he couldn't recognize. Over the six-foot-high fireplace, the head of a twelve-point stag was mounted.

The bartender saw him staring up at it. "That is the largest stag ever killed in the area."

Stack was lost in concentration when he heard a faint knocking on the window near his chair. He turned and saw a girl, face pressed against the window, motioning with her gloved hands for him to come outside.

Startled, he almost dropped his brandy. Another surprise tonight might just tip him over the edge. Still, he gathered himself, and after a quick look around the lobby, rose and walked across the lobby to the heavy oak door.

"Herr Yellow Bird." Her whisper was low and throaty. "I'm a friend of Ashton and Canaris. Come. Let's walk through the city."

Anxiety thundered through every nerve in Stack's body. *Go—Don't go!* Just a couple of hours ago—no, less—he'd sworn to be careful, more judicious. But this girl knew the code name he'd been assigned the last time he'd been in London, and it was natural to come upon friends of Ashton in deepest Europe. What if she had a message for him, something important?

He followed the girl outside.

The girl was wrapped in a heavy wool scarf and a large wool coat. Her feet were covered with high boots that looked as if she'd pulled them off the feet of a dead paratrooper. Strangely, the bulky clothes and short hair made her more impish—attractive, even. As she walked alongside Stack, he guessed her to be a charwoman who worked nights and made extra money from the last bar room customers. She didn't look older than twenty-one.

"Who are you?" he said after a few moments of silence. "How did you know my name?"

"Call me She-Bear. I work for the Abwehr, mostly in Poland and Germany, some for the British."

"Seems like most of our information gathering is done by double agents."

"It's always difficult to know the pros from the amateurs," She-Bear said. "I pray someone will bring order to the business one day." She gave him a sideways look. "The Americans, perhaps."

Sirens blared in the dark. Each time he caught the echo of jackboots hammering down stone streets, his breath stopped—then the sounds began to move off and fade away, before starting up all over again a few minutes later.

"I saw you when you arrived but could not get to you," She-Bear said. "That was an act of real bravery out at the loading platform. Also, very stupid. You could easily have been shot."

Stack shivered—his feet were already going numb. "Any more tips for an amateur?"

"This way." Holding his elbow, she guided him down the quiet, vacant streets. He realized they were heading toward the river.

"How did you get your code name?" Stack asked.

"She-bears are scarce, and little she-bears are scarcer," she said. "I grew up with Polish parents in Southside Chicago. My father knew it was a tough place, and he gave me a name that would make bad boys thinks twice. Where are you from, Yellow Bird?"

"Carthage, downstate from Chicago."

"I know where that is." Her teeth gleamed as she flashed a quick smile. "Not far from the Mississippi River in one direction and a short hike to Champaign-Urbana, home of the Fighting Illini." Then she looked serious. "You need to be more careful. I don't want to work with impulsive agents—it could get me killed. This isn't a cowboy movie, so get tough and keep your emotions under control."

Stack looked her in the eyes and saw softness along with her strength. "I will."

She looked doubtful, but nodded. "Now, Yellow Bird, I haven't got much time, so listen closely. The Nazis will want to know what happened to that officer at the rail station. If suspicion falls on you, Canaris can cover for you."

"But I didn't kill him." But he'd tried—and he might've succeeded, if Valzic hadn't been there.

"Do I look like I care?" She shook her head. "For God's sake, don't try to explain, and don't feel like you need to be exonerated. This is a war, not a trial."

Up ahead, a few lights rippled, reflected on the water. "Berlin is our central communication post for the time being. I'll send you a message with codes so we can work together. I don't know what they told you, but if you get exhausted, Lisbon is the R&R city—Portugal is neutral, so we tend to loosen up there. But we're always working and don't monkey around . . . much."

"So, I've noticed," Stack said. "I've had some experience with that brotherhood."

At the riverbank, She-Bear leaped down three feet from the street to the docks, landing on her feet. Stack followed more slowly as she found a dry place for them to sit with their backs to the stone wall. She pointed to the rising moon and shuffled over so their bodies were touching. She looked at the moon, then at Stack . . . and then kissed him.

It was a deep, hungry kiss, full of longing. She pulled him toward her, leaning back until he was lying on top of her. They kissed again as they rolled on the planks of the dock. Bottled-up tension rose to the surface as they clutched one another.

She-Bear laughed. "It's hell getting my pants down."

"Me too." Stack was breathing heavy now, struggling to shove aside the bulk of his own pants.

"Oh—that's better . . ." She sighed as he penetrated her. After a few more minutes she shook all over. "Oh, God. That's wonderful—"

"Yes—yes!" Stack stopped moving, then after he caught his breath, he rolled over and lay panting on the dock alongside her. He'd never felt so light, compared to the unbearable weight he'd felt just moments before.

She-Bear sat up first and began to wiggle her hips, pulling her pants back on.

"You need to get back before they start wondering where you've gone," she said. "Come on."

She jumped to her feet, grabbed his hand, and pulled him down the dock. After a few yards she stopped, spun around, and kissed him on the cheek. "You're cute."

She started to skip away but he grabbed her arm and pulled her toward him for one more kiss, one with real passion.

When they parted, she jumped down into a flat boat with an outboard engine. She cast off and let the boat drift toward the middle of the river before she started the engine, a loud rumble that settled into a steady putt. She threw a kiss to Stack, grabbed the tiller, then disappeared around the river bend.

Stack was light-headed. He'd never imagined this type of encounter, one that began with so much fear and ended with so much excitement, such a sense of relief.

He thought back to the rail platform. She-Bear was right—it had been a stupid thing to do, even though it had been Valzic, technically, who'd stabbed the man. The only good reason to kill a man was to save a life, and he couldn't have done that.

••• •▬▬• ▬•▬▬

The next morning, the officer's mess was abuzz with the news of the dead officer. Stack tried to look surprised while staying alert to any potential changes in Heydrich's behavior toward him. But Heydrich didn't seem to even see him, much less suspect him of anything.

"How was your evening?" Heydrich asked eventually over breakfast. "Did you like the ancient city?"

"Yes, Herr General, it is marvelous. I sense that you made significant plans last night—I only hope they pave the way for a Nazi victory."

"Worry not, my young friend. All is indeed well. In fact, we were able to identify a traitor."

"Oh?" Stack gripped his knees under the table to stop his hands from shaking.

Heydrich nodded. "He will be taken to Berlin. The Reich remains healthy."

The officers from last evening's meeting drifted into the room, most of them smoking, and took their seats around the large dining table. After slicking his hair back and putting out his cigarette, Heydrich stood and proceeded to give his men the verbal scorching of a lifetime for sloppy performance at the rail station. Heydrich had been given orders to get in, get the children on the train, and get the hell out of town.

Stack spotted General Werner von Bloomburg sitting among the officers. He didn't remember seeing him at the meeting yesterday. The man looked tense, rigid.

Around noon, Stack was notified that Heydrich wanted to leave for Berlin promptly at one p.m. He packed his bag and was standing outside the hotel by 12:50—he didn't want to seem as if he were avoiding Heydrich. Surely the man wouldn't have been so cordial this morning if he thought Stack was a traitor. At precisely one o'clock, Heydrich's car arrived. Three men got out, including Werner von Bloomburg. When Heydrich came down, everyone—including Stack—piled back into the car.

The ride to the airport was silent.

After boarding the plane, the men arranged themselves in the eight passenger seats and awaited take off. Most read newspapers, except for Bloomburg, who simply sat staring at his knees—as he had for most of the drive over.

Stack unfolded his own newspaper and buried himself in it.

An hour into the flight, Heydrich finally turned to Bloomburg, who was seated across from him.

"You and your filthy wife are an embarrassment to the Reich and to the German people."

Stack peered over the top of his paper. Apparently, he wasn't the traitor after all.

"Your filthy whore has been spying while she's entertaining her clients," Heydrich continued. "You—I will not call you General—are just as bad. You can't exist in the Wehrmacht, much less command it."

Bloomburg's eyes bulged.

"No, no, please, Herr General—"

Heydrich yanked opened the fuselage door and pushed Bloomburg out. His scream faded out quite quickly.

"We must all monitor one another," Heydrich said after he had closed and relocked the door. "The Reich has no place for those who are not dedicated to it and the Führer."

Stack didn't have to fake the slight tremor in his voice. "What did he do?"

"Bloomburg's wife was found out to be a stripper." Heydrich straightened his uniform and resumed his seat. "You might be interested to know that he was convinced you are a spy." He chuckled. "Of course, I have discounted that—I trust Canaris to manage his people, even contractors." He tapped his temple. "But be careful that you are always thinking of our greater good."

••• •▬▬• ▬•▬▬

Back in Berlin, Stack met with Canaris to report on the trip. When he told him that Heydrich would like to add the Abwehr to his command, Canaris grinned.

"Good reason to keep your eyes open and your mouth shut. The bestial behavior of Heydrich can't be excused. But, having seen it at its worst, you should be motivated to be very, very careful."

"He said Bloomburg though I was a spy."

Canaris shrugged. "I wouldn't give it much consideration. Heydrich's goal is to advance himself. If you have any opportunity to help that along, don't hesitate. Otherwise, stay out of his way and you'll be fine." His eyes narrowed. "Now, what happened in Prague? I got a note from Valzic saying I 'owe him one.'"

"I was about to be shot." Stack straightened himself. "Valzic saved me."

"What were you doing?"

"SS troops were throwing young children into rail cars. Some were hurt . . . There was a trooper in a hut . . ." Stack remembered She-Bear's advice: *don't explain.* "Valzic was right behind me. The trooper attacked me and Valzic killed him."

"I see." Canaris said. He picked up something from his deck and handed it to Stack. It was a beautiful broad-bladed knife with a swastika on the handle, encased in a metal scabbard. Stack drew it. *Eisen und Blut* was engraved on the blade—*steel and blood.*

"In the future, you will have to clean up your own trail." His eyes forbade any further discussion.

CHAPTER 14

The spring blossoms in Berlin in June 1939 were remarkable, as the weather turned warm earlier than usual. Nostalgia for his family farm flooded over Stack, as it would for every spring the rest of his life.

Physically, he'd changed little, except that he'd taken to combing his blond hair back, aided by a bit of oil, as was the German style. But still he had a tousled look. He now owned two suits and a sport coat, but no uniform. In his mind and heart, he'd gone from a young man to a mature, seasoned veteran of life. His only regrets were that he hadn't read a book in over a year and that he saw no hope to change things.

Anton had made a date for dinner with Martha at nine o'clock and asked Stack to attend. Seeing more than blossoms blooming, Stack refused at first. While she'd been helpful in the past, he found Martha too capricious. Then again, what if she had something big to pass along? In the end, he decided to accompany Anton.

Wearing light-colored herringbone jackets in deference to the spring weather, Stack and Anton made their way to the same little café in which Stack had first met with Canaris. Their felt hats were a perfect fit for Berlin.

They were seated at the window table, the most interesting spot in the house. They saw Martha arrive by limousine, all aflutter. Though she hadn't approved of the café, she preened as she exited the car, wearing a black satin halter-top evening dress. Without a doubt, she was the most striking woman in all of Germany.

Inside, she paused to scan the room, and when she saw Anton and Stack she shrieked in happiness.

Stack flinched but managed a smile and a small wave. The last thing they needed was to draw undue attention. And for all he knew, she could be even more embedded in the Communist party since the last time he'd seen her. Whatever Anton's intentions might be, Stack's were to get as much information out of her as possible.

"Boys! This is so wonderful; it's just like old times." She dropped into a chair, looking graceful even when she was flushed. "How have you both been? I have been having a *wonderful* time, and I've learned so much—I'm *so* glad I decided to stay!"

Stack glanced at Anton. He was smiling and calm.

"May I offer you a cocktail?" Their waiter bowed from the waist, then took a pad and a pencil from his starched white jacket.

"Well of course, young man, champagne all around." Martha clapped her hands. "What do you think of the new ambassador, Stack?"

"I think he's a bit of a bore."

"Not as bad as Daddy, I hope. Honestly, there was never a hope of him doing something constructive. Writing his damn book was all he cared about, and he couldn't even find time to work on that. And he never really understood the European cultures." With that she turned to Anton and started speaking in German.

"See!" she said in English, after a brief exchange. "I have learned the language. Well, not as well as Stack, but we all know he's a bit of a bore too, don't we?" Smiling, she leaned over and kissed Stack on the lips. Conflicting emotions rattled Stack's brain. *Better not get entangled with this one*, he chided himself.

As the champagne flowed, mostly in Martha's direction, she began to speak more freely. She was now the lover of both Ernst Kostring and I. G. Farben. The first was an aide to Göring at Luftwaffe, who remained in Berlin on the energy committee; the second was a civilian automobile executive who also served on the energy committee. Stack shuddered when he heard Martha speak their names so casually. Having seen the demise of Bloomburg, he knew full well how ruthless the Nazis were.

"Hitler . . ." Martha laughed. "Do you know, he was so stupid he didn't realize he'd run out of gas if he invaded Poland? He says he's got a plan to use the oil of every country they invade, but if Czechoslovakia is any indication, it's going to be a disaster."

"What happened?" Stack asked.

"Production's decreasing, just like everyone said it would—except for the increase in Austria, and even that will decrease with more military activity." She rolled her eyes. "Göring is hiding all this from Hitler, of course." She waved at the waiter. "More champagne! Let's have a real reunion party."

"Not for me tonight," Stack said. "I have an early morning." This wasn't true, but he desperately wanted to be away from Martha. He'd never met anyone so reckless. "You two go and have fun." With that, he discreetly jotted a note on the back of a receipt and slipped it to Anton as he left.

Get her to shut up. SS will kill.

••• •▬▬• ▬•▬▬

Europe continued its downward spiral through June and into July. Speculation ran wild as to the Nazis' next move, and Canaris called a meeting of his senior officers. Stack was asked to attend.

As they entered the third-floor conference room in the Abwehr headquarters, some of the group started guessing the reason for such a short-notice meeting. Following the others, Stack tossed off a quick salute to Canaris, then went directly to the hat rack. After hanging his hat, he greeted those he knew and nodded to those he didn't.

Stack was the only civilian present, and his navy-blue suit stood out among the gray uniform jackets and black jodhpurs, all pressed and polished. He pulled a pack of cigarettes from his suit coat, lit one, and inhaled deeply, exhaling a cloud of smoke. The others watched him carefully. They didn't know exactly who he was, but it was obvious Canaris thought highly of him.

Despite the tension-filled atmosphere, the spring day had brought out a buoyancy in everyone. Light banter dominated the room, though Stack was too tense to join in. Eventually Canaris cleared his throat, which was the signal for everyone to settle down.

Stack had been told what was coming. He was shaken, but knew he needed ice water in his veins.

Canaris remained standing as he spoke. "Gentlemen, I suppose it is no surprise to any of you that the Führer wants to take the Sudetenland. You also know that General Beck has opposed the taking of more territory, believing it will start a world war, which it probably would. It now looks like Hitler is gearing up to take not only Sudetenland but Lithuania as well. His patience has run out, and he is angry at the lack of agreement that we are one and the same with Sudetenland. The invasion of Czechoslovakia this March has encouraged him, so he has given the order to prepare to invade Poland as soon as possible."

Every head turned at the last statement, disbelief written on their faces.

"But, Herr Reichsmarschall, we are not in a position for such an action," said Joachim von Ribbentrop, the Nazi foreign minister. "We can expect an immediate declaration of war from

England, France, and possibly others."

A few heads turned toward Stack, though most kept their eyes on Canaris.

"Yes, that would seem so," said Canaris. "On the other hand, Göring's committee assures us that with the grain Russia is sending, we will have a total of two and a half million tons off-loaded and ready for distribution by the time we invade. As for oil, it is estimated that we have enough to last through 1941."

"At this rate?"

"We expect to garner some oil from our conquests," Canaris said. "The Galician fields in Poland, for instance. This should take us well beyond 1942, at which time the war will be won . . . by us."

Stack sat quietly, taking notes. Canaris had said he should be the scribe for the meeting. *Yes, I'll bet Hitler believes that. And I bet he expects everyone else to buy in too.*

Canaris held up a report. "We are in very good shape with machinery and rubber. Hitler's charge to us is to verify the status of these supplies. Then, I would guess, we will strike Poland. Questions?"

"What can we do if supplies do not prove out?" said von Kleist, one of the oldest members of the Abwehr staff.

"We will have to become more aggressive in developing synthetic oil."

"And in stealing it from our Russian friends," someone else muttered.

Canaris held up one hand. "Let's all hope events go well. Quite frankly, gentlemen, the success of the war depends on acquiring the Galician oil fields in Southern Poland very quickly. Russia would like to control them, but under the current treaty, the fields are within our sphere of influence." He paused. "Therefore, as Oster and Vogel have pointed out, it is our job to sabotage as much of that production as possible."

Stack watched as glances were exchanged around the table.

"Sounds crazy?" Canaris smiled. "Consider that with those fields, Russia could dominate us as well as Western Europe, while continuing the Eastern campaign. So that leaves only one option. We must control the oil fields, and the only way to do that is to disable them until the Russians lose interest. Then we get continental control." He rapped the table. "Gentlemen, we are dismissed."

Stack's mind was turning over several thoughts in rapid succession. Donovan had given him the understanding that Hitler had promised to keep his hands off the Sudetenland and Poland. He'd never put much stock in that, however. He had far more confidence in the information he'd been getting from Anton, who confirmed that Germany was dangerously close to war with Russia.

Goddamnit! He felt genuine anger, and a thread of real fear. *This crazy bastard is going to run all of Europe right off the road.*

Once the room had emptied from the meeting's conclusion, Canaris settled himself in the chair across from Stack.

"This is not your field, I know," Canaris said, "but from your perspective, are we sufficiently equipped? I'm talking about oil, weapons, ammunition, food—do we have enough to win the war?"

"Sir," Stack said, "I couldn't even begin to guess."

"I know, I know," said Canaris, waving his arm as if batting an insect. "You are not qualified to respond. But I want as many opinions as possible." His cold blue eyes bore into Stack. "You will be the one to shut down the Galician oil fields."

"Sir?"

"You will have a small team," Canaris said. "Including Johnny Jepsen and a man named Claus von Stauffenberg. You will go to the Galician oil fields and sabotage them with explosives." He stood. "Come with me."

Canaris left the office so quickly Stack had to jog to keep up, snatching his hat off the rack at the last moment. They went down the hall to another, smaller room, where Johnny Jepsen and another man, presumably Claus, were already waiting.

Canaris lit a cigarette and started speaking.

"Here is some background information. The unspoken truth is that Germany has been importing oil throughout the 1930s. It is only in the last couple of weeks that an attempt has been made to develop a coherent energy policy. In short, if any of the estimates or projections fall off the mark, the Nazis are in one hell of a mess."

"That could be to our benefit," Stack said. "It'll give us more time."

"Yes—except with Hitler alive, there can never be peace. There are pockets of Nazis all over Europe who would drop everything to fall in behind Hitler. Right now, we need a plan to sabotage the oil fields in order to slow the pace of conquest."

"How so, Admiral?" said Stack.

"This is an unexpected opportunity." Canaris looked at Stack. "Certainly you've seen it. Our sabotage efforts could set the Nazis back at least six months of production time while they retool. If, on the other hand, Hitler has the benefit of the Galician oil, he could take all of Poland before Stalin can react. That means Hitler will get a foothold in Eastern Poland. It also means that Russia might attack Germany."

"The man is insane," Claus said with some passion. "He needs to go!"

"That brings me to another point," Canaris said. "Stack, some time ago we spoke about a public relations campaign . . . something to open the eyes of the German people, to lessen support for the Nazi party." There was a gleam in his eye. "I think perhaps you were onto something."

••• •■■• ■•■■

Later in the evening, Stack and Anton sat down for drinks in the British Embassy.

"Anton, I need you to see what you can find out about the current Nazi inventory of tanks, U-boats, planes, and artillery."

"Do you need basic figures or long-range estimates?"

"Basic stuff now, but anything your greedy little eyes can file away will be helpful," Stack said. "I'll contact Donovan and fill him in. I'm also going to try to get him to send Hank over here."

"Who the hell is Hank?"

"Guy I know in Chicago," Stack said. "He's good at ad campaigns, and he's got a great eye. Canaris thinks if we can show the people how unstable Hitler is, they'll abandon the Nazis like rats on a sinking ship. Don't know if we have enough time to make it work, but it's worth a try. In the meantime, I think we'd better start getting our ducks in a row. Let's all meet here in three days and outline a plan of action."

••• •■■• ■•■■

Using the embassy's secure phone, Stack dialed London.

"Donovan."

"Stack here. Just wanted to fill you in on our situation." He perched on the edge of the desk. "Just got out of a meeting with C. He thinks the timing is perfect for an attempt at the Galician oil fields. You know what that means?"

"You're damn right I know what it means," said Donovan. "We have an opportunity to earn a merit badge."

"In addition," Stack said, "C thinks we should follow up with a media campaign—something to make the people aware of the realities in Europe."

"Interesting idea. Who's going to handle that?"

"I have someone in mind," Stack said. "A friend of mine back in Chicago. I was hoping you could reach out."

"Okay, but he better be damned good."

"He is. Besides, he speaks Polish—if the campaign's a wash, we can always make an agent out of him."

Later that night, Stack lay on his bed, thinking things through. His heartbeat accelerated and his breath quickened. This was the real thing. It wasn't exactly fear—more like shock, brought on by an understanding of what it meant to be a leader. If their mission in the oil fields failed, the consequences would be awful. Death by explosion or pistol—and death to millions if they couldn't stop the German war machine. Never had he seen such high-tension circumstances. The thing he'd liked about studying law was the clear consequences: there was a punishment for every crime, and a system to see that justice was done. But here, the rules of life no longer seemed to apply. He had to rely on his wits and his teammates, all of whom had their own axes to grind.

CHAPTER 15

On August 10, 1939, Stack's team—everyone but Jepsen, who would be meeting them in Prague—met in Canaris's office.

"I've given a lot of thought to what we should be doing, so let's start with the basics," Stack said. Even as the youngest man on the team, he looked like the leader of the team in his felt fedora, gray pants, and Harris-tweed jacket over a light black sweater. "Things are moving fast, and we're the best assets in the field. So we're going to bomb the Galician oil fields."

"You're comfortable with the organization that's been set up?" Ashton had shown up in Berlin suddenly, and Stack had thought it best to include her, though she hadn't been thrilled about Jepsen's involvement. "The team you've assembled?"

"Yes," Stack said with some hesitation. "Jepsen is known as the best double agent in Europe."

"Jepsen is entirely trustworthy," Canaris said. "He is of Polish nobility, a highly emotional patriot. He will do anything to cripple the Nazis and help Poland's people. And without him, we could not attempt this operation—not without at least six months' reconnaissance."

"Why not?" asked Stack.

"Because without him, we don't have the information we need," Canaris said. "It would take at least six months and some lives to acquire it."

"If any of us is caught, we will be executed," Anton said. "This is a very dangerous mission, and care and good judgment must be exercised."

"I know." Anxiety was beginning to seep through the edges of Stack's mental armor. He forced himself to remember that the soldiers on the field of battle would be barely out of their teens. No one was giving them the option to back out.

Time to suck it up.

Canaris spoke next. "The Galician oil fields lie between the towns of Boryslav and Drohobych, roughly 550 air miles from Prague and over the Carpathian Mountains. You will fly to Prague the morning of August twentieth and go directly to the Hotel Turka, where rooms will be held for you. Jepsen will fly in a day prior to secure the explosives and other equipment. He will instruct you on the use of the explosives. From Prague, you will fly to the fields."

"Will that be possible?" Anton said. "A direct air approach?"

"You will need to jump three or four miles west of the oil fields—the spot will be determined just before takeoff. Since the Boryslav fields are the flattest, aim for that area. Maintenance equipment, storage drums, pipeline replacements, and repair and transportation hubs are all potential targets. It is imperative that the explosions go off at the same time—we must not allow them time to mobilize."

"Our goal is to cripple the fields and cause a hell of a lot of confusion," Stack said. "That'll be our getaway cover."

Canaris nodded. "Once you've bombed the Boryslav fields, Jepsen will take you to Drohobych, where the show will be repeated. Hitler will then have a severe leak in his war-making capacity. Since the Polish engineers have proven to be inept at running an oil field, repairs should take quite some time."

Anton said, "Admiral, none of us has been trained to perform the tasks you've outlined. I don't mind trying to go through Heydrich's luggage, but jumping out of airplanes and sneaking in and blowing up oil wells?" He folded his arms tight and leaned back in his chair. "This is a job for local resistance."

"I am sorry you do not find the job description to your taste," Canaris said. "You may lack the experience, but no other team is better positioned."

"He's right," Ashton said. "Most operatives in Europe are, what is it you Yanks say? Loosey-goosey. This outfit has structure and can be highly effective. It depends on dedication. We learn on the job. She-Bear?"

"Good." She-Bear said.

"This isn't what any of us signed up for, I know," Stack said. "But I've got a feeling we can make it work."

After a moment, Anton nodded.

"Very good," Canaris said.

"The drop will be scheduled for just after dusk, about six p.m." Stack glanced at Canaris for confirmation. "It should be dark when we come down, so we won't be seen. We meet up with Jepsen again at the hotel in town."

"At twelve thirty a.m. you will be picked up at the end of the block by a truck loaded with packaged explosives, then driven to the fields," Canaris said. "The guards should be asleep at the fields, but if not, you tell them—in German, please—that you are checking security. Then you walk through the oil fields dropping packages in the targeted spots."

There was a loud knock on the door. Everyone startled, and Canaris moved to open the door.

"Hello!" Hank smiled. "Am I late?"

Seeing Canaris's confused look, Stack quickly stood. He knew the Nazi mentality was shaken by surprise.

"This is Hank Burner from Chicago," he said. "He's here because he wants a chance to get shot at, just like us. He speaks Polish and German, and he's a marketing whiz."

"I see," Canaris said. "And who invited you to this quiet little war?"

Before Stack could explain, Hank spoke.

"I was asked by Colonel Donovan." He looked uneasy, but he seemed to be rallying. "He thought we could work out a relationship similar to the one you have with Stack."

Stack managed not to cringe. As it was, he put the tips of his fingers together and went into a slight rocking motion. Sending Hank here was a power play by Donovan, clearly—and even though Donovan had never told Stack he was following through on Stack's suggestion, it was his job to back the decision.

"I know I'm a bit of a surprise," Hank said, "but Donovan wanted me in on the oil mission as soon as possible and skipped the formalities. I would assume that my language skills and ethnic background had something to do with it."

"And what are those, precisely?" Canaris asked.

"I speak Polish, German, French, and English. I was raised in Gdansk and am now a US citizen."

"So, you think you may also be a help to us." Canaris smiled. "I suppose if you are not, we can always shoot you and claim you were a double agent."

Hank went pale.

"He's joking," Stack said, though he wasn't too sure himself. To Canaris, he said: "I think Hank will be a strong asset on our team." Then he turned back to Hank. "When did you get in?"

"I flew in from Lisbon," Hank said. "Just a small plane with six other men, who I'm pretty sure were all spies for the Nazis."

Stack chuckled, but no one else laughed.

"Were you fully briefed?"

"Don't know what 'fully' is, but they told me I'm up to date," Hank said.

"One more thing," said Canaris. He leaned across the table and slid each of them a new Walther P38 pistol. “Keep it with you at all times.”

••• •▬▬• ▬•▬▬

The mid-August weather, which was normally cool in the Carpathian Mountains, turned warmer and more humid. Scattered thundershowers dogged a bumpy ride to Prague. Stack felt more queasy with every little midair jump of the plane.

When they landed, She-Bear jumped out and ran for a small ravine parallel to the runway. Stack followed suit. He finished heaving and got back to the tarmac just in time to see the small plane taxi toward takeoff, turning into the wind and picking up speed down the runway before finally lifting off and leaving them behind.

The mission had started.

Stack reached into his memory for some kind of courage, something useful from a previous situation, but he came up empty. He'd never been in a situation like this. He took a few more breaths to clear his head and settle his stomach. He felt like he was beginning to understand which things he could control and which he couldn't. He knew he was going to die sometime, but death alone without anyone to know you'd even lived was a very different and deeply lonely thought.

At the hotel they met Jepsen, who explained the explosives and how they were to be used.

“As you can see,” Jepsen said, “each backpack has a fuse sticking out of the top. Each of you has a map just like the one on the table.” The map on the table identified each drilling rig in relation to the town and environs. “Each of you is responsible for bombing two rigs, one in each village. The green fuse is the slowest and should be lit first. The red one is next.”

"Hold it," Stack said. "Green first, then red. Right?"

"Right," Jepsen said. "Now, this is very important. Entry to the rigs will be achieved by showing a false ID to the gate guard and asking for entry in German. If they don't understand you, switch to Polish."

This left Stack as odd man out, because he didn't speak any Polish. *But hell, there are three Poles here to lean on.*

"If you encounter resistance, move quickly to eliminate it," said Jepsen. He nodded at the pistols they all carried. "You've got the tools."

After the bags were dropped, the team would meet Jepsen at the truck, drive to Drohobych, then repeat the operation. Afterward, She-Bear, Anton, Hank, and Stack would be driven to the outfields outside of town to lie in wait for an opportunity to steal a truck and head north to set flares showing where they would land. Jepsen would go back into Poland, after a rendezvous with Ashton in Prague. Hank wanted to go with him to get up to speed with the Polish spy network—a good idea, unless he was spotted by the Germans.

Stack said no to this idea. "You need to get your ass back to Berlin and check in before Canaris decides you've deserted and has you shot."

••• •▬▬• ▬•▬▬

Once more, the team boarded the small plane and headed east. None of them had much experience with parachuting, but it was the only way to get close to the targets without being seen.

The landscape that stretched from the village was covered with lavender. From their height, it looked like a feather bed of purple and white.

The copilot organized the bail-out, shoving them one at a time out the open doors. Stack shivered at the thought of Heydrick kicking the general out of the plane over Prague. Surprisingly, the descent to the ground was exhilarating. The ground wasn't as soft as it looked—there was a jolt on landing, but they rolled forward as they'd all been taught, reducing the shock to manageable. Each quickly folded his parachute and stuffed it into a bag that had been brought for that purpose. Then the bag was discarded in a shallow hole in the adjacent woods.

The walk to the hotel turned out to be longer than anticipated, but after such an adrenaline rush, no one complained about the distance. In the hotel, they gathered in a room that had been reserved for Jepsen. The town, while in Russian territory, was close enough to the border that most of the citizens spoke Polish.

Jepsen asked for attention. "First, any questions?" No response. "Are we going to unify Poland?" he asked.

"Yes!" they yelled in unison.

"Okay! Let's get something to eat," said Jepsen. "Then it's time."

••• •▬▬• ▬•▬▬

At twelve thirty a.m. on September 1, 1939, German military might was unleashed on Poland in a blitzkrieg. Stack's group could count on resistance in getting into the oil fields and depositing their loads. They all understood the implications.

The truck rumbled down the street. Stack, She-Bear, Jepsen, and Hank came out of the hotel, dressed in black, and found themselves jostled by the crowd out on the streets, where news of the Nazi invasion was spreading.

Jumping into the back of the truck, they were grateful for the canvas covering that hid them and the explosive packages. Twenty-four hours ago, the Polish people in the streets would have looked on the saboteurs as German allies—now, they were enemies.

"What do we do now, boss?" She-Bear sat beside Stack and looked him in the eyes.

He knew he needed to show some leadership.

"This complicates things," Stack said. "But we need to keep moving and get the job done with as little sloppiness as possible—then we get the hell out of here. The Germans haven't changed our mission goals. We'll worry about the other field once we see if this cake bakes."

With Jepsen driving, they reached the gate of the target oil field at Boryslav quickly. She-Bear and Stack got out, as did Hank when he realized they might need his language skills.

BAM! BAM! She-Bear pounded the door to the gatehouse. Slowly, it opened, and a large soldier wiped the sleep from his eyes.

"What the hell is going on? Who are you? It's the middle of the night."

"The Nazi armies have invaded Poland," Hank said. "We're here for an inspection."

"What are you talking about?" The angry guard pushed Hank out of the guard shed. "Get out of here. Now."

"Don't be stupid, mein Herr," She-Bear said in perfect German. "We are under assignment to test the oil rigs for function and performance capacity."

"I don't know about this," the guard said. "You better show me your orders."

The three men and the woman all crammed into the gatehouse, creating more confusion than clarity. They all took out their false passports and authorization papers and handed them to the guard. He was still sleepy, but he was establishing his authority.

"Hurry, please," Jepsen said. "Hitler needs this oil and we need to report."

The guard frowned, shook his head.

"I must call my superiors," he said as he turned and picked up the phone. *PIT-TOON!* came the sound of the Walther P38 that She-Bear held in her hand.

The guard's body dropped to the desk, then slid to the floor. The other three team members found the keys and propped the guard up in his chair so he looked to be taking a nap. Hank ran to the truck. As soon as he signaled all clear, the team began to gather the explosives and proceed to their assigned oil well.

Each packet had a rig number. Each person found their corresponding rig, made the drop, then dropped their extra packets in unassigned rigs. Stack felt like they were running up the face of a clock, but in truth, the mission was accomplished in under ten minutes.

Behind them, in near perfect sync, several explosions signaled success. The staccato noise built to an ear-shattering sound. Stack, having never been in a battle zone, was sure the explosions equated to the damage being done.

In the nearby buildings, lights came on. Guards who'd been dead asleep stumbled out in their underwear, clutching their rifles.

"Hey! Stop! Who are you?"

They broke into a run, and behind them gunfire erupted.

As the team huddled safely back in the truck, the last of the explosives detonated.

Jepsen wheeled the truck around under full throttle. Machine-gun fire followed them all the way to the road.

••• •▬▬• ▬•▬▬

The September 1 blitzkrieg hadn't been wholly unanticipated, but it had come much more quickly than expected, causing chaos all through Europe.

Trucks loaded with half-dressed German soldiers passed them

on the road, clearly on their way to respond to the bombings at Boryslav. By the time they arrived in Drohobych, there was nearly no one left.

With the second round of bombs planted, Jepsen drove like a man possessed, passing other vehicles, riding through ditches and fields, swerving but never slowing.

Suddenly an overturned truck appeared in front of them. Soldiers were scurrying to get the truck back on the road and themselves in the truck. They started waving their hands, while screaming for the Jepsen truck to stop and help.

"They're Polish," hollered She-Bear.

Stack knew what that meant. Even though they were going fast, the Polish troops could see the swastika on the truck. Sure enough, within moments, the Poles opened fire.

Stack jerked and moaned as he felt a searing pain in his side. She-Bear leaned over him and began looking for the wound.

"Shoulder," Stack said. Blood was seeping through his shirt in the area of the clavicle. "Look in the glove box."

"Bingo!" said She-Bear. "Gauze pads and tape. Will that hold you together, hot shot?" She smiled at Stack. He didn't have the strength to smile back.

After about an hour of breakneck driving, the truck slowed and turned to the right onto a gravel road. They drove for only five or ten minutes, but to Stack it felt like a week.

The truck stopped.

Jepsen reached into the dashboard box and brought out a small short-wave radio. After thirty minutes of nothing but static that enveloped them like fog, Jepsen began speaking in German.

"Mission good. I heard. Caused some problem. Mostly helped till now. We're splitting up to meet in Vienna. New boy and I to Poland. Others work it out, but keep in German territory so we're not detained by Nazi troops. We have a casualty—Yellow

Bird was hit in the shoulder. Where will the plane pick us up?"

Jepsen turned to his fellow team members. "That was Oster, Canaris's aide. They'll send a plane. But we have to walk about fifteen miles to meet it."

"Let's get going," said Stack, "There's flat land for the next fifty miles. We can walk fifteen miles easily."

"Jepsen's back," said She-Bear. "I thought he was cutting out on us."

"No," said Jepsen. He stuck his head out the window. "Get in the fucking truck." He waved his arms at them. "Come on."

"We can't take a plane now," Stack said through gritted teeth. "The SS troops will blow us out of the sky."

"Shouldn't we wait until we know where we'll be picked up?" Anton said.

"Goddamnit! Haven't you been listening?" said a highly agitated Stack.

"We have to keep moving," Jepsen said. "We can just head west."

Stack knew they were used to working alone, and their nerves were raw. If he tried to force the issue, Jepsen might leave and take the truck with him.

"Okay," he said. "Let's go."

"Looks like you'll have to suffer until we're picked up," said She-Bear.

... .--. -.--

They looked like Nazi Storm Troopers as they drove slowly behind the inhabitants of the small village, who'd gathered to watch the bright lights of the explosives.

"We need to patch up Stack," said She-Bear. They'd worked their way down to the river near a small dock surrounded by what appeared to be cottages. “Maybe one of these cottages has some supplies.”

“You really think they’ll help?”

She shrugged. “I’ll tell them we’re Polish.”

She knocked on a cottage door. No answer. More knocking. No answer. She slowly opened the door—inside, a woman screamed.

“I come in peace,” said She-Bear. “I’m Polish. Don’t be afraid. We need help.”

“Are you soldiers?” the woman asked.

“No, No,” She-Bear said. “We’re trying to escape the Nazis. One of us is wounded. We need a bandage and a boat.”

... .--. -.--

The lady of the cottage bandaged Stack better than a hospital could. As they prepared to leave, he pulled She-Bear aside.

“Thank her,” he said. “And tell her to forget she ever saw us.”

She-Bear helped Stack outside, where the others were waiting.

“Hurry,” said Hank, who was standing in the bow of a long boat of sufficient size for all of them.

“Where’d this come from?” Stack said.

“We’re borrowing it.”

“Bingo,” Stack said. “This can take us a few miles up the river.”

She-Bear checked the gasoline can, which was almost full. They poled the wooden vessel away from the banks and into the current. Paddles stacked in the bow helped them guide the boat until it was safe to turn on the motor. Hank worked his way to the stern to help She-Bear get it started, then Stack felt the boat pick up speed.

Being trapped there, at the mercy of the river, created a strong sense of fear, but Stack was slightly consoled by the knowledge that the Nazis would never find them. There was too much activity between the two countries, and because they could speak the languages, they could pass as locals in either.

"What do we know?" Stack looked at Hank and She-Bear, who were talking too quietly for him to hear. "Where's the war right now?"

"My guess is the Nazi army invaded Poland from the East German border and marched toward Krakow and Warsaw," Hank said. "That means the troops are to the northeast of here."

Stack tried to picture this, based on the maps they'd all memorized, but he was exhausted, in too much pain to keep a single thought for more than thirty seconds.

They were all hungry, thirsty, and lacking in humor. After what could have been an hour or more, Stack looked toward the stern and saw Hank with his head between his legs.

"Let's pull over and try to get some sleep," he said. "It must be close to dawn."

"Hey, boss," said She-Bear, squinting into the distance, "I think there's a farm up ahead. Looks like chicken coops and cows, right on the river. We can pull over there and see if the farmer will sell us some food."

"What if he says no?"

"Then I'll shoot him."

"Can't see you in stealth work," Stack said. "But I'm betting you can make a deal. We'll hang back until you signal us."

The farm was a welcome sight. In addition to food, they could get directions—it would help to know where they were and how far they'd come.

As Stack hauled himself up and started to climb out of the boat, he put his hand on She-Bear's arm to stabilize himself. She shook it off and growled.

"Get the hell out of the way," she snapped as she jumped out.

"What's eating you?"

"Leave me alone. I have a lot on my mind."

Stack stared after her. He wanted to say something but held his tongue. This was less a team than a collection of strongly independent individuals, and any one of them could say to hell with it and bolt at any time. Stack wasn't sure how his encounter on the docks with She-Bear had affected her, but he knew damn well how it affected him.

Everyone was hungry and tired, but Stack asked if they'd be willing to wait until dawn to approach the farmer. All agreed, but Stack could see She-Bear wasn't happy.

They got Stack out of the boat and laid him on a grassy part of the river bank. He was sleeping on and off. She-Bear had been changing his bandages so often they were nearly out of supplies. Soon they'd have to start tearing strips off their shirts, or maybe something off the farmer's drying clothesline.

The others flopped down on the bank and fell asleep. She-Bear lay next to Stack and covered them both with jackets. Cautiously, he reached out and touched her arm.

"Do you really think Canaris will send a plane for us?" she asked Stack.

"He's a pretty honorable guy," Stack said. "If he said he will, he will."

He dozed off, then felt She-Bear shaking him awake.

"I think we better get going," she said. "How's your shoulder?"

"Doesn't hurt as bad is it probably should," he said. "When I think of a bullet so close to ending my life . . . what have I done to deserve being alive?"

"Hush," said She-Bear. "You don't know what you're talking about. You're a good man, but life is cheap in war."

Stack whispered in her ear. "I want to see you more often. Can you come to Berlin?"

"Poland is my country and Germans want to hang me," said She-Bear. "Stack, I'm a Jew. All my efforts are to liberate the Jews and destroy Nazis."

"I know," he said. "But I still want to see you."

"We will see each other in the field, if we live." She smiled. "How's your shoulder now?"

"Hurts like hell."

"Good sign," she said.

He opened his eyes and found himself staring directly into hers.

She kissed him warmly and held him close. Three or four minutes passed as they lay quietly without any movement. Then he shifted, inviting her to climb on top of him.

Like an infant crawling for warmth, she easily slid onto him. She opened his pants and wrapped her fingers around him. When she felt him hard, she pulled him out and straddled him. But the movement sent a sharp shock of pain through his side, and he soon went limp.

She was still, then she slowly moved down his body until her lips were level with his hips. The warmth of her mouth soon brought him back, but the pain returned as she started moving faster. He ran a hand through her hair and gently tugged her up for a kiss. She obliged, moving her body rhythmically against his until she quivered into a motionless orgasm.

He writhed in pain. But he found comfort with the thought of her needs being fulfilled.

••• •▬▬• ▬•▬▬

Just after dawn, the farmer and his wife crept out of the cottage. She-Bear joined them, and after speaking with them quietly for a while, she waved the rest of the team over.

The farmer's wife provided a breakfast of boiled eggs, hard

bread, and milk. Stack was feeling better already, and after his bandages were changed once more, he almost felt renewed.

"Have we heard anything from Canaris?" Stack asked She-Bear.

"Yes," said She-Bear. "We're to meet about five miles upriver where the plane can land."

"Thank God," Stack said.

Hank thanked the farmer, and the team returned to the boat, preparing to set off for the rendezvous with Canaris in Berlin. Stack, Hank, and Anton would take the plane back, while She-Bear and Jepsen planned to disappear into Poland.

"Good luck to you," Stack said. "Don't forget to touch base with Ashton in the next week and get to me before you start to make plans for Polish resistance."

"We will." She gave him a quick kiss, then left.

••• •▬▬• ▬•▬▬

At last, on the plane, Hank rubbed his eyes. "This has been a real learning experience for me," he said. "I thought of Europe as a bunch of countries close together, cooperative, with cultures that weren't too different from each other. But this is like a neighborhood where everyone speaks a different language. It's worse than the Red Sox and the Yankees."

"That it is, old friend," Stack said, and he closed his eyes, hoping to sleep his way back to Berlin.

CHAPTER 16

Stack was put in the hospital and his wound tended. It was more serious than he'd thought: the bullet had had a downward trajectory and had just missed severing his carotid artery, but it did fracture his right humerus, creating pain so constant he found it difficult to think clearly.

He had to talk with Canaris—not just about the mission, but about the other team members. Even though he knew there was a loose relationship between agents and their runners, the natural desire to control the rest of his team was maddening, especially when his entire team was out of reach (with the exception of Hank). Pain sharpened his anxiety, knowing Canaris was waiting to debrief him without a hint of his evaluation of the mission.

Briefing Donovan was high on his list also. That meant getting in front of the wireless in Fletcher's office in the American embassy. The escape route from Berlin to Lisbon to London was still open, as long as the US didn't enter the war—but here Stack sat in a Berlin hospital, without any means of communication.

In the quiet of the hospital, when Hank came to visit him, Stack motioned him close and spoke softly. "I've got something weighing on my mind, and I need to unload."

"What is it?"

"I haven't been quite honest with everybody," he said. "She-Bear told me before we all split that the British MI6 met with her and pushed her to find an Enigma machine—specifically the one held by the Poles. They seemed to know a lot about her: knew she was a Pole; knew she'd served as both a British agent and a Nazi agent in Poland. We knew all of that about her when we asked her aboard. We respected her mindset and passion for freedom. But she's probably a very high risk in the thinking of some of the team. So I've kept it from them."

"Ashton told me about the Enigma machine," Hank said. "She knew where it was, but no one knew where the codes were kept."

"That's where she wants to go," Stack said. "To find the codes and bring back the machine."

••• •▬▬• ▬•▬▬

When Stack was released from the hospital later that week, he and Hank went to Canaris's office. Canaris motioned for them to sit before settling in. His face was completely unreadable.

"So, Herr Stack, you had quite an adventure in the oil fields."

Stack's stomach tightened with tension—he was always apprehensive when Canaris addressed him formally.

"You could say that, Admiral." He badly needed a cup of coffee.

"Tell me what you have done to further our efforts," Canaris said.

"Our mission was a success," Stack said. "We were able to destroy 75 percent of the oil production."

"The Führer thinks we can crush the rest of Europe in short order. Do you have any information that would contradict this idea?"

Stack began to relax. Any concerns that the team hadn't met Canaris's standards were beginning to dissipate.

"Sir, I don't see how. Like I said, the mission was a success—we blew the hell out of those fields." He cleared his throat. "There remains enough oil in the Galician fields to support a limited offensive, but there's little to no stockpiling capacity. We saw no tank farms, and the staff was half asleep when we arrived."

"We were lucky," Hank said.

"That's good," Canaris said, "though Hitler may hang me when I tell him how little oil is available to him now." He paused to light a cigarette, his face somber.

If Canaris was out of favor, Stack's protection was gone. He felt his nerves winding up again.

"What's the official story?" Hank said. "Terrorist? Polish patriots?"

"I expect blame will fall immediately on the Polish Jews, at which point Hitler will begin to step up activities against them." Canaris tilted his head and gave Stack a look he had never seen before. It had the chill of death in it. Until this moment, he'd never felt the man looking at him was the real Canaris.

"What about Heydrich?" Stack still wasn't sure what Canaris's place within the Abwehr was since the invasion.

"Heydrich is a hungry savage, poised to absorb the Abwehr into the RHSA and SS fold," Canaris said. "With me here, Himmler and Heydrich have been held in check. We need to keep it that way." Then he straightened, all the chill gone in a moment. "How did your team perform?"

"They were great," Stack said. He slapped Hank on the shoulder. "Hank was a real asset in the field, and he and Jepsen got along quite well."

"That may be to our advantage." Canaris allowed himself a slight smile. "As you know, Herr Stack, Jepsen is very effective, but he is damned hard to keep track of."

"Yes, sir. I think we made a very effective team, and I think we can use this experience to breed additional teams."

Canaris focused on Hank. "We need to know more about the situation in Poland. Do you think you can help us if you team with Jepsen?"

"Yes, sir," Hank said. "But what about She-Bear? She speaks Polish, and I think we worked great together."

Stack gave Hank a look. When had he gotten so cozy with She-Bear?

"I have another job for her." Canaris pointed his cigarette at Stack. "If I team her with you, can you work well together? I'm prepared to make it very profitable for you."

"I think so," Stack said, trying not to look too pleased. Nazis assumed that everyone was as motivated by riches as they were. "What's the mission?"

"You are familiar with the Enigma machine?"

Hank and Stack exchanged a quick glance.

"Yes sir," Hank said. "As a matter of fact, I was under the impression She-Bear was already working on plans for a mission to recover the Enigma."

"You'll have to hurry to intercept her."

Turning to Canaris, Stack said, "Can you track her down from this office?"

"I think I can do that."

"You may need to arrange paid vacation for Anton," Stack said. "He's running out of excuses for missing work, and he's too valuable for us to let him go. I wish that photographic memory of his was mobile."

"I wish that also," Canaris said. "I have observed that he is a man of many skills, very valuable both in the field and out." He clapped his hands and stood.

"I think that's all I need to know, gentlemen. You are free to go."

••• •–––• –•––

"How's your shoulder?" Donovan asked when Stack arrived back at the American embassy and called London on the secure phone. "I assume it's in pretty damn good shape for you to be up and about already."

"The weapon was a high-powered rifle, so the bullet went straight in the front and out the back clean." Stack tugged on his shirt collar—everything was rationed now, including fabric, and it was a big step down from the suit he'd bought with Jack Kennedy. He looked less like a soldier of the secret war and more like a man who'd fallen on hard times. "The doctors gave me the all clear yesterday."

"Glad to hear you're back among the living," Donovan boomed.

"Boss, you know the Enigma machine that Ashton was telling us about?"

"Sure, what about it?"

"We've got a chance to get our hands on it."

"How in the hell are you gonna pull that off?"

"No details yet," Stack said, "but don't forget we've got the heart of Poland on our team. Getting in and out shouldn't be a problem. She-Bear is the information center of Poland."

"I hope that works out," said Donovan. "Keep me posted. Meanwhile, we've had some developments. Word is Russia is preparing to invade Finland and Norway. We need someone to go there and check out the number of men and armaments Russia's dedicated to those efforts. I was thinking of asking Jepsen when he resurfaces. Trouble is how to keep him on a leash."

"Boss," replied Stack. "It might be better to send Anton. He's familiar with armaments, and he speaks Russian."

"Good thinking," said Donovan. "Just don't tell Canaris."

"Sir?"

"We're helping each other," Donovan said. "But that doesn't

mean we're on the same side. If an operation goes tits up, he'll flip on us."

Stack was silent.

"I want you to meet me in the American embassy in Berlin in two weeks," Donovan said. "Hitler's ramping up, and I expect things to move rapidly. We need to know our options. Pull the whole team in. I want to talk to them too."

"That might not be possible," Stack said. "We don't know exactly where She-Bear and Jepsen are right now."

"What? What the hell do you mean? I thought you said she was hunting Enigma."

"Yes, sir, that's the plan, but, well . . . It's hard to understand the depth of feeling She-Bear has for Poland," Stack said. "She and Jepsen are still there, doing what they can to undermine the invasion."

"Goddamnit!" Donovan shouted. "No matter what you say to them, European spies work by their own rules. How're they gonna get out of Poland?"

"We just have to wait till they contact us."

"Operations can't always wait," Donovan said. "If we need to move quickly, I need someone ready to go at a moment's notice."

Stack heard a steady tap-tap-tapping on the other end of the line—Donovan drumming his pen against the desk, no doubt. Then: "What about Valzic?"

"Sir?"

"I know it's radical, but think about it. He knows Europe inside and out. He's an excellent asset who can show up anywhere at any time. A real pro."

"He's good, that's for sure," Stack said. "But I don't think we have a snowball's chance in hell of getting him to switch sides."

"Well, try." Donovan said. "You're close to Canaris. See what you can find out."

••• •▬▬• ▬•▬▬

The next time he was in the Abwehr headquarters, before he met with Canaris, Stack went to the men's room and asked a man at the next urinal where he could find Valzic.

"Third floor at the end of the hall," he said.

Stack hurried up the stairs. He found the door, knocked twice, then went inside. Valzic was indeed there, leaning back in a chair with his feet up on a small table, smoking a cigarette.

"Valzic," Stack said. "I never did thank you for helping me in Prague."

"My job," Valzic said in German.

"Still," Stack said. "You know I work for Canaris?"

Valzic shrugged.

"Then you know we're working to reduce the Nazi stranglehold on Europe—and get the US into the fight." He took a deep breath. "You could be a very important part of that."

He shook his head. "I report only to Canaris."

"He'll be running the show," Stack said. "But—"

"NO!" said Valzic. "I do nothing he doesn't ask me to do." He glared at Stack. "I owe him."

"I get it," Stack said. "Just . . . keep it in mind, okay?"

He left the room, Valzic's eyes still on him, and hurried to Canaris's office.

••• •▬▬• ▬•▬▬

"I have been to Poland," Canaris said. "I have seen the atrocities, including the mass executions of Catholic priests and bishops. It has left me quite sick at heart." He walked around the desk, bent low, and whispered in Stack's ear. "We desperately need to influence Hitler's thinking."

"How?"

Canaris made his way back to the other side of the desk. "I believe you know Valzic?"

"I do."

"That's our plan," said Canaris.

"He's very loyal to you," Stack said. "Why is that?"

"He owes me a debt that cannot be easily repaid," said Canaris. "He is a very efficient tool if used correctly."

CHAPTER 17

June 1940

Stack sat drinking Zywiec beer with She-Bear, Jepsen, and Hank at a table in the bar of a small hotel in Plonsk, outside Warsaw. She-Bear and Ashton both knew the owners of the hotel, so they were making the most of their local assets. It had been more than six months since She-Bear had started looking for the Enigma machine, but she had yet to get her hands on it.

"Jepsen," Stack said. "Glad you could make it."

"Of course," Jepsen said.

"Okay, She-Bear. You've been on this for months. What can you tell us about this machine?"

"It's the key to the war, Stack. It can decipher all the German messages coming and going. This one was stolen from a German U-boat and the Nazis want it back badly."

"No doubt," Stack said. "If we can get our hands on the code as well as the machine . . ."

Jepsen excused himself and headed to the men's toilet. Stack's instinct kicked in. Counting to five, and seeing the others relaxing, Stack turned to Hank and said, "Keep your eye on Jepsen." Stack then followed Jepsen. He stood outside the door to the facilities, listening.

"What's the bounty?" Jepsen said.

Stack couldn't make out the other guy's response.

"Good!" Jepsen said. "I'll see you there."

Damn, Stack thought. *This could be a real problem.*

The door swung open and Jepsen emerged. "Stack! I didn't know you were out here."

"I know you didn't." Both men moved out into the hall. "Who were you talking with?"

"None of your fucking business."

"You'd better not throw a monkey wrench in this operation," said Stack. "If something goes wrong, I'll be looking to you."

"Don't think you can tell me what to do, kid. I've been in this game for a long time."

"Do you want to go back to Berlin and tell Canaris you just can't get along with the rest of the team?"

"I'll think about it," said Jepsen.

"No thinking. You're either in or out, 100 percent."

"All right, Mr. Big Shot. I'm in till we get back to Berlin."

"I'll be watching you the whole way," said Stack.

••• •▬▬• ▬•▬▬

At the station in Warsaw, She-Bear, Stack, and Jepsen jumped off the train onto the concrete platform before it came to a full stop. People were still in a state of panic over the invasion, and the crowd jostled them in every direction. They saw several pickpockets, who moved off the moment they realized they'd been spotted.

"This is worse than I thought," said She-Bear. "For God's sake, don't let your guard down—you might lose everything in your pockets."

They followed Jepsen to the set about finding the Hotel Europejski. The crowds made it nearly impossible for the authorities to verify papers or passports. They'd be relying on that when it came time to exfiltrate. She-Bear suddenly grabbed Stack's arm, pulling him around to face her. He raised his brows, but stopped. She put her arms around his neck and her lips against his ear.

"That bastard at the counter knows my face," she whispered. "Wait until he leaves."

Any other time he would have been thrilled to be holding such a beautiful woman so closely. Even though she was dressed as a field hand, her bright blue eyes and golden hair made his pulse skip.

"Okay," she said after he stroked her hair for a while. "He's gone."

Bumped and jostled, they made their way to the counter.

"We have no rooms," said the desk clerk.

She-Bear leaned across the counter. "Do you have a message for Princess Juliana?"

The desk clerk turned and reached into one of the mail cubicles. He pulled out an envelope, and with a bow and a half-smile, he gave it to She-Bear. "Anything else, Princess?"

She gave him a wide smile. "No, thank you."

She-Bear stepped aside and tore open the envelope. It was empty. She flipped it over, and something fluttered toward the floor. Stack grabbed it. It was a small piece of paper that said only *222*. "What the hell does that mean?"

"Well it must mean something." She looked tired but tapped her cheek, thinking. "Let's go see what's in room 222."

They climbed the steps to the second floor and started down the hall.

"Here it is," She-Bear said. They both pulled their pistols and stood to the side of the door and knocked.

"Come in," said a voice in English.

Carefully nudging the door open, they saw Hank's smiling face.

"Hank!" they said in unison. "How did you get here so fast?"

"Well," said Hank, "Canaris thought you might need some help. There's a plane waiting for you at the Nazi airfield, when you're ready to leave."

Jepsen frowned. "How did he know we needed one?"

Hank shrugged. "A lot has changed since the invasion."

"Are you going with us?" She-Bear asked.

Hank shook his head. "I'm just supposed to get you from the pickup to the plane." He smiled at Stack, then turned to She-Bear. "Plus, I thought I'd come see you off."

"Stupid," she muttered. But Stack didn't think she actually looked upset.

Jepsen rolled his eyes. "Fine, we have our exit strategy. What about getting inside?"

"We have a map of the inside of the Citadel where the machine and codes are kept, courtesy of Ashton," Stack said. "She'll be sending us an update on the usage of the Citadel, and one of her people will meet us outside before we go in. Once out, Ashton will take the codes and the machine to the British command staff—and she's given us the combination to the safe."

"Sounds like we have everything pretty well in hand," Hank said.

... .--. -.--

It started to mist, which turned to a light rain, quieting the crowds and moving them off the streets. Jepsen, Stack, and She-Bear followed the Vistula River to the Polish Army Headquarters, located in the Citadel about three miles upriver. The Citadel was a large pentagon-like building made of rust-colored brick, big enough to house twenty thousand troops. It was the headquarters of the Polish Army and had been built by Czar Nicholas in 1830. Jepsen had been through it many times, as had

She-Bear. During the shock of the invasion, the troops stationed inside the Citadel had forgotten to close the massive oak doors.

"Let's go over to that street light and take a look at the map of the building and grounds," Stack said.

"Won't someone see us?" Jepsen said.

"The bulk of the army left to respond to the invasion," She-Bear said. "The remaining troops are maintenance people."

"So where in all this is our target?"

"Right here." Stack put his dirty finger on a room just off the interior platform, a structure that allowed soldiers to move easily around the circumference of the Citadel.

They slipped through the unlatched door, then sprinted across the courtyard toward the walls, which, according to their hand-drawn map, supported a firing platform in true medieval style.

Stack quickly identified the location of the army headquarters, occupied by the commandant—right in the middle of the widest part of the property. Squinting at the map, Stack saw that within those headquarters was a reception room, a large bedroom, an office, and newly added baths.

She-Bear leaned over his shoulder.

"The Enigma machine and the codes are in a heavy safe in the office," she whispered.

There was hardly anyone else in the entire building except the guards posted outside in the cold. However, one lower room had a fireplace, and occasionally one of the guards would peel off and duck into the warmth for several minutes before returning to his post.

They ran to the central building and crept up the stairs. Still tense, adrenaline flowing, they moved quickly but quietly. With the Enigma machine and its codes, the tide of a war would dramatically shift. The acquisition wouldn't end the war, but it might shorten it.

Slowly and in total silence, She-Bear slipped a key into a deadbolt lock and turned. There was a faint click.

They pushed open the door, filed inside, and began spreading out, searching for the safe. She-Bear located it, and when she did she turned on her flashlight and turned to Stack.

"Do you want to try first?" she said.

"I doubt we'll get more than one chance," he said. "Go ahead."

Jepsen held the light and She-Bear crouched. Suddenly Stack grabbed her arm. "What was that?" he said.

"I didn't hear anything."

"I did."

Jepsen clicked off his light. "What do we do?"

She-Bear stood up. "Stack, take off your pants."

"What the hell are you talking about?"

"Just do it, and fast." She glanced at Jepsen. "Get out of sight—under the desk."

Stack unbuttoned his pants and pushed them down around his knees. She-Bear pulled off her shirt and was just unhooking her bra when the door swung open.

"Oh! I thought I heard noises in here." The soldier grinned. "Looks like the room is being put to good use!"

She-Bear put her hands to her face and turned away. She said something in Polish to the guard, who laughed, threw Stack a sloppy salute, and closed the door behind him.

Stack and She-Bear quickly pulled their clothes back on as Jepsen crawled out from under the desk.

"I'll try the combination," She-Bear said. "Keep an eye out for more guards."

She held a small flashlight in her teeth and tried the combination. Her hand slipped and she swore.

"Let me hold the light," said Jepsen.

He held the light over her shoulder. She focused, took a deep breath, and went through the series again. This time the lock clicked, the handle turned, and the door swung open.

"I think the tumblers were sticky." She reached in and pulled out a machine about the size of a typewriter and handed it to Jepsen. "Here's the machine. Hang on." She gathered a file and some loose papers to her chest and stood. "I've got the codes."

"How are we supposed to carry all this?" Jepsen said.

Stack poked his head into a coat closet and came out holding an empty satchel.

"Put it in this."

They'd just packed the machine and codes into the satchel when they heard another set of footsteps in the hall.

"Alex!" An angry interrogation in Polish followed.

"What's going on?" Stack whispered. All three of them were huddled behind the desk.

He heard the voice of the young guard who'd interrupted them earlier.

"He's saying he found a young man with a . . ." Jepsen glanced at She-Bear, who rolled her eyes. "A Polish whore."

Out in the hall, the second voice was loud, clipped. Stack didn't need to speak Polish to know the young guard was being chewed out.

"Shit," Jepsen said. "He's asking how we got in."

A mumbled string of Polish, followed by a curse and shouted orders.

"They're going to lock the doors," She-Bear said, "and search the fort."

"Then we need to get the hell out of here," Stack said.

The huge doors were so heavy they needed two men each just to swing them closed. They were halfway shut when the three snuck back down the stairs and into the main courtyard.

"We'll have to run," Stack said.

"We'll be shot!"

"It'll be worse if we stay," She-Bear said. "Come on—run!"

They bolted across the open space. A guard shouted, then another.

"Faster!" She-Bear panted.

Stack heard a single shot, and the clamor behind them became even more chaotic. He frowned, slowed, and glanced back over his shoulder. The guards were running—not toward the doors, but toward the walls and the firing platform.

Another shot—not a pistol, he realized, but a rifle.

The gap between the doors was so narrow Stack had to turn sideways to slip out. He heard bullets strike the wood behind them, and from the walls above, a few shots pelted down.

Jepsen grunted and fell to the ground.

Stack fired up, blindly.

"They got Jepsen," he yelled. "Get the hell out of here!"

The doors were slowly being pulled back open, and a few soldiers spilled out. Before they could fire, Stack started shooting. The two men dropped.

From behind the door, he heard more shots being fired.

Stack shouted to She-Bear, "Which way?"

She hoisted Jepsen up over her shoulder in a fireman's carry. "Left!"

Stack started running. He glanced back once.

A figure dropped to the ground—they'd gone over the wall, not through the doors. Whoever it was had a rifle slung over his back.

The figure stopped, turned, and stared directly at Stack.

Valzic?

Then he was gone, racing up the sidewalk in the opposite direction. A few more bullets struck the concrete, and Stack realized he had to keep moving. He ran after She-Bear.

He saw a taxi, opened the door, and flung himself into the backseat. Between them, he and She-Bear managed to get Jepsen inside.

"Hey, *nie mam obowiązku*!" The cabbie turned and looked over into the back, his eyes widening when he saw Jepsen.

Stack stuck the barrel of his P38 in the cabbie's neck.

"You're back on duty," he said. She-Bear quickly spoke to the driver in Polish, presumably translating. "Get us to the Nazi airfield, and hurry." He paused. "And remember, I can drive—if you cause any trouble I'll kill you. Now get going." He leaned back in the seat and looked at She-Bear.

"Hi," she said.

He smiled. "Hi."

"You didn't get shot?"

"Not this time."

"How's your shoulder?"

"Useable, but hurts like hell."

"Damn lucky." She-Bear muttered and started the car. "How's Jepsen?"

"Still alive," Stack said. There was blood all over the backseat. "But we don't have much time."

The moment they arrived at the airport, the driver's door opened and the cabbie jumped out, sprinting up the street and around the nearest corner. She-Bear jumped out and into the driver's seat. She looked into the backseat and gave Stack a crooked smile.

"Come on," She-Bear said, hopping out of the front seat. "Let's get him . . ."

Stack shook his head. "I'm sorry. He's gone."

"Jepsen's dead?"

He left the body in the back of the cab. "Come on, let's find Hank."

••• •▬▬• ▬•▬▬

Hank met them just outside the plane.

"How far can you take us?"

"According to the pilot," Hank said, "we can't leave German airspace."

"That makes things difficult," Stack said. "I think we can get picked up from Belgium. But what to do with the Enigma?"

"I'll take it," Hank said. "It's too dangerous for you to keep hauling around. I'll take it back to Canaris."

Stack stood still. "It's supposed to go straight to Donovan."

Hank shrugged. "I'm just telling you what he told me." He lowered his voice. "I think the pilot has his own orders. And I don't want to find out what happens if you try to take that thing off the plane and into Belgium."

She-Bear said something harsh in Polish, and Hank flinched. Stack held up his hands.

"The machine isn't going anywhere," Stack said. "We'll stash it just inside the border, then come back and retrieve it when things cool down."

CHAPTER 18

"Stack, what a sight for sore eyes." Donovan enthusiastically embraced each man at the curb outside the embassy in London. "Hank, good to see you again." Donovan turned to Stack. "You guys did a hell of a job in Poland. My hat's off to both of you. Come on in and let's debrief."

Putting his arms around both Stack and Hank, Donovan guided them to the large meeting room.

Stack took him through the mission step by step, which was exhausting.

"Where is the Enigma?"

"We stashed it at an airfield just over the border," Stack said.

"Why there?" asked Donovan.

"Because the German plane wouldn't cross the border for fear of being shot down. We waited in a shed at an old airfield and hid the machine in a bush ten paces southwest from the shed. We told Canaris where it is, but pointed him northeast instead."

"Bill Stephenson is hot to get it in his hands," said Donovan. "We'll have to hightail it over there and get it."

Hank looked from Stack to Donovan. "Who in hell is Bill Stephenson?"

"He's a genius at organization and has an imaginative mind to boot," Donovan said. "Churchill talked him into taking the job of head of all allied intelligence. He brought me in. You may have heard of SOE, or the Special Operations Executive? That's him." He paused, took a breath. "Time I brought you up to date on the Nazi-Soviet situation. The grain shipments Russia promised have been far less than expected. The invasion of France went off well enough, and that's given Hitler confidence. He may try to move on Russia."

"Damn," Stack said. "Does it ever get better?"

"Not until the German people see the truth about the Nazi and Jewish situations. Right now, according to the Abwehr, they're pretty firmly behind Hitler—the high rate of employment under his watch keeps him in people's favor."

"Because they've got everybody building arms," Hank said.

Donovan nodded. "You and Stack have sold Canaris on a public-relations sales game. It's time to show the German people and the world the truth about the Nazis. It's more likely to turn some heads today than it was yesterday. That's the speed of change in the world now."

"Where do you think we should be concentrating our efforts? Considering that we're still not at war?" Stack looked Donovan in the eyes without blinking. Donovan smiled slightly.

"Stack, in this room we're always at war." He slapped the table. "As for your efforts, we've now seen how important it is to think on your feet and be creative. We need to go to Poland and knock around. Same with Estonia, Lithuania, Romania. We need to be in France to aid their resistance, but that will come after they organize a resistance, if at all. But most of all we need to know what's going on in Russia."

Stack nodded. "Agreed."

"What do you think, Hank?" Donovan asked.

"With my limited experience, I think that makes sense."

"How do you feel about going back now to pick up the Enigma?"

"I'm ready, boss," said Hank, "but with Jepsen gone, we really need Anton."

"I'll bring him back in from Norway."

"Colonel, I had a thought," Stack said.

"Well, spit it out, Stack. What is it?"

"Let's revisit the unified small team concept. To use target management, we need to establish targets and prioritize each one. Suppose we could do the same with intelligence gathering. I like the small team approach."

"I like the idea, Stack, but I need time to ponder the success ingredients. If I'm any judge, we're going to be in this war before another six months goes by. We probably need to beef up our team. But let's talk with Stephenson and the army intel guys and see what they know. But in no circumstance do you take any action without getting a clearance from London. Understood?"

They all answered, "Yes."

"We'll meet again once you've got it in hand," Donovan said. Oh, and Stack, you might want to check your mail before you head out again."

••• •▬▬• ▬•▬▬

Stack had received over thirty letters since his last trip to London, most of them from Mary Jane. He felt guilt like lead when he realized how self-centered he'd been. But it sure felt like he hadn't had much time to focus on anything besides not getting killed.

And then there were his nights with She-Bear, and his feelings for her.

He could have made the time to write, but he hadn't. Was he truly in love with Mary Jane? He desperately wanted to see her, he knew that. He thought of writing a long letter describing his activities, but the censors would eliminate most of it.

The last of Mary Jane's letters said only, "Tell me you love me, and I'll wait until hell freezes over for you."

He didn't need to write a long letter to answer that—and it was one thing, at least, the censors wouldn't cut.

> *Dear Mary Jane,*
> *I do not deserve the feelings you expressed in your last letter. The depth and loyalty of your love is beyond understanding. I've been consumed by recent events, but that is no excuse for not taking the time to say "I love you."*
> *I have been in places I never knew existed, places strange and beautiful and terrible, and in every one of them I was thinking of you. If you still have love for me, I promise to be yours till we die.*

Days after he'd sent his letter off to Mary Jane in a diplomatic pouch, he was still thinking about what he had written. Every time he thought of her, he remembered her fondly, and he felt a swell of affection. He was certain he loved her, and he missed her, but at the same time, he didn't need her—or at least, he didn't feel crushed without her there, didn't feel like he was going to waste away if he didn't see her. Wasn't that how people in love were supposed to feel?

••• •▬▬• ▬•▬▬

Two weeks later, Bill Donovan stood looking out of the open window at the unusually warm day. Behind him sat Anton, Stack, and Hank. They'd successfully brought back the Enigma, and Stephenson's team had had a few days to work with it.

"Do you realize how big this is?" Donovan's jaw was firmly set, a sure sign of high intensity. "From the one double agent, we recovered over seventeen hundred messages between Berlin and the various Abwehr stations, none of which we'd have been able to translate without that machine. Knowing what's coming is the heart of the war. We will be long forgotten, but not the Enigma." He turned to face them, hands clasped behind his back. "One of the messages we intercepted states that Hitler wants to eliminate England by invasion, target date September 5. This is to be preceded by bombing London."

"Bet that woke up British intelligence," Stack said.

"I think they may have found their voice, yes," said Donovan. "You've met Stephenson. Churchill has put him in charge of all intelligence operations."

"What about the States?"

Donovan shook his head. "The US still hasn't moved." Disappointment showed on the men's faces. "On the brighter side, Churchill is mobilizing to meet all threats."

"So, you're saying that with the proper information we can sabotage their plans," Hank said, sitting on the table and swinging his legs. "What's first?"

"Think of yourselves as free agents working for whoever rings your bell—though in this case, it damn well better be the Allies." The weight of the job was clearly showing on Donovan's face. "Of course, we'll be in close communication with the war intelligence as we proceed."

"Bill," said Stack, "I think I should go back to Berlin and check in with the situation there."

"Damn right," said Donovan. "Get over there and snuggle up to Canaris. Which brings me to the next subject—Heydrich. Thanks again to the Enigma, we've learned that Heydrich has new and expanded responsibilities as ruler of Czechoslovakia, and Hitler has stepped up his efforts to eliminate the Jewish race."

"You mean mass murder."

"My point is, be careful," Donovan said. "If I'm any judge, Heydrich is highly suspicious of you. Word is, he wants you out of the picture. If Canaris is in the can, you're naked."

"I know," Stack said. "Do you have any way of getting in touch with She-Bear? We may need her information, her contacts."

"I think she may be in Warsaw. We should contact Ashton—she'll know how to get in touch."

"Maybe we could try placing an agent in Warsaw," Anton said.

"We're in good shape in Poland, even without Jepsen," Stack said. "What we need is more presence in Spain, Lisbon, and other European cities."

"And I guess I need to report to work," Anton said. "I know Canaris is covering for us, but I think there's some real engineering work I could do. Might even be able to sabotage some plans."

"Good idea," said Donovan. "Hank, why don't you go back to Berlin with Stack and Anton? This is the perfect opportunity for you to get with Canaris on the anti-Nazi campaign."

"Okay, boss," Hank said.

"A final issue," Donovan said. "Canaris replied to my message informing him that Stack and Hank were in London. He said rule of law was disappearing fast in Germany, and that he's been able to consolidate all the intelligence operations of the Reich into one bureaucracy—with the exception of the Abwehr. And while Heydrich reports to Hitler, he does not report to Canaris, who I'm sure is really pissed off about this."

CHAPTER 19

Hank, Stack, and Anton were driven to the airport by an American embassy official who clearly had no idea who in the hell they all were. They flew from London to Lisbon, where they spent the night. In the hotel they met Johnny Jepsen's good friend, Ian Popov, for several rounds of drinks and a large dinner.

"Johnny would've liked that," said Popov, who had a habit of hanging around Lisbon while not otherwise occupied.

They were halfway through a third round when Popov caught Stack's eye.

"Do you see the large man sitting by himself near the door?"

Stack nodded.

"Hitler has launched a campaign to enlist a large number of spies with the goal of sabotage," Popov said. "That man is one of the chief recruiters. He's been bouncing around the Mediterranean for years, selling his secrets to the highest bidder. And he knows all about you, Yellow Bird."

Stack kept his voice even. "How do you know this?"

"I have sources," Popov said. "You better buy a hat." He gave Stack a tight smile. "He needs to be eliminated. He knows that Heydrich wants your balls nailed to the wall."

Stack kept his eyes away from the large man near the door. "So, what now?"

"Don't worry." He patted Stack's shoulder. "I'll take care of it. As a favor to Johnny."

Before brandy was served, Popov rose and excused himself.

Stack watched him go to the desk and speak with the clerk. Then he went around the desk and disappeared from sight. He turned—the man at the door was gone.

Casually, Stack made his way to the desk.

"Excuse me," he said, nodding back toward his table, "but I want to let my friend know I'm leaving. Can you tell me where he went just now?"

The clerk peered at the register. "Ah . . . room ten, sir."

Stack made his way upstairs and down the hall to room 10. He wrapped his hand around the pistol in his pocket and prepared to kick the door in.

Then the door opened. There was a single bed that was wrinkled, but no one in or on it. He stepped inside and found Popov leaning against the wall.

"What happened here?" asked Stack.

"We need to get out of here. You are a wanted man in this quarter of the world."

"Did you kill him?" asked Stack.

Popov didn't answer.

••• •▬▬• ▬•▬▬

It was a smooth flight to Berlin, and warm—the men all had their coats slung over their shoulders as they disembarked from the plane.

"Jesus—soldiers marching all over the airport," Stack said.

"It's frightening," Hank said.

"Like Russia in the purge," Anton said. "I don't know which is worse, being a Jew or being a spy."

They took a cab to the American embassy. The closer they got to the middle of town, the more oppressive the atmosphere seemed. Stack knew the marching soldiers were death squads.

"What time is dinner?" he asked, though he wasn't remotely hungry.

"Seven sharp," Anton said.

"Okay, see you then," Stack said. The men dispersed to think and rest.

··· ·▬▬· ▬·▬▬

Stack was sitting in the embassy's reading room when Anton burst in.

"I've just stolen the Luftwaffe production plans and numbers," he said, still breathless.

"Then why the hell are you talking to me?" Stack said. "Don't you need to return them before they're missed?"

He tapped his temple and smiled. "No need," he said. "Photographic memory, remember? Took me fifteen minutes to memorize the whole thing."

Stack whistled. "Give me an executive summary. Anything critical?"

"It looks like activity is at the boiling point. Most of the manufactured product is shipping out to countries surrounding France and Russia."

"How should we proceed?" Stack said. "What do you want to tell Donovan?"

Anton shrugged. "You're in charge, aren't you?"

"Then we keep doing what we're doing," Stack said, "with one exception."

··· ·▬▬· ▬·▬▬

"You think they'll make a good team?" Donovan sounded skeptical of Stack's plan, which had Hank working with She-Bear to collect the latest Enigma codes.

"What about the propaganda program?" Donovan asked.

"It's done," Hank said. "Newsreels, movies, voiceovers. They're all in production."

"Wow!" said Donovan. "Hell of a job with all that's going on."

"Not too hard when you get Canaris excited," Hank said. "He rolled out the budget and the manpower, and bingo, here we are."

"Then as far as I'm concerned, you can be on your way to Poland tomorrow morning," Donovan said. "You'll have to change trains in Frankfurt, and then it should be smooth sailing. You know your way around; you just need to look for Ashton and her contacts."

... .--. -.--

Stack and Hank sat down to dinner with Ambassador Kirk, who had succeeded Wilson's brief tenure in the office. After nearly two years, Stack now felt secure in dealing with the older man.

"Just what are you boys up to?" Kirk fixed his gaze on Stack.

"I don't know what to tell you, sir," Stack said, "except that we have our orders and I assume you have yours."

"You could say that," Kirk said. "FDR himself told me not to touch that transmitter in Fletcher's office. Like I was some dirty little boy who'd break the furniture."

"Roosevelt should have filled you in." Stack exchanged a look with Hank, who only shrugged. "We're part of an intelligence operation to help Britain stay ahead of Hitler."

"But that's illegal," said Ambassador Kirk.

"In a sense, maybe," Stack said, "but the president thinks Hitler needs to be stopped, and until the country recognizes that, he wants to help England. If you have difficulty with that, you should take it up with the president."

"I would like to discuss this with him," said Kirk.

"Feel free," Stack said.

••• •▬▬• ▬•▬▬

Walking with Canaris toward his office, Stack sensed the inevitability of death. The Nazi dictatorship was in full bloom. The once-sweet air around the Tiergarten was rancid with smells of military hardware, and the sound of troops in jackboots echoed on every street.

Canaris was on edge. In his first sentence, he even stumbled over the pronunciation of a word or two, the first time Stack had ever heard him do so.

"I'm afraid our leader has bitten off more than can reasonably be digested," Canaris said. "The Balkans, Scandinavia, and France, all before breakfast. The operation I mentioned to you before has been cancelled. And the plans to attack Britain have been postponed to this fall." He sighed. "I would very much like to make peace, my friend, but it seems this will not be possible."

"Why cancel the operation?" Stack took advantage of the unusually candid atmosphere. "I don't see why a sniper couldn't knock him out with one stop."

"His security is too tight," Canaris said. "The assassin would be caught immediately. Valzic has given me his opinion on the matter." He shook his head. "No, now is not the time. But we are pursuing many paths. Oh—and I am truly sorry to hear of your loss in the American embassy."

Stack was halfway out of his chair before he realized it. "What loss?"

"I am sorry," Canaris said. "I thought you had heard. The former ambassador's daughter was always a bit of a free spirit, but being out with Ian Popov was not good judgment." He shook his head. "Popov did some work for us, on and off. It is truly a significant loss."

"When did this happen?" Stack said. Certainly, he hadn't been close to Martha, and most of the time he hadn't even liked her, but this? "And how?"

"Car wreck," Canaris said. "They were on their way home from a party in Paris."

"But we just saw Popov, in Lisbon."

Canaris held up his hands, shrugged. "You must be careful who sees you—and with whom you are seen."

Stack didn't say a word about the Enigma, and Canaris didn't ask.

"Do you think now that America will enter the war?" Canaris asked Stack.

"Not yet," Stack said. "How's progress with the propaganda campaign?"

"There are so many plans on the table, I have trouble keeping track," he said. "But this one I have followed closely, and I think it's going to be a wonderful asset."

As Canaris walked him down the stairs, they passed Heydrich heading up.

"My old friend Stack." Heydrich didn't smile. "You have been absent from many of our meetings, and I have been so busy with my new responsibilities that I had forgotten to ask after you. But here you are, good as new! We must get together and catch up." He saluted. "Heil Hitler!"

Once Stack returned the salute, Heydrich executed a perfect about-face and marched the rest of the way up the steps.

"Wow," Stack said.

"While you are being alert," said Canaris, "be especially wary of that one. He's a viper."

PART III

CHAPTER 20

1945

Much of the energy and vision of the European people had been drained by the time the US entered the war, though as far as Stack was concerned, they'd been waging a secret war for a very long time. The Allies had won the secret wars, and it was finally becoming clear that their armies could win on the battlefield.

In April, Donovan called Stack into his office at the American embassy in London, where Stack had been stationed for nearly five years, since it had become clear that there was a target on his back as long as he stayed in Berlin.

"I have some news."

Stack tensed and felt a pang in his shoulder—though long since healed, it still gave him trouble.

He detected none of Donovan's bluster, which was always present even when delivering bad news.

"Go ahead."

"Canaris is dead."

Stack held the phone for a long moment, feeling short of breath. Canaris had been a good friend, and the implications of his death were so numerous and far-reaching he thought he might drown if he tried to absorb them all at once.

"How?"

"He was found hung, nude, along with his pal Dietrich

Bonhoeffer." Bonhoeffer, a German pastor and theologian, was a spy and a staunch anti-Nazi dissident. Stack had heard of him but never met him.

"When?"

"The Allies found them in the woods three days after the camp was overrun," said Donovan.

"He was a good man." Delicate as their relationship had been, Stack knew that to be true. "A hero."

"I know." Donovan cleared his throat. "Allen Dulles wants you to call him in Bern."

"What does he want?"

"I suspect that he wants you to help figure out what's next for the OSS."

The Office of Strategic Services, or OSS, had been created in June 1942. It was a brainchild of both FDR and Donovan, and Donovan had come to rely on Stack to play a large role in getting it off the ground. By now, Stack had become invaluable to Donovan.

"Why me?" asked Stack. "You're the one who came up with the whole idea."

"I'm too busy," Donovan said. "But I know you think like I do, so you're the man. And with Canaris gone . . ."

"I know," Stack said. A hundred minor projects had just come to an end. "I assume I'll be working with the SOE?"

"Maybe not. But whatever the case, we need to have a relationship with Britain that is tighter than a lion trainer's ass. Have that in the back of your mind always. Don't go wandering off the reservation," Donovan said.

"I won't," Stack said. "But Boss, I don't think I can be in there shaping government agencies. First, I don't know the scope. Next, I'm not an organization man."

"Stop right there. Damn it, Stack," said Donovan, "the one

thing we don't want is for these Yale bureaucrats to start reinventing the wheel. They'll fuck up any chance we have of the winning against the Russians. Just go see what Dulles has to say, and we'll jump in from there."

"I don't see any blue sky," said Stack.

"Come on, Stack. Where's that can-do attitude that will win us a war? Get the fuck out of here, and don't forget to call me," said Donovan.

··· ·–– –·––

Germany surrendered soon after this, but the war in the Pacific continued, with US troops capturing one island at a time, still losing thousands of soldiers. In August 1945, President Truman gave the order to drop the atomic bomb on Japan. Surrender was swift, and the terrible war was finally over.

Around this time, Stack was sitting in his office going over the list of operational materials when the phone rang. "Stack!" It was Donovan. "Can you come to my office right now?"

"Sure, be there in a minute." Stack shook his head as he stood up—had he forgotten a meeting? He racked his brain all the way down the hall, until he opened the door to Donovan's office.

"We meet again!" The deep, throaty voice was that of Winston Churchill, who pushed himself to his feet as Stack entered the office. "Allow me to introduce Gerald Attwater of the BBC, and Edward R. Murrow of CBS in America."

After everyone shook hands, Churchill motioned them to sit.

"As you know, I will be leaving office soon," said Churchill. "But before I go, I want very much to recognize two men who answered the call to service and, without any hope of commendation or acknowledgment, took up arms as soldiers in the secret war. You all know General Donovan. But you probably don't know that in Europe's darkest days, he joined with me in developing plans of action to hold Germany at bay until our allies signed on."

Churchill gathered his breath and, leaning on Donovan's desk, continued. "Much must be kept secret for obvious reasons, but as the years go by I want the names of these two men to be remembered. Therefore I, along with US General Marshall, am nominating General Donovan to lead us forward in our ongoing joint intelligence efforts."

••• •▬▬• ▬•▬▬

In the cold of December 1945, Allen Dulles, station chief of the Bern, Switzerland, office of the OSS, came to London to meet with Bill Donovan. As Donovan's aide, Stack was invited to attend.

"We've been able to create and operate a highly successful intelligence network," said Donovan. "And now that the hot war is turning into a cold war with the communist countries led by the Soviet Union, we need a much more sophisticated organization."

"We have all the support in the world," Dulles told the group. "Congress is for us a hundred percent. And President Truman wants it done now."

"Well, it's about time," said Donovan. "He's the one who got rid of the OSS."

"He's not wrong to be cautious," said Dulles. "From Washington, it looks like we have a lot of agencies to say grace over. And there's too damn much duplication. But we have been in the field since the beginning of the war, and we're ready to be expanded into a leadership role. We've got the manpower. Now's the time to put it together and do it right."

"Well, Allen, you know how I feel," Donovan said. "I'm all in."

"I will let you know," Dulles said, "that President Truman has made this operation one of his highest priorities. But MacArthur and Nimitz are against us. They want to run their own operation, not one that works with Washington. They can't stand the competition."

Donovan looked at each man at the table before speaking again. "I'm going to be working full-time in Nuremburg. I suggest we come up with someone we can all back to head up this new unit. The man I have complete confidence in is Stack. All through the war, he was the most efficient agent of the intelligence operations in Europe. He was better known in the Nazi world than in the US. That will be to our advantage as we establish our intelligence presence in the Allies' minds. Reputation counts. Remember, experience and imagination are key."

Stack was shocked by this turn of events. Flattered, of course, but wary. He had not been expecting this level of responsibility, but if duty called, he would do his best to answer.

CHAPTER 21

1946

Stack couldn't help but compare his life now with what it'd been like when he was prowling Berlin, Lisbon, and Gdansk, an agent in the field, instead of a coordinator in an office. He never imagined he'd miss the excitement, but he did.

He also had more time to think. Mary Jane flowed into his mind, and the thought created a tightness in his stomach. He hadn't heard from her in a long while, and given that he'd been delinquent in writing, didn't expect a letter. Knowing she'd moved on hurt, but he understood. He became depressed, and even with a job to occupy his time, he felt bored and lonesome. Whenever he had an opportunity to get out in the field, he seized it.

On an inspection of one of the bombed-out buildings in Paris, Stack slipped on some crumbling stairs and twisted his knee.

"Sir," said his aide. "Are you hurt?"

"Nothing serious," he said—then flinched when he tried to put weight on his left leg. "I can't stand, though. Better have the doctor wrap it up."

His aide hailed a non-com passing by in a jeep. "How about a ride to the field hospital?"

••• •▬▬• ▬•▬▬

At the field tent that currently served as a hospital, Stack was relegated to a waiting area, where he picked up a year-old magazine and began to read.

A woman's voice—familiar, and one he hadn't heard in a very long time. "Well, look who finally decided to show up."

He looked up.

Mary Jane stood there, hands on her hips. She was smiling, but her lips were quivering slightly. She looked older, and it suited her—as did the crisp white nurse's uniform she wore.

"My God!" Stack tried to stand and stumbled, nearly falling to the floor. He managed to catch himself against the wall. "What are you doing here?"

"Let me help you," she said.

She slung his arm over her shoulder, but he stumbled again. They ended up sliding to the floor, in each other's arms.

Mary Jane looked him in the eye.

"I missed you," she said. Stack was shocked to find his own face covered in tears, and his hands trembled as he hugged her back.

They walked out of the large tent, with Stack leaning on Mary Jane. She guided him into a smaller tent with a cot—as a senior nurse, he found out later, she had the freedom to go where she pleased.

"I heard you were here," she said, "but I didn't really believe it." She pulled up a chair next to his bed. "And now here you are." She dabbed the corners of her eyes with her sleeve.

"I don't know what to say."

"Don't say anything," she said. "I'm so happy to have found you."

"There's so much I want to tell you. . . . I don't know where to start."

"I know where you are now, at least." She took a deep breath. "Don't worry—we have each other now."

••• •▪▪• ▪•▪▪

Stack returned to his London office, and Mary Jane began the process of transferring there. While he lived for the few precious moments they spent together, bitter emotions slowly surfaced as the novelty of reunion wore off.

"I'm truly sorry I couldn't keep in touch with you," Stack said. "Honestly. I went from pillar to post in Poland, Germany, and England. Just getting through the day alive was hard enough. I know it sounds awful, but I was thinking more about me than you—I had to."

"I accept that." She took a long, shaky breath. "But I'm not going to go through not hearing from you again—I don't think I could handle it. I spent all my time worrying—about you, about me, about whether we were ever in love, about whether you'd ever even cared for me. No, I'd rather split up now, for good." She teared up. "Four letters in eight years, Stack. What do you think I thought? I'll tell you—that you didn't give two damns for me. I don't know how I got through those years."

"Mary Jane . . ."

"I met a soldier who asked me to marry him," she said, "before he left for the front. Deep down I knew I loved you, so I turned him down. But how can I feel secure like this? How can I know you won't just disappear on me again? I'm so damn mad I could spit!" Mary Jane pushed the table away from where she was sitting.

"I understand," Stack said. "I feel like I haven't had a moment to breathe in eight years. I had you on my mind, but I always found a hundred reasons not to write, and . . . I was so damned immature. Will you forgive me? For me to be as in love as I am after such a long time is truly a sign," Stack said.

"I don't know." She sounded so sad. "I want to. I think. But I'm not sure. I've got to learn how I feel about you all over again." Mary Jane looked at Stack with her soft, steel-blue eyes. She shook her head. "We planted these seeds eight years ago. I still love you, I think, but . . . is that enough? Enough to make up for eight years of neglect and humiliation?"

"I spent those eight years knowing my life could be over in a flash," Stack said. "All I want now is to be with you and settle down."

"We'll see." She backed away. "I have to get back to work now. I have a job to do too, you know."

"Yes, I know," replied Stack. "But think about it hard."

"I will. I promise," said Mary Jane. "I've got a long drive with a private driving, so my concentration may not kick in until later."

"I hope I can get my work done, too," said Stack.

••• •▬▬• ▬•▬▬

Donovan ran into Stack in the hall late that afternoon.

"Boss," Stack said, "have you got a minute?"

"Sure," said Donovan. "What's on your mind?"

"Come on into my office," Stack said. "This might take a second."

They both took seats and Donovan folded his arms. "What's up, Stack?"

"First, I just want to tell you I'm flattered, more than I can say, to be in this position," he said. "It's an honor I could never have imagined."

"Yeah, yeah, yeah," said Donovan. "What's the issue?"

"It's Mary Jane," he said. "We're having one hell of a time reconciling after eight years. It may not work, but dammit, I want to give it all I've got, and I honestly don't know if there's enough of me to go around. I want to get back to the girl I wanted to marry. We've put this off since 1937."

Donovan nodded—he was familiar with young men experiencing a sudden desire to be with a woman when hostilities subsided.

"Tell you what," Donovan said. "Why don't you go back to the States, get married, then fly back here with your new wife?"

Stack brightened at the idea. "If she says yes, then I think that's one hell of an idea."

"Come on, Stack," said Donovan. "Who else needs to approve it?" Donovan rose from his seat on Stack's desk and came to Stack with a smile and his hand out. "Congratulations," he said.

••• •▬▬• ▬•▬▬

The next day, Stack tried to reach Mary Jane. "Damn it to hell!" Stack swore into the phone. "Doesn't anything work the way it's supposed to?" He beat the table. "It's only two hundred miles to the field hospital. I could walk it. Shit." Stack's frustration overflowed. He was so anxious to tell Mary Jane the plan and get her approval.

A pretty English secretary paused. "What's the problem, sir?"

"I can't get a connection."

After a couple of minutes, the line began to ring, and Mary Jane answered.

"Mary Jane, thank God."

"Is that you, Stack?"

"Yes, and I've been having a hell of a time reaching you."

"I've been busy." She sounded cool. "How are things with you?"

"Well, I got some great news," Stack said. "I was thinking—

we should go back to the States, get married, then fly back to London for a year or two."

"Is that so?" Mary Jane replied. "Well, I can see you've got it all figured out. You didn't even need to consult me at all."

Stack said nothing. For the first time, he saw himself not as a brave young spy, but a self-centered boy. Minutes of silence seemed to go by. His heart dropped.

"Mary Jane, are you still there?"

"Yes," she said, her voice business-like.

"I love you and want to marry you," Stack said. He ran a hand through his hair. "I know this isn't perfect, but I'm trying to show you how much you mean to me. I really want to commit to this—to us."

Another long pause.

"Why don't you come up here and we can talk about it?" she said. "I'm not going to give it another thought until I see you face-to-face."

"Done," he said. "I'll head up as soon as I can."

"It's just a train ride," Mary Jane said. "I've got to go now. Keep in touch and let me know what you decide to do."

She hung up.

··· ·−−· −·−−

You are the most insensitive man I have ever known, and in the last eight years, I've known quite a few, Mary Jane wrote in the letter she sent after their phone call.

He knew she was right, but he wouldn't be sending any more letters. She'd said it herself—she wouldn't give it another thought until they were face-to-face.

He stuck his head in Donovan's door.

"Boss, I need to head to Manchester."

"Why?" said Donovan.

"To talk to Mary Jane. The phones are on the blink." Stack replied.

Donovan waved a hand without looking up from his paperwork. "Go get her, kid."

... .--. -.--

The marriage of Mary Jane Armstrong and Milton Stack in the spring of 1946 became an eclectic reunion. The wedding was held in London, with the Armstrongs and Stack's parents in attendance. It was the first time he'd seen them since 1937, and nostalgia flowed like honey. A surprise guest was the congressional candidate from Boston, John Fitzgerald Kennedy.

"My God, Stack. You look great," said Jack. Look at you. No more rags, but still country-boy plain."

"Screw you," said Stack. "Jack, you really do look great, even if I hate to admit it."

As they moved toward the church, Jack held Stack's arm and whispered, "I want to talk to you when things settle down."

"Great. I've got a couple of things to talk to you about too," said Stack.

Stack saw Hank and Juliane, formerly known as She-Bear, walking up to the country chapel where everyone was gathering.

"My God," Stack whispered.

She-Bear and Hank ran to Stack. She-Bear was crying, and Hank hugged his long-missed buddy.

"I can't believe you came!" Stack said. "I had no idea where you were, or what you've been doing."

"We missed you too," Hank said. "Where's Anton?"

"He thought it might make trouble to attend a wedding this side of the Iron Curtain," Stack said. "But we can get in touch if we're careful."

Hank and She-Bear were introduced as old colleagues. Stack learned they'd gotten married and now resided in West Berlin.

"Hank, Juliane," Stack said. "This is more than a reunion. This is a rebirth. I'm so filled with warmth—it feels like the bonds are stronger than ever. Remember that time in the Citadel when you made me drop my pants?"

They all chuckled.

"We could have defeated the whole German army with our attitude," Juliane said. "No problem was too big."

"I miss Anton," Stack said. "I hope this isn't the last we see of each other."

"Every time I visit other cities and governments," said Hank, "I become impressed all over again at how terrific our team was."

"You know, I even miss Canaris," Stack said. "I was always impressed by how clever he could be. He gathered the tools needed to do a job for the benefit of mankind."

"And Jepsen." She-Bear looked wistful. "He was a good teammate, and a friend. I'll never forget him."

"Let's make a pact right now," Stack said. "Let's get together somewhere in June of 1950 for another reunion."

"Hear, hear," Hank said. They raised their glasses.

••• •▬▬• ▬•▬▬

Later that afternoon, Stack found some time to be alone with his parents. He wrapped his arms around them, grateful they hadn't had to experience the horrors of war-torn Europe.

"I know you're relieved the war is over," said his dad, "and I know you probably don't want to think about these things, but . . ." He shook his head. "You hear about the bomb, and Russia . . . it's hard to feel safe."

What could he say to alleviate their fears—without saying too much?

"Let's not worry about it today," Stack said. "I know it's hard, but we should take these moments when they come, and appreciate them as much as we can."

... .--. -.--

The parents of the bride and groom were anxious to know how and where the newlyweds were going to live. Stack assured them he had an excellent government job that would keep them in London for a year, and then they'd return to settle down in Washington, DC.

"I'm committed to helping set up this new agency," said Stack. "And I'll delay making a definite decision on my future employment until I talk to my best advisor."

"And who's that?"

He pulled Mary Jane close to his side with a smile. "My wife."

Donovan attended the wedding, but to all the other guests he was just a nice-looking major general who didn't want to talk about the war. They had no idea the crucial role he'd played, nor of his current undertaking.

... .--. -.--

"This year is going to be hard, you know," Stack said to Mary Jane one evening. "Food is scarce, and so are jobs. And we may never get used to English food."

"Even if all I'm doing is helping wipe away tears, it will be worth it," Mary Jane said. "But there's something else, isn't there? You're tense, and good news doesn't seem to help."

He gazed several feet ahead, eyes fixed on something beyond

the present moment.

"Things will get better every day," he said at last. "But the fact is, the secret wars are still going on. The A-bomb only makes things worse. I haven't talked to Anton since he left Berlin, and that makes me antsy. I know he's up to his ass in alligators, somewhere behind the Iron Curtain. I couldn't even get word to him about the wedding."

"Are you sure?" Mary Jane stopped, and laid a hand on his knee. "Could something have happened to him?"

"I hope not," Stack said. "I keep an eye out every day, but nothing so far."

... .--. -.--

Working in London gave Stack opportunities to learn the fates of people from the old OSS.

"Most of the British have gone into MI5 and MI6," said Donovan over lunch with Stack.

"You remember Valzic? Any sign of him?"

"How could I forget Valzic? Creepy son of a bitch. But no, haven't heard about him in a long time," said Donovan. "Why?"

"I've been wondering about him ever since Canaris told me Ian Popov was shot—that's why his car went off the road that night."

"Where are you going with this?"

"I've been keeping an eye out for Anton and some of the others, but Valzic is one name that's fallen through the cracks completely. Nobody's seen him since Canaris died; nobody seems to know what happened to him. But I know he and Canaris were tight. He owed Canaris some kind of favor, something big." He shrugged. "Just wondering . . ."

"Well, as far as I'm concerned, Valzic is one I wouldn't mind never seeing again," said Donovan. Then he chuckled. "Maybe I told you to use your imagination a little too often."

Just then, Hank strode over to their table.

"Why wasn't I invited to this little get-together?"

Stack and Donovan both stood to give Hank a hug and a slap on the back before inviting him to pull up a chair.

"We were just reminiscing," Stack said. "Past days."

"Great days," said Donovan.

"Damn right," Stack said. "I haven't regretted one moment of it. Have you?"

"Not for a second," Hank said.

"So, what's in your future?" Stack said. "Now that you're married—and I don't recall getting an invitation to the wedding, pal."

"It was a spur-of-the-moment thing," Hank said with a smile. "Juliane and I may live in West Berlin, but we live in Poland in our hearts."

"That puts you in the heart of the East-West struggle," said Donovan.

"That suits us fine," said Hank, "We can do a lot of good from there as long as we operate closely with the Central Intelligence Group."

"I sense you've gotten a whiff of the administrative overlay the USA requires," Stack said. "It ain't the good ol' OSS."

"Well, if anyone can handle it, big guy"—Hank grinned—"it's you."

"Which brings me to my favorite subject." Donovan pointed his fork at Stack. "We need to talk about you."

"What about me?" said Stack, his shoulders already tightening up.

"You've been a saving grace in the transition from OSS to CIG," Donovan said. "You've got the most experience with the niceties of the organization."

"Well . . ."

"No kidding, Stack. We need you more than ever."

"Mary Jane's ready to go home," Stack said. "And I am too. Souers already talked to me about Bern and London, and it's just not appealing. Donovan, I know you've dedicated your life to serving your country. You make me feel like a worse man sometimes, honestly. But the fire just isn't in my belly anymore."

"Think about it," said Donovan. "That's all I ask."

"Still no word from Anton?" said Stack. "Hank, you hear anything?

Donovan shook his head, as did Hank.

"I'm worried about him," Stack said.

"It's certainly worrisome, I'll give you that," said Donovan. "Anton has a mental library the size of an aircraft hangar, and it looks like he's turned it all over to the Soviets."

"He wouldn't," Hank said. "Would he?"

"You don't know Anton," Stack said. "But I don't think we need to worry just yet. Also, notify our agents to be on alert regarding him. We won't all be fixtures where we are now."

••• •▬▬• ▬•▬▬

When they returned to the embassy, Stack was glad to see his old friend Jack Kennedy talking with a group in the lobby. Stack stepped over to speak to Jack.

"Stack, you know I've gone into politics?" said Jack.

"Yes, but I've been too busy to congratulate you."

"I don't need any of that bullshit," Jack said. "Besides, I haven't won yet. But I do need help. Someone who can get things done. And that person is you."

"What are you talking about, Jack?"

"No rush, but I really need you." Jack was earnest. All the frivolity was gone from his face.

"Jack, I don't know how I could help. My experience does me no good," said Stack.

"Nonsense," Jack said. "The team that is coming to me are academics or political pros. I need a thinker and a doer. You're a guy I can depend on. Furthermore, you now know the lay of the land in Europe. And Europe is where we are going to fight the Russians. I'll talk with you in a week," said Jack.

"You are very persuasive. I guess some things never change," Stack said, recalling the early days of their friendship. "Remember how young we were just a few years ago, and how much experience taught us?"

"If we're to have a country we want our children to live in, it's in our hands to help young people develop and grow. Never forget that the future in in the hands of the young."

CHAPTER 22

November 24, 1963

As soon as the funeral procession was over, Stack hustled Mary Jane back to their apartment off Dupont Circle.

He went into his tiny office and shut the door.

He needed to think.

On his desk was a typewriter he'd never gotten the hang of using, a few papers, and an old prewar cable machine. It was long since obsolete, but he'd kept it up and running—partly for sentimental reasons, and partly because it was his last line of communication with Anton.

Which gave him an idea.

••• •■■• ■•■■

Thirty minutes later he came out with a folded paper, which he tucked in his breast pocket next to the polaroid of Valzic.

"Stack, what's going on?" Mary Jane said.

"I'll explain later," he said. "Right now, I have to get to Bobby's office."

"But why?" she said. "Who was that man?"

"Mary Jane, I promise I'll tell you everything," he said. "But right now, I've got to go."

"How long will you be gone?" she asked.

"I'm not sure." He paused. "I'll see you later."

••• •▬▬• ▬•▬▬

The cab took Stack directly to the attorney general's office, where he was surprised to find a receptionist at her desk on Sunday afternoon.

"Good afternoon, Stack."

"Good afternoon, Linda," he said. "I'm here to see the AG—it's urgent."

"He'll be right out."

Stack had just found a comfortable seat when Bobby Kennedy flung open the door.

"Stack," Bobby said. "Damn good to see you."

"Thanks, Bobby. I know how sick at heart you are, and I'm sure you know I feel the same."

He followed Bobby into the office and hung his jacket over the back of a chair as Bobby took a seat behind the desk.

"So, what's on your mind?"

Stack grabbed the back of the chair. "I know who shot Jack."

Bobby stared. "What are you . . . ?"

"I was on the curb watching the funeral procession," Stack said, "and I saw, not ten feet away, a Soviet assassin—I've seen him before. He saw me, too, and recognized me. This guy is a thug and a sharpshooter."

"Jesus! Got a name?"

"Valzic Krewcheski."

"Doesn't sound Russian."

"He's Polish," Stack said. "He became a spy and an assassin for the Nazis during the war, then went freelance. Since the early fifties he's been one of Russia's top killers." He handed over the Polaroid.

Bobby studied the snap. "But you do think this was a Soviet assassination attempt?"

"Maybe, maybe not," Stack said. "There's something else you should take a look at." He pulled the paper out of his pocket, unfolded it, and slid it across the desk.

"What's this?" Bobby asked.

"I have an old cable machine," he said, "and so does my friend Anton, who's now on the other side of the Iron Curtain—remember him? No one cables anymore, which gives us a clear wave of most of the time. Just read this and give me your first take on it."

> *The Soviet Union was in no way involved in the regretful assassination of President Kennedy. We have a high regard for the quality of the police forces of the United States and will cooperate with them in whatever way they would like for us to. It appears that this act was a conspiracy, as one man could not coordinate and execute this type of operation. We recognize that the suspect, Oswald, spent time in Russia and that his wife is Russian. But we had no contact with him except that he tried to join our military. He also did time in the US Marines.*
> *Reviewing the events in the six months leading up to the tragedy, it is not surprising that this happened.*
> *Our sincere condolences.*

The letter was signed by the general secretariat of the politburo.

"Well?"

Bobby skimmed the paper, frowning. "Not to be blunt, but my first thought is that you and the sender are close friends, and the sender is a Soviet spy and a communist. But that's just my gut reaction."

"Bobby, I trust Anton with my life," Stack said. "This looks like the Soviets wanted to make sure they were not a target in any investigation we instigate. And remember, this is the same guy who gave us the straight dope on the Cuban missile issue. Saved us going to war."

"Agreed." Bobby called to his secretary. "Linda, please put this memo on file." As soon as she'd taken the memo and shut the door, he shook his head.

"Boy, this must be urgent for him to go around their State Department and directly to you," Bobby said, with a quizzical look on his face. "They really don't want the shadow to fall on them."

"Once rumors start, they never stop." Stack looked at Bobby for a reaction.

Bobby was staring blankly at him. Then he shook his head with an attempt to focus. He finger-combed his mop of hair, pushing most of it from his forehead.

"Sorry, Stack," he said. "I'm having a hell of a time thinking straight. I'm not surprised the bastards started shooting, I just always thought it would be me they shot at. Christ, I wish we could call Jack up and get his opinion." He sighed. "What are the implications of this for my family?"

"I don't think it was the Russians alone," Stack said. "But they do need to be investigated. Jack was hated by several groups. Your tough performance at the Mob corruption hearings and looking for communists under every stone ruffled a lot of feathers too. And in a very touchy area, our own CIA and air force were both involved in the Pigs fiasco. Dallas itself was a cauldron of Kennedy hate. But the city didn't do this. It's possible a key local could have aided and abetted, but there's no other evidence. So the case is building against Oswald."

"And look at Oswald," Bobby said. "Typical mob formula—first they get a guy like him, who's got no hang-ups about killing the president and who's too dumb to realize he's being set up. The guy was probably a pretty good shot, too, and took a lot of pride in that. So, the Mob trains him, sets him up in the school book depository, and waits. As soon as the deed is done, they have Ruby eliminate him."

"Or the Russians train him, then turn him over to the Mob, who sets it up," Stack said.

"Air transportation courtesy of the US Air Force and General LeMay's staff," said Bobby. "They continue to fuck up. I'll personally shoot LeMay if it turns out that his folks let this guy go."

"But I'm convinced it was Valzic who pulled the trigger," Stack said. "Here's a theory: the team has someone shadow Oswald in case he doesn't shoot or misses. In either case, number two shooter hits the target *and* Oswald. Jack Ruby was the mob's plant to be sure they got Oswald."

"Makes sense," said Bobby. "This guy Valzic was the shooter, Oswald gets the credit, and Ruby does the boss's bidding but is too removed from the mob to be a threat. The key is finding Valzic. Shit!" He burst up out of his chair and started pacing. "He could be miles away by now."

"Damn, Bobby, sit down," Stack said. "You're making yourself a wreck."

Bobby gave Stack a wry look and settled on the edge of his desk, but only for a moment. Then he was back to pacing the length of the office.

"Look, Bobby," he said. "I'm here, and I'm not a politician. I can help you the same way I helped your brother. But you have to trust me, the way Jack did."

"Okay, okay," said Bobby. "We're in this together."

"So! First order of business," Stack said. "I don't think we should show Anton's communiqué to anyone just yet. Not LBJ, not the CIA, no one. I'll see if I can touch base with some old contacts—they might be able to give me a picture of what things look like a little closer to our friends in the USSR, without us leaning too much on Anton."

"Lyndon is putting together a commission to be headed by Chief Justice Warren to look into the murder," Bobby said, "but that'll be nothing like what we can do." He paused, then walked to the door and grabbed his coat. "Let's keep our powder dry, Stack. I'm going home for now. Let's talk this through after the funeral."

"Good idea," Stack called after him. "See you tomorrow, Bobby."

Stack was putting on his own coat when Bobby stuck his head back in the door.

"Stack, I'm sure in my gut that this is an extension of the conflicts we've been having with the Cubans, the Mob, and our own CIA and military hawks."

Stack sighed and slid his coat back off. "Should I sit down?"

"You know all this, but I think we need to go over these events so we have a combined fact base to direct our investigation." Bobby slipped his coat back off, shut the door, and loosened his tie. With hands in his pockets, he circled the desk.

"I talked with Jack before he went to Texas—tried to talk him out of going. I've had a feeling for some time that someone was going to kill one of us, but with all the shit I've been throwing at those right-wing and Mob guys, I was sure they'd come after me. Then when we failed to send in the second wave of air support for the Pigs invaders, the military and CIA started their 'grooming for death' talk."

"How can Americans go around killing other Americans over policy and strategy disagreements?" said Stack. "I saw it in Europe during the war, but never in the United States."

"Ever hear of Huey Long?" asked Bobby.

"Sounds familiar," Stack said. He had an odd prickling sensation on the back of his neck—he'd heard the name, a long time ago, but where?

"He was the representative of the little man until he got in the way of the bosses, and out he went," Bobby said. "It all goes back to Ethel and Julius Rosenberg giving our A-Bomb to the Russians. Communists seem to be the main object of people's fear, and with Russia having these weapons, communism becomes more of a threat. The racketeer hearings gained me a hell of a lot of hate from powerful Mob bosses. The military hated Jack after the whole Pigs fuck-up, and civil-rights efforts have ignited more hatred. Those newspaper articles warning Jack not to go to Dallas have really pissed me off, too."

Stack loosened his tie and rubbed his neck. "I did see Drew Pearson's column responding to the Dallas articles, but it didn't really sink in. Something about a paramilitary group called the Rangers?"

"So did I," said Bobby, "but I thought it came from inside." Bobby rubbed his eyes with both hands. "Damn, I'm tired."

"Bobby, go home and help the family. I'll start putting together a profile on the kind of people we'll need to run our own little investigation. Then, after the funeral, we can sit down and create a strategy. That sound okay?"

"Good advice. I'll ask Linda to call you and set it up."

"Bobby."

Bobby stopped and turned around.

"Just so there are no surprises," Stack said, "I think we need an in-depth planning session before we start pulling anyone in."

"There's just too much going on to have that luxury," Bobby responded.

"I don't see it as a luxury, I see it as mandatory." Stack pulled his coat on for a second time. "We can't have guys running around stepping on each other's neckties. And we need evidence."

"What we need is to get in there before the clumsies stomp all over the crime scene or bury the evidence any further."

"I agree we need to move while the trail is hot."

"So, you're with me?" asked Bobby.

"Always," Stack said. "But we'll talk about it more after we both get some sleep."

··· ·–·–· –·––

Stack walked down the Mall, leaving the Justice Department behind him. In the OSS, they'd moved on problems and usually had the solution in mind. This situation was rekindling old memories. He hated whoever had killed the president as much as he'd hated the Nazis on the rail platform in Prague.

Whoever was behind the conspiracy—whoever was ultimately responsible—they were dominated by arrogance. Everything was about what *they* wanted, and to hell with anyone else.

When Stack returned to their apartment, Mary Jane was glued to the television. The whole country was running on adrenaline, but he didn't feel that things were in chaos. He'd seen true chaos, and this was still a long way from it.

"Stack! Thank God." Mary Jane ran to him and wrapped her arms around his waist, holding him tightly. "How was your meeting?"

Stack squeezed her once, then took a hanger from the closet and hung up his coat.

"The game is on, and we can't lose." He sat on the love seat and stared out the window. From the eighth floor, the view over Georgetown was stunning: to the southeast they could see the Potomac River, the Washington Monument, and the Lincoln Memorial. No wind disturbed the vibrant leaves on the trees encircling the Tidal Basin.

"What did Bobby want you for at a time like this?" She smoothed her skirt, joined him on the love seat, put her hand over his, and looked into his eyes patiently.

"He's convinced the murder was part of a conspiracy," Stack said. Pausing to let that thought sink in, he took a deep breath and continued. "And he wants me to find out who, and why."

Her brow creased. "That's a pretty big job."

"It's not that, so much. It's more . . . I don't know what it is right now." He put his head in his hands, elbows propped on his knees. "I'm tired."

She stood, still holding his hand. "Then come to bed."

CHAPTER 23

November 26, 1963

Both men arrived at the Justice Department at nine the morning after the president's funeral.

"I haven't gotten any further with this," Stack said. "But I think everything we talked about before is solid. It makes too much sense."

"Here's my thinking," said Bobby. "First, I'm convinced this was a conspiracy; at the very least it was a group effort."

"What makes you so sure?"

"Like you said—it makes too much sense."

"Then let's move on that concept for starters," Stack said.

"You said you were going to put together some profiles," Bobby said. "What have you got so far?"

"I do know a couple of fellows over in Langley I worked with in Europe both before and during the war," Stack said. In truth he wished Donovan was still alive—his old mentor would be bound to have some advice. "And some people I've worked with who aren't on the books. Frankly they're the only ones I think we can trust. Langley is infamous for leaks."

"CIA scares me, but I'll start the wheels turning," said Bobby.

Bobby kept talking, but Stack's attention drifted. *Who in the Company is high enough and thinks like we do?*

"We need to find these guys through Justice while I still run it," said Bobby.

"Why Justice?"

Bobby circled the desk. "Because chances are slim that a CIA guy will be so loosely tied to the Company as to become loyal to us," he said. "The profile will be a malcontent due to intercompany politics. We need a quality, loyal team from the start."

"I agree," Stack said. "Bobby, you need to trust me on this—if I can find some old friends of mine, we'll have everything we need."

••• •▬▬• ▬•▬▬

The paths in Rock Creek Park were littered with fist-sized rocks, but Stack could pick his way between them if he took it easy. That suited him fine—he needed time to think. Being in that wooded park in late afternoon on a clear day reminded him of walking through the Tiergarten with Anton, or Canaris.

As Stack followed the leaf-covered path, he turned over everything he and Bobby had talked about.

Who's making all this mischief? Stack wondered as he turned back up the path and toward home. *What if we're wrong?*

••• •▬▬• ▬•▬▬

Stack decided his best move now was to contact Hank, who'd kept in contact over the years and now worked at the FBI.

"It's been a while." Hank sounded cordial but cautious on the phone. "What's going on in your life these days?"

"Well," Stack said, "things have been difficult lately, as you can imagine." He took a moment to sort out his thoughts. "Hank, I've got a problem. And I think—I hope—that you can help me."

"You only have to ask," Hank said.

••• •▬▬• ▬•▬▬

Stack had been a part of the intelligence landscape for years, but had never been inside the offices of the FBI. Jack had warned him about Hoover and his disciples. He had no experience with the culture of the greatest investigative organization in the world, Mr. Hoover's Kingdom. But things were different now. Stack knew a hell of a lot about the European Intelligence agencies. Agencies had divvied up their territory, and they didn't like to share. The last thing he needed was a bunch of agents running into each other in the field and bungling each other's operations.

It had turned colder since the funeral. Stack grabbed his navy-blue topcoat out of the closet and, on instinct as much as anything else, took down the snap-brim felt hat he rarely wore, hoping it would help him fit in at the agency. This trip needed to be as low-key as possible.

Out on the curb, he hailed a cab driver heading in the opposite direction, who was able to execute a U-turn and get to him. The pace was stop-and-start all the way to the agency, and by the time they arrived, Stack was a nervous wreck.

He paid the driver, slid across the seat to open the curbside door, and jumped out. Moving quickly to the massive doors, he entered the marble lobby and walked directly to the welcome desk. The receptionist called to confirm that he was expected, then sent him upstairs to Hank's office.

"Hey, Stack, old man." Hank was smiling and enthusiastic as he came out of the elevator. "Great to see you."

Before the elevator doors closed, a second person stepped out.

"Juliane!" The years had lavished softness and beauty on She-Bear, and Stack was taken aback by her loveliness. "It's good to see you again," he said. "Thanks for coming in on such short notice."

"Don't give it another thought, pal." Hank was a rail of a man who hadn't gained a pound in twenty years, but his hair was turning gray at the temples and he had heavy wrinkles in his neck. He was made of solid stuff.

Hank put his arm around Stack's shoulder and guided him from the elevators, Juliane trailing behind. Once in the office, off came the suit jacket, and he loosened his tie. Hank said. "Hell of a shame what's happened, Stack."

"Terrible," Juliane said. "We're so sorry."

"Sure has this place in an uproar," Hank said. "I've never seen a criminal caught so quickly."

"Does it make you wonder, Hank?" Stack took off his hat. "I mean, is that really the long and short of it?"

"Well, I hear the president has the director putting together a commission to investigate," Hank said. "And Congress is doing the same thing."

"What do you think?" Stack asked.

"Here at the FBI, we're not supposed to offer an opinion until we have all the evidence."

"Between us, I don't see how it could be just one man," Stack said. "But before we go any further, you should know I'm here on behalf of the attorney general."

"Well, then there's nothing to stop this conversation," Juliane said. "Let's get to it."

"Feels like the old days with Donovan," Hank said. "Don't let anything get in the way of results."

"Fair enough." Stack filled them in—on spotting Valzic at the parade, on Bobby's theories about the conspiracy, everything.

"Holy shit," Hank said. "He was just walking around watching our president's funeral parade? Let me check the files and see what we've got. You need anything? Coffee?"

"Coffee would be great."

"Okay, be back in a minute."

Juliane said, "Stack, it's great to be working with you again."

Returning, Hank said, "Sorry, pal. We've got a file on Valzic, but all it says is that he's from Poland and a known assassin. But I need to inform the CIA and Interpol."

"Okay," Stack said. "You know where to find me. And here are some photos you can send to other agencies. You may want to make copies."

"Thanks," Hank said. "I'll jump right on it."

... .−−. −.−−

Running through the names of personnel he knew in the Justice Department, Stack began to establish criteria for the next team members.

"I don't want an old hand from the Company for a couple of reasons," he said when he brought Bobby up to speed. "First, the closer they are to the top, the more likely it is that they're aligned with Company thinking."

"Agreed," Bobby said. "If it's anything like the FBI, their brains are rusted over after years of not using them. All they know how to do is follow the director."

Stack knew Robert Kennedy was the power behind this effort in terms of money, authorizations, and people. But if Bobby were no longer the attorney general, the team would disband. President Johnson had asked all staff, cabinet members, and others to stay on. But if LBJ and RFK crossed swords too often, that could change.

They'd been able to secure Hank and Juliane on a temporary basis after Bobby talked with Director Dulles.

"This is basically an indoor job," Stack told his friends. "No James Bond stuff, except in rare instances. We need to all be on the same page always. Juliane will be our coordinator, and she'll have an office here in Justice. She'll report to me and Bobby. Still interested?"

"Sure," Hank said. "How many people are there in this operation?"

Stack smiled. "The team is small—I'll only add people if I absolutely have to. This is so tight, a casual word could land us all in jail. It's going to look like we are working with Valzic, not against him."

••• •▬▬• ▬•▬▬

It was time for everyone to meet, so Stack brought Hank and Juliane to the AG's office.

"Hey, Linda," he said. "Is Bobby around?"

"Not at the moment, but I expect him back soon. In the meantime, Stack, you have a coded message. We went ahead and decoded it."

"Shocking."

Linda smiled and handed him the message. Stack took a seat and tore open the envelope.

> *Arrive tomorrow morning Delta 335 from Berlin. Representing the Soviet Union in honoring President Kennedy.*
> *Anton*

Turning in his chair, Stack looked at Hank and Juliane. "Have you ever met the attorney general?" he asked.

"No," they replied in unison.

"Well, it won't be long," Stack said. "Oh, and it sounds like Anton is on his way to pay respects to the fallen president."

In about ten minutes, the door opened, and Bobby Kennedy

walked in with a scowl and his bangs hanging over his forehead. He barely glanced at Stack's little gathering before waving his hand in a follow-me motion and heading into his office.

In the AG's office, Stack stifled a smile as Hank and Juliane stared at the total mess in front of them. Papers and files were scattered on every flat surface, including the floor.

Bobby rolled up his sleeves and grabbed an armload of files.

"Linda, no interruptions," he said. "Hold all my calls."

"Gotcha, boss."

"Mr. Attorney General, meet Henry Burner, known as Hank," Stack said. "And this is Juliane Burner, formerly known as She-Bear." Bobby gave a slight smile while turning his eyes from his desk to She-Bear.

"Okay," Bobby said. "Let's talk."

Stack moved to the side of the attorney general's desk.

"Do you understand how secret this operation is?" asked Bobby. "Congress and the White House are both launching investigations. But I believe that Jack's death can be laid at more than one doorstep, so we're focusing on that."

Hank instantly became the picture of concentration.

"I understand, and for the record, I feel the same way."

Bobby smiled, the slow, broad smile that changed him in a second from a cold, unforgiving and penetrating person, into a warm, open man of great sincerity.

"Looks like we've putting together a great team, Stack," he said. "Are we planning to bring anyone else on board?"

"We may have hit pay dirt. Anton sent me a message—he's on his way here."

"Shit, Stack," said Bobby. "I thought he was a communist. And doesn't he live in Moscow?"

"Right on both counts," Stack said. "But given the message he sent me, if the Soviets *did* hire Valzic, it's starting to look like they'd just as soon be done with him. I think Anton can help."

Bobby nodded. "If you trust him, so do I." Then he looked to Hank and Juliane. "This is a sealed operation, and Stack will have to run it. Any problem with that?"

They shook their heads.

"Great." He shook hands with them. "Well, we're here, so we might as well start on a plan."

"Right, boss," said Hank, smiling.

"We're with you," said Juliane.

Bobby nodded to Stack. "Why don't you walk us all through it?"

"For starters," Stack said, "we need you in Langley looking at files—try to identify the agents who were part of the Pigs operation. The assassination idea may have started there. But we need proof. We can't expect them to tell us, but they may tip their hand by saying something meaningful to us that's old hat to them."

At that moment, the door opened, and Anton was ushered in.

"I've heard his name so much I was sure he must be important to you all," said Linda. "So I decided to let him through."

They all jumped up and gave Anton a hearty hug.

"We are skating on thin ice using this office," Anton said. "Anyone recognizes me here and the game will be over."

"It's not as dangerous as you may think," Stack said. "We have an office in the building next door that can be sealed with all automated equipment. Anyhow, we'll wrap this up quickly now that you're here."

The phone rang, and Bobby excused himself to go to the outer office.

"We got some action," he said when he returned. "A pilot on Pan Am saw the photo of Valzic as he was boarding his flight to Berlin. He called the FBI and they put him on the phone with Linda, who took down all the information. Valzic was turned away from the flight because he had a rifle with him, but now he's vanished. We need to move with dispatch."

"We need to make sure hotels, bus lines, and rail companies get Valzic's picture," Stack said. "We found him that way once; we might get lucky again."

"I don't want him getting out of this country," said Bobby. "Hope everyone cooperates. If Lyndon stops us, I don't know how we go forward."

CHAPTER 24

Stack had asked Linda to see if Hank and Juliane would be able to meet with him and Bobby at four o'clock in the afternoon. They both agreed and were prompt.

Stack leaned back in his chair. "It looks pretty much like Oswald was the perpetrator. But it's too pat a hand for my liking."

"Facts are facts," said Hank, "but sometimes they aren't."

"And Ruby showing up before Oswald could be questioned?" Juliane said. "That's rather convenient."

"Who else was around that might have a motive?"

"Pretty much everyone," Hank said. "Including the Dallas newspapers."

"They certainly add to the negative atmosphere," Stack said. "Any word from Anton?"

"He just stepped out," said Juliane.

"Damn. I just wish we could get somewhere new with this," Stack said. "We know who the shooter is, but somehow that's not enough."

"Regardless, we need to move quickly to take advantage of the negative atmosphere," said Bobby.

The door opened and Anton came in.

"Where have you been?" snarled Stack.

"To take a leak. Is that a problem?"

"Sorry, pal," said Stack. "We just can't be too careful. Anyway, Hank came up with some logic based on what he knows of the Mob and the info the Bureau has on file. The Mob offered up Oswald, but the Russians felt he was too flaky and hard to control. So they brought in Valzic to keep an eye on Oswald. The rifles found in Oswald's apartment were Russian issue. Valzic must have lost Oswald in the confusion, so Ruby stepped up."

"But who benefits?" asked Bobby. "I don't just want the man who pulled the trigger, damn it, I want the ones pulling the strings."

"The Mob benefits because it gets the Kennedys off their backs," Stack said. "LBJ benefits too. And Castro gets revenge for the failed Cuban invasion."

"Hell of a theory," said Bobby. "But that doesn't narrow it down."

"Hank, can you get the rifle Valzic was trying to bring with him on the plane?"

"Sure."

"Then check it for fingerprints," Stack said. "See if any are a match for ones found in Oswald's apartment or the book depository."

... .--. -.--

Stack received a back channel message that Valzic had been spotted in Cuba. He instructed Juliane to send Valzic's bio and photo to all FBI field offices, Interpol, the NSA, CIA, and other agencies. "Identify him as an international killer. I'll get approval from Bobby."

As soon as he hung up, Stack called Linda and left the briefest of outlines to get Bobby's okay for the distribution of the Valzic notification.

"I'd like to have a government plane to get back quick and avoid all the airport red tape. Also, we may need it again soon." Stack said.

Stack had been in Cuba for less than twenty-four hours before Bobby called.. "Well, pal," he said. "The man who can do anything has just kicked up the biggest hornets' nest in over a year. Are you having fun yet? The FBI and the whole Justice Department are in a twist because they think I have inside information on the assassination. And the AG never uses government airplanes."

"Screw you, Mr. Know-It-All."

Bobby laughed. "Come on home, pal, and we'll talk about the next inning. This is like the Yankees and Red Sox games. By the way, I approved your requests, including the plane. Did you want the stewardess to wear spiked heels? If so, I'll have to tell Mary Jane."

"Again, Mr. AG, go screw yourself."

"What did you find out down there?" Bobby said.

"Nothing to hold on to. Yes, they have a couple of assassins under wraps. No, they have not been out of jail for a year. And the president of the University of Havana pledged his everlasting support and help," said Stack.

"I'm glad we didn't spend any more time on that lead," said Bobby.

••• •▬▬• ▬•▬▬

As the government plane taxied to its hangar, Stack looked out the window and saw a black limousine pull out of a parking spot and fall in behind the plane. As soon as they were cleared to disembark, the door opened and a young man in a dark suit came on board. He was as tall as Stack—maybe six feet—but he was broader in the shoulders and wore his hair closely cropped. His voice was sharp, professional.

"Mr. Stack?"

"Yes?"

"I'm Wilson with the Secret Service, sir. I'm here to take you where you need to be."

"I thought I was going to the AG's office."

"You were, sir. But the attorney general was reminded by his wife that *The Pink Panther* was opening in Washington tonight. I'm told they have Mrs. Stack in tow, and you're expected to meet them at the theater."

"Well, I'll be damned!" Stack smiled, but it was half-hearted. Of course, he'd rather spend the evening with his wife and friends, but he knew he should be sitting in Bobby's office going over recent events.

Still—a night out was long overdue. And if nothing else, he owed it to Mary Jane.

At the theater, the Kennedy family was already seated. Stack was ushered to the assigned row. Though he tried to be unobtrusive, he bumped several knees and stepped on a few feet, making children laugh.

He finally reached Bobby and his wife. He smiled at Ethel and patted Bobby's shoulder.

"What's the size of this clan now?"

Bobby's smile covered his whole face, in stark contrast to his normal scowl.

Just past them sat Mary Jane. With care, Stack picked his way across the seats and joined his wife. He received a kiss on the lips. Ethel, sitting on his other side, patted him on the arm. Apparently, his late arrival was forgiven.

Mary Jane slipped her hand under his and held it tightly. "I'm so glad to see you," she whispered. Wearing a black straight pencil skirt and white silk blouse, she was beautiful.

He finally relaxed—though he suddenly wished they were alone together.

"Me too." He smiled and squeezed her hand back.

When they got home, the Stacks sat on the love seat and held one another. He found his hands sliding over her skirt, slipping underneath her blouse.

"Would you like to go to bed?" she whispered.

That night, he slept like a man with a fish on the hook.

••• •−−• −•−−

He was woken by the telephone.

"Stack, ol' man!" It was Hank. "I was expecting a call last night."

Stack rolled out of bed and rubbed his eyes. It had snowed in the early morning hours, and the ground outside glistened where the sun touched down. Holding the phone in his left hand, Stack pulled the drapes shut with his right. Too early.

On the bed, Mary Jane stretched like a cat and reached out, her hand grazing the back of his thigh.

"Sorry, Hank. Bobby got a little caught up with the family." He glanced back at Mary Jane, who smiled. "So did I, to be honest."

Hank chuckled. "Don't worry; Linda let us know. Really I just called to tell you the flyers are out."

Stack took a seat on the edge of the bed while Mary Jane pulled on a robe and slipped into the kitchen.

"I don't know exactly when we can get together with Bobby, but I think we need some time to bring things together before we stumble into his office."

"I think that would help me a lot," Hank said. "Remember, sooner or later, I have to own up to the director." No matter that he was on assignment to the attorney general's staff, Hank was still an FBI Agent.

••• •−−• −•−−

The third floor of Justice was as relaxing an environment as could be found in the nation's capital, but still Stack felt the tension harden around him like a suit of armor. Most classified meetings took place at Langley, but since the CIA was exempted from this meeting, that wouldn't be necessary.

Looking both ways as he entered the room, Stack grinned when he saw Anton and Juliane. He dropped his bundle of papers and files on the table, took off his suit coat, and dropped it on a chair.

"I know you all remember this," Stack said. "But a little recap never hurt anyone." He took his seat. "I first saw Valzic outside Canaris's office in Berlin in 1938. I ran into him again on a rail platform in Prague."

He glanced at Juliane, who met his gaze and offered a slight smile.

"I didn't actually see him again until JFK's funeral procession," he said. "But I always had a hunch I saw him outside the Citadel the night we retrieved the Enigma machine."

Hank looked surprised. "What would he have been doing there?"

Stack shook his head. "Whatever he was doing, he was there on Canaris's orders." He looked around the table. "This whole operation reminds me of the pre-OSS days in Europe."

"Never enough information?" Anton said.

"Always flying by the seat of our pants?" Juliane asked.

"Terrible food?" Hank suggested.

They all laughed.

CHAPTER 25

September 1964

Stack arrived at Bobby's office early. "Linda, will you help me round up some legal pads and pencils for the meeting this morning?"

As always, she was cordial and relaxed. "You don't even have to ask."

There was a knock on the outer door. Stack was expecting the team, so he called out, "Come on in."

But the man who stepped in wasn't a member of his team. It was J. Edgar Hoover.

"Good morning."

"Good morning, Mr. Director." Stack kept his face blank. As Hoover strode past him, he raised both brows at Linda, who only shrugged.

"Where do you want me, young man?" Hoover said. Stack, thinking quickly, pointed to the chair at the head of the table. "Thank you."

The door swung open again, and this time Bobby Kennedy strode in, nodded his hellos, and took a seat at the table.

Juliane and Hank arrived next.

"Come on in," Stack said.

Finally, the door swung open and Anton stepped in. He noticed the others in the room and quietly took his seat.

"Thank you all for coming," Stack said after he'd introduced each person to the group at large. "Bobby, do you want to start us off?"

Bobby nodded. "Sorry I've been tied up," he said. "But I've read the summary of the investigation to date. You've all been very busy. Tell me what you're thinking now."

"Sure," Stack glanced at his teammates. "Your input is valuable, so jump in anytime." He turned his attention back to Bobby. "Well, Mr. Attorney General, it seems that there was a conspiracy, but not the kind we assumed. There's a lot we don't know, and proof is elusive, but we believe the Mob, with Russia's help, ran the operation."

"Enter Valzic, the shooter," Anton said. "The Mob—the Outfit—says they want to use their own man, but they're okay with Valzic being a backup. In the warehouse, Valzic watches and waits. Any hesitation by Oswald, and Valzic blows him away and shoots Kennedy himself. Ruby was an Outfit member assigned to kill Oswald before he could be interrogated."

"And now," said Bobby, "the Outfit only has one Kennedy to deal with, and a president who doesn't give a damn as long as he has total union support."

Stack looked at each person sitting around the table. He could see that they were all listening intently.

"I firmly believe what Anton has proposed—that Valzic was the backup shooter and that the Mob was running the show," Stack said. "We got a hit from some of the flyers we sent out, so we know Valzic is still in the US."

"And what do we do when we find him?" Hank said.

"I think we have no choice but to eliminate him." Stack watched Bobby as he spoke. "I've made a life of not being recognized. I could disappear. You, Bobby, cannot."

Bobby hesitated. "If I agreed to the elimination of Valzic, I would be responsible for a crime—and if anyone ever found out, it could sink the Democratic Party."

"On the other hand," Stack said, "if we just let Valzic be reabsorbed into the Soviet Union, he could show up anywhere and anytime and cause tremendous harm to others."

"Also, such a move would prevent the JFK investigation from ever becoming public," Hank said.

Bobby shook his head. "It makes no difference what the Warren Commission comes up with, as long as we're right. I'm more worried about us being able to muster the evidence we'd need to convict him at a trial . . . which is why I think you're right, Stack. We need to be judge, jury, and executioner if we catch him."

••• •▪▪• ▪•▪▪

By November, Hank, Juliane, and Stack were still trawling through documents, interviews, and shaky evidence. Anton had given them what he could before returning to Moscow. Bobby popped in and out, just enough to run his ship and keep abreast of progress. "I want Valzic's ass hung from the wall," he said during one meeting. "I can't accept that he's beyond reach."

Leaning backward into his soft leather club chair, Stack let out several deep breaths. He'd reactivated the World War II encrypting machine and notified Anton of the team's strategies, thinking they might've missed something. He got a reply of hedged concurrence. Stack only hoped Anton would continue to help by knowing who and where the international criminals were.

It was Bill Donovan's old files in the CIA history archives that yielded the name of Dick Ellis. Ellis had been one of the founders of the OSS along with Bill Stephenson, and had gone on to be integral to Churchill's British Security Coordination. Both Brits were extremely knowledgeable about every operation in Europe from 1935 to the present.

Stack called Hank, Juliane, and Anton in and brought them up to speed.

"BSC has been closed since the end of the war, but many of their people and records are still with the American CIA. I think if we could find a way to get in touch with Dick Ellis, he could be a help in finding Valzic."

"Hell's bells," Anton said. "Why do you think he would remember a sniper from the war, much less know how to find him now?"

"Ellis kept a file of specialists on hand," Stack said. "Anyone we ever tried to recruit went in there, and I even tried to recruit Valzic myself."

Anton nodded. "I'll see if I can track Ellis down."

"Meanwhile," Stack said, "I think I'll take the shuttle from Washington to New York and see what's what in the old BSC offices."

••• •▬▬• ▬•▬▬

Driven by adrenaline, Stack quick-stepped to the cab line and was able to spot a driver who seemed to be relatively sober and knew where Rockefeller Center was. The cabbie was wrapped up in jackets and scarves, which made him look like a sausage, and didn't need any encouragement to keep the heat on full blast.

Staggered by the sudden chill when he finally got out of the cab, Stack leaned in the window of the passenger side to pay. His feet were cold, and already wet.

As expected, there was no listing for the BSC. Now feeling the chill throughout his body, Stack went across the plaza and found a seat in a restaurant overlooking the ice-skating rink, which hosted a swarm of skaters. If he were Ellis, where would he be?

Suddenly, he remembered the cover for the BSC was the British Diplomatic Passport Office.

Finishing his coffee, he hustled back into Rockefeller Center and found the British Passport Office on the forty-fourth floor. He knocked—no response. He knocked again—nothing. Expecting the floor to be vacant on Sunday, he turned the knob and was surprised to find it unlocked. He let himself in.

He found himself looking directly into the startled eyes of a lovely young lady sitting behind an oak desk.

On the wall behind him was another oak desk, at which sat a well-groomed man wearing a dark gray suit and vest. His hair was combed back from his forehead. No one else was visible.

"May we help you?" the woman said with a light English accent.

Stack experienced a rush of déjà vu and weakness in the knees. He was back twenty years in post-war England and in the spartan offices of the BSC.

"Are you always open on Sunday?" he asked.

"Occasionally," the man said—he also had a British accent. "Why?"

"I need to get in touch with a man named Ellis," Stack said. "I used to work with Bill Donovan."

"What is your code name?" the lady asked.

"Yellow Bird."

She disappeared through the only other door in the room. It took thirty minutes, but she eventually returned.

"May I see some identification?"

Stack produced his driver's license and his White House pass.

She studied them both. "Hm. You're real, I think. What can we do for you?"

"I'm tracking a man who used to work with the Abwehr," he

said. "I think he may be in New York."

"A Jew killer?" she said. "We get a lot of those inquiries."

"Not this time," Stack said. "But a killer just the same."

"Yes," said the Englishman, who had come around the desk and was now flipping through Stack's file. "I see you accomplished quite a bit under Donovan and Stephenson."

Stack eyed him. "You know who I am, but who are you?"

"Is this a security issue?"

"It would certainly fit in that category," Stack said. "The US government urgently needs to find this man." He reached into his pocket. "Here's a photo that might help."

"Please take a seat, or go downstairs for a cup of tea," said the Englishman. "This will take some time."

"How long?"

"Oh, about fifteen minutes."

... .--. -.--

Fifteen minutes turned into an hour, and one cup of coffee into four. Stack watched the skaters on the rink while his stomach tied itself in knots. He knew he should be thankful to have found anyone at BSC so many years after the war.

After another two hours with intermittent reports from the young woman, who identified herself as Agent Silver, she finally appeared with a broad smile.

"Come on up, Agent Yellow Bird. We have contacted Intrepid, and he was rather eager to speak with you."

... .--. -.--

"Stack, what a bloody surprise to hear from you." Stack smiled on hearing the voice of Bill Stephenson. "If you're in New York, you have less sense than I used to give you credit for. Hop over to visit me in Bermuda, and tell me everything."

"No time, boss," Stack said. "We have a situation that's very dangerous and must be brought to a conclusion as quickly as possible." He then brought Stephenson up to date on the current activities, including his unproven gut feel conclusions.

"I see," said Stephenson. "You really do have a dicey situation there. Give me some time, and I'll get back to you."

"How long?" Stack asked.

"Well, given that Dick Ellis is living in Manhattan, I should be able to talk with him today or tomorrow," said Stephenson. "Then it's a matter of file searching. But Dick knows the field, so to speak, and I'm quite confident he'll be able to get to the heart of the matter."

••• •▬▬• ▬•▬▬

It took two weeks before Stack received a call from Ellis.

"According to my contact," said Ellis, "Valzic is currently in New York."

"That's what I had hoped," Stack said. "But how did you know, if you don't mind my asking?"

There was a pause. "My contact has been in touch with Valzic over the years."

As far as Stack knew, Valzic had only one skill set. "I see."

"The bad news," Ellis said, "is that he's still in the country."

"It's good for us," Stack said. "I don't know how the hell we'd pull him out of Russia."

"If he's still here, it means he's working on a contract," Ellis said. "Otherwise he'd be long gone."

"I'm just glad to have a shot at him."

"Let me remind you," said Ellis, "that we are not at war, and anything you do will probably be outside the limits of the laws of at least two countries—three, if you count the Soviet Union. You will be jailed and tried, if caught, and you could get a life sentence. The CIA and the US Government will do nothing to intervene."

"I understand that."

"Well then," said Ellis, "in that case, I wish you good luck."

··· ·▬▬· ▬·▬▬

The first thing Stack did was call a meeting with Bobby and the rest of the team. He flew back to DC the next morning. Outside the airport, as promised, a black limo pulled over to the curb and stopped. Bobby himself opened the door, snowflakes covering his head in seconds.

Stack quickly got in the car, though his mind was turning fast. Why had Bobby come to pick him up personally?

"Having second thoughts about this mission, Mr. AG?"

"Hell no," said Bobby. "I just want to be sure I have all the facts right. Are you heading back to New York after this?"

"Yes," Stack said. "We're going to set up observation points while we bring the FBI into the loop."

"Well, keep me posted," said Kennedy. "And don't make Mary Jane a widow."

"I'll try."

"What do you think our actual chances are of just capturing Valzic?" Bobby said.

"Not too good," Stack said. "I have no idea how I'd get close enough to bring him in."

"Remember," Bobby said, "I still want to confirm Oswald's role in my brother's death, and I need to know if there are others." He hesitated. "Do you think it would be smart to call in the NYPD?"

Stack rubbed his temples. "You know Valzic isn't a static figure. We won't have time to spot him, call for help, and wait for them to come. If he's sighted, we have to nail him before he gets lost in the crowd."

"All right," Bobby said. "But if we don't get him by the day after Christmas, we'll call in the police. How's that?"

"Fine," Stack said. "Let's get cracking."

CHAPTER 26

Christmas Eve 1964

It had been snowing in New York for over a week. The team met on the fourth floor of a nondescript building on Madison and Fifty-First Street—according to Anton, the Manhattan headquarters of the KGB.

"Post a lookout here and we'll see Valzic eventually," he said.

Content to stay indoors for now, Stack organized a planning session, and from there the team devised a plan of action. Valzic had been lying low in facilities secretly owned by Soviet Union Intelligence on Madison and Forty-Ninth. Normally, Anton explained, they would see he was a radical and toss him out as a threat to security, but he apparently had powerful friends, and they wanted to let events take their course.

"We need to be alert to the fact that we're most likely being watched," Anton said. "Every time you go out, understand that someone is on your tail. Use tradecraft or anything you can to ditch them. And stay away from the British Passport Office—from this point on, they're no doubt monitoring the building on a twenty-four-hour basis."

Phones were installed in the conference room and folding cots brought in. The team began a twenty-four-hour surveillance operation broken into four-hour watches. Stack, walking the neighborhood, identified four restaurants that would deliver food and one coffee shop that would supply pastries at all hours.

Everyone was jumpy, snappish. Over several days, sidearms were smuggled in and one assigned to each team member.

"Remember, no cowboy actions," Stack said. "This is a strictly clandestine operation. Spot, follow, verify, and report back. I'm a little too excited after all our hard work to be within capturing distance."

••• •■■• ■•■■

Stack buttoned his topcoat all the way up, tugged his wool hat down over his ears, and stepped out of the building, merging with the Christmas shopping crowd. He needed fresh air, and it was several hours before his next shift.

From the curb he looked across Fifty-Ninth at Fifth Avenue. Cabbies, families, beautiful people . . . and Valzic.

Stack turned away and patted his coat pockets.

"Shit," he muttered—no pistol.

He joined the herd and crossed the street. No sign of Valzic—maybe he'd been wrong.

God knows we've been on high alert long enough to start seeing things.

He started back across the street to get his pistol—if he did run into Valzic, he might as well be prepared.

But as he passed the GM Building, he saw him again. And this time, he was absolutely certain. *It's him.*

Valzic was moving east on Fifty-Ninth. Stack tailed him to the entrance of Bloomingdale's, where Valzic entered the revolving door and was swallowed by the crowd.

Stack swore, but kept walking around to the Third Avenue entrance, then strode past the door to watch from a short distance.

The crowds were overwhelming. The throngs of last-minute

shoppers were five deep on the sidewalk. Stack's hunch paid off; he turned to look back at the Bloomingdale's entrance—and straight into the eyes of Valzic, who pointed his index finger at Stack like a pistol and smiled. He knew Stack wouldn't risk gunfire or attempted arrests in this crowd.

Stack moved as if jolted with the crowd crossing Fifty-Ninth. He lost sight of Valzic, then spotted him up ahead—he'd beaten the traffic across the street. Stack moved quickly to a waiting cab and jumped in.

"Hey, Mac, we ain't goin' anywhere with this crowd."

Stack slid across the backseat, opened the door on the other side of the cab, and slipped straight out.

"Thanks, pal," he said as he shut the door.

Moving as fast as he could, pushing and weaving through the crowd, he headed west on Fifty-Ninth. Looking back, he saw Valzic moving toward him.

The tables had turned. Valzic was now the hunter, and he was damn good at it. The game of life or death was on.

Stack circled around and went into the Oak Bar at the Plaza Hotel. He sat in a corner booth and ordered a beer. Looking out the street level window, he could see most everyone moving by. Unfortunately, they could also see in—he turned away just as Valzic walked by.

Stack left five dollars on the table and left through the lobby and jumped into a cab right out front. The cabbie took him up along Central Park to the Guggenheim Museum. He paid the driver and went into the museum. He looked around—he'd remembered there being a pay phone behind the coat room.

It wasn't there.

"Where's the pay phone?" he asked the guard.

"Third floor, next to the men's room."

Stack sprinted up the circular ramp to the third floor, found the phone, and dug through his pockets for change. He dialed and waited for the phone to ring.

"Hank?" he said the moment someone picked up.

"Where in hell are you?" Hank asked, worried.

"I've had eyes on Valzic—but he's had eyes on me too. Last saw him outside the Plaza Hotel, and I'm hoping he hasn't gone far. I'm at the Guggenheim and heading back down to the GM Building. Can you get over there quick?"

"Okay. Leaving now."

Looking out from the phone booth, Stack saw no signs of Valzic. He slowly wandered down the ramp toward the door, then scanned the first floor, edging toward the door and finally passing through it. He jogged along the outside of the Fifth Avenue sidewalk crowds toward the GM Building.

All clear. Stack slowed to a walk as he crossed the street, then circled the frozen fountain in front of the Plaza Hotel.

Hank will pick Valzic up or he won't. In either case, I've got to keep moving.

He left the fountain and walked west beside the Plaza on Fifty-Eighth. He turned left on Sixth Avenue he passed a couple of all-night grills and the Warwick Hotel. Slowing his pace, he began to catch his breath.

Suddenly he saw Valzic coming toward him. Stack lunged into the street, getting clipped by a cab that screeched to a stop. He kept running, but the cab blocked his view.

Did he see me back there?

He ran north toward Fifty-Fourth then down to Fifth Avenue. There he turned south and slowed to a walk.

Christmas chatter filled the air. No sign of Valzic.

The sound of a large choir singing "O Holy Night" was being piped from the Fifty-Third Street entrance to the St. Thomas Church on Fifth. The sidewalk was packed with people pushing in and out. The going in tide took him in, and he didn't resist.

The sanctuary was dark except for the high altar, which rose over two stories.

A white light broke through the hall just as the music began again, this time "The First Noel." Stack sat next to a column one row from the rear and partly hidden by a heavy tapestry. He looked around. Most of the cathedrals he'd seen in Europe had been bombed out.

The music intensified as the brass section joined with the strings until it reached a crescendo. Though he'd heard Christmas music his whole life, the very power of this music filled his chest and gave him new strength.

As Stack began to relax, Valzic appeared.

The sniper walked slowly up the left aisle, looking into every pew. At the fourth, he stopped and sat in the left side, watching the crowds for Stack.

Stack felt his whole stomach cramp. *Damn, he's good.*

He knew the chase would end tonight. Breathing deeply and slowly, Stack began to prepare for a confrontation.

More people drifted into the church and out again just as quickly, seeking God's blessings on this holy night. There were gaps, though, between the crowds, and Stack saw his opportunity in one of those gaps.

Again, killing. This is Prague all over again. He'd been unprepared on the rail platform, reacting on emotion rather than sense. But this scenario was in his hands totally. He could kill or be killed, but he couldn't back away.

Stack moved to Valzic's pew and sat on the opposite end. As worshippers left and Valzic turned, Stack slid closer to his prey. He took a knife from his jacket and opened it. Acting as if Valzic were a friend or family member, he smiled as he slid over to him.

Valzic's eyes widened as the knife plunged into his ribs, immobilizing him long enough for Stack to put his arm around Valzic's neck and his hand over his mouth while he quickly cut the carotid artery on the sniper's neck.

Blood began to flow. Stack wrapped Valzic's coat and scarf closely around his neck as the Polish vigilante gurgled into unconsciousness. He appeared to be just another man sleeping off too much Christmas cheer.

As he let the crowds take him out of the Fifth Avenue entrance, Stack prayed for forgiveness.

••• •▬▬• ▬•▬▬

"**W**here in hell have you been?" said Hank as Stack stumbled back into the office. "You're one hell of an evasive soldier. I followed two or three men thinking they were you, and I was wrong every time." He took a breath. "At least Valzic didn't turn the tables on us. Do you think he knows about this office?"

"Doesn't matter," Stack said. "It's over." He took off his beat-up topcoat and wool hat and hung them to dry.

"What the hell do you mean, it's over?"

Stack, exhausted, slumped in a chair. "It's over. Valzic has been eliminated."

"How? What happened?" Anton asked.

"I'll put it in my report to Kennedy and you can read it." He met Hank's gaze, then Anton. "Come on, guys, it's Christmas. Let's go get some dinner, sing a few carols, and forget about this for a while."

They looked at each other.

"Everything's closed," Hank finally said.

"I know a couple of places on Sixth Avenue that are open," Stack said. "Follow me."

They sat at a table for six and spread out.

"You guys are working damn late on a Christmas Eve," said a potbellied, balding man in a white apron. "On a deadline?"

"Yeah, and we just put things to bed. Hope we can beat the kids getting up in the morning," said Hank.

"When you going home?" asked Anton

"Not till seven," said the waiter. "So, whatcha want, or are you just waiting for Santa?"

"Hell no," said Stack. "Let's eat. How about three eggs over light, plenty of bacon, hash browns, and wheat toast?"

After everyone ordered, the waiter said, "How 'bout I just fix ten or twelve eggs, bunches of toast, and bacon all on one plate?"

"Sounds good." The decision was unanimous.

CHAPTER 27

"So, all the bad guys are accounted for." Bobby brushed back his hair and thought a moment. "The Mob is still in business, but there's not much we can do about that. You're sure it was Valzic?"

Stack slid over a piece of paper. "Look at this."

The New York Times, December 25, 1964
The FBI has revealed that they have solid evidence that the man found with his throat cut in the St. Thomas Church on 53rd Street on Christmas Eve was Valzic Krewcheski, a terrorist from the USSR. He was wanted for a series of assassinations in Eastern Europe. New York police agreed with the FBI that there is one less dangerous person in the US. Police speculate that his death was Mafia-related.

Then Bobby stood up and went around the room, thanking each agent personally. He stopped when he reached Stack.

"You know there can never be public recognition of what you've done for this country, but on behalf of my brother, and the United States of America, I thank you and want you to know that I am fully aware of the details of your service."

Turning to the others, he said, "You've served with a legend. I hope you'll use his example to guide you the rest of your life."

There were many lessons to be learned, but not the ease of murder, Stack thought. He felt the satisfaction of doing a job successfully. The relief of removing a threat to the country. A sickness of seeing the winds of war attack a whole race. Yes, he was much older now. Forcing himself to be positive, he drew satisfaction from working successfully and well with others. There was now a free world, and he had been part of its creation. Stack felt proud of that.

God bless us and forgive us.

••• •▬▬• ▬•▬▬

Choosing to walk home from the Justice Department, Stack dusted snow off a bench and sat in reflection. What was the justification for killing without a war? But it *was* a war, a secret war that stopped humanity when it couldn't stop itself. Stack was proud to have contributed to this effort. But he did feel guilty for the chaos that he had participated in. He had learned a lot about the effectiveness of individuals coming together for a common cause. These lessons would work well on the farm, for which he longed. And he needed no recognition for the role he had played. It was a secret, and one he could live with.

Acknowledgments

Foremost among the people that facilitated the writing of this book: Tom Hall, whose skills and literary feel kept me from drowning in computer technology. Betsy Thorpe took me under her wing and gave me the guidance that I needed to proceed. Maya Myers and Diana Wade rounded out her team and added additional expertise.

I am finally thankful for my wife Judy and her sharp prodding when it looked to her like I was slacking off. Her trust in me when she didn't know what all was going into the book is wonderful.

CPSIA information can be obtained
at www.ICGtesting.com
Printed in the USA
LVHW030331040119
602694LV00003B/21/P

9 781732 995819